'Letters and Secrets'

by Richard Ayres

 New Generation Publishing

Chapter 1

Shropshire, Friday 27 April

Computer technology, when we understand how to use it, can open up new worlds. At the click and slide of a mouse we can view the earth from on high. We can swoop over hills and valleys, mountains and plains, forests and deserts, lush pastures and teeming conurbations. We can zoom in, zoom out, view from directly above, or from a low angle. The whole world is beneath us.

It is easy to be tempted by majestic scenery of foreign parts, but let us instead hover over a small part of England. Examine it closely: it is a patchwork quilt of fields and hedgerows, the quintessential English landscape of all our imaginings, the green and pleasant land evoked by Blake. There are no dark satanic mills here.

If we zoom in more closely we will see there are areas of dark blue amongst the various shades of green: areas of water probably; and yes, they are lakes. The lakes are surrounded by woods, but close to one of them, at its north-western edge, is a small town.

Cutting through the woods which surround the lakes is a narrow blue ribbon. It isn't straight, but it doesn't meander like a river would in these lowland parts. It is, in fact, a canal: the Llangollen Canal, which runs from Hurlestone in Cheshire to the town of its name. It is the most popular canal in the country for boating holidays.

We have a particular interest in the Llangollen Canal, but this is where Google Earth fails us. We are unable to zoom in closer, and the technology does not yet exist to show us how places are in real time. No doubt, some day soon, the entire country will be covered with aerial CCTV cameras to allow our masters to see what's happening everywhere at any given moment. But we don't have this facility: we must therefore imagine that we can track the movement of a man who is running along the canal towpath.

He is slim and dressed in a t-shirt, shorts which reveal thin sinewy legs, and trainers. He has a head of thick grey hair, cut short: his face is deeply lined, but close observation reveals a fine bone structure despite the slackening jawline and the dark shadows under the eyes, eyes which are a penetrating blue. His nose is aquiline. He is probably in his sixties, but it is evident that he was once a strikingly handsome young man. The fact that he is jogging points to his being one of those who fight a rearguard action against the looming threat of old age, an uncomfortable prospect for most of us, but so much worse for one whose trademark was his good looks.

Who is he, this man on whom we are spying?

His name is Derek Bailey. Like all adults, especially those no longer youthful, he exists in the present but carries the past around with him. Sometimes memories drag us down; sometimes they bear us up. 'Baggage', these are sometimes called, but without a past we would be adrift: without memories we'd be nobody. Derek is no different, but his past has been more traumatic than most; so traumatic that parts of it, in his darker moments, rise up to torment him. Because of this he is considering embarking on a course of action that may change not only his life but the lives of many others.

But of course this is all surmise. None of it is evident from the view that we have of him as he reaches a junction of the canal, where he stops running and starts to walk along the short spur that leads almost to the town centre. Tracking his movements is no longer enough: we need to get inside his head.

*

He'd woken that morning still undecided whether to send it. Lying there in bed, Gabrielle snoring softly beside him, he'd embarked once more on an attempt to analyse his motives for the action that he still hadn't decided he would take. Curiosity about what had transpired, perhaps? Or a way of seeking forgiveness, an act of atonement? Or was he just finding an excuse to indulge himself by writing his memoirs? Or even ... he dared hardly articulate to himself the other reason.

He'd found no answer to these questions, so he'd got up without rousing Gabrielle, and had set off on his morning run. Now, walking the few yards from the canal spur to the street of Victorian terraced houses where he lived, he knew he'd come to a decision whilst jogging. After breakfast he'd go into town and post the letter. If nothing came of it – well, he could live with never knowing. He'd been doing so for nearly 25 years.

He reached his front door, removed his trainers before opening it, and padded into the kitchen. He was greeted by the aroma of freshly ground coffee and an embrace from Gabrielle.

'Sweaty!' she observed. She pinched his backside. 'Go and have your shower.'

He kissed her and made his way upstairs.

As he stood in the shower he felt the adrenaline rush that always came after his morning run. Working-out indoors, something to which he'd been restricted for so long, had never resulted in the sense of well-being that came from sustained exercise in the open air. His body wasn't bad for a 69 year-old, but there was a small roll of loose flesh around his waistline which he was unable

5

to shift. He was glad that it was now acceptable, even *de-rigueur*, to leave shirts untucked. It had taken a while for him to get used to that, along with many other things. He was still having to acclimatise to the culture of the 21st century. It was all so different from the 1980s. Hartley was wrong, he thought: it's the present that's a foreign country.

He towelled himself briskly, pulled on a pair of old jeans and a tee-shirt, ruffled his hair, and ran down the stairs. The caffetiere was ready to pour. Gabrielle manipulated the toaster. The early summer sunshine streamed through the windows, highlighting the shabbiness of the kitchen. He didn't care that it needed a makeover: he still relished its peaceful homeliness after years of eating in the echoing clamour of an institutional canteen.

He leafed through *The Independent* as they sat and breakfasted. Eventually Gabrielle spoke. 'Well, have you made up your mind?'

He put down the newspaper. 'Yes. I'll go and post it after I've washed up.'

'You're absolutely certain you're doing the right thing?'

'Absolutely.'

'Well, just as long as you haven't set your hopes too high. He may not reply.'

'Oh, he won't, not immediately.'

'How do you know that?'

'I haven't given him my address.'

'Why ever not?'

'I don't want him to feel under pressure. I want to give him the chance to learn what I was like before ... before it all happened. I don't want to spook him by putting questions in his mind, not immediately. So I've just told him about my childhood. I'll tell him more in later letters. It's a way for him to get to know me gradually.'

'When did you get that idea? Why didn't you tell me?'

'I only got the idea a few days ago, when I started to write. I didn't tell you 'cos I wasn't sure I was going to send it.'

'But hasn't he got your email address?'

'No. I made contact through Facebook and got his home address through *192.com*, remember? Quite easy with a name like his. And now, I've taken myself off Facebook.'

Gabrielle's look was a mixture of exasperation and affection.

'Sometimes I think I'll never understand you,' she said.

He grinned. 'Man of mystery, me. That's what turned you on in the first place, wasn't it? That, and my good looks, of course.'

She flicked a toast crumb at him. 'The conceit of the man! You weren't so hot when I first saw you, were you?'

'But you could see my potential. And you don't regret it, do you?'

'No. God knows why, but I don't. Shift yourself; I want to clear the table.'

As they stood, he put his arm round her and pecked her cheek. Had he believed in heaven, he would have said that theirs was a partnership made in it. He loved her, not with the fierce intensity of youth, but quietly, and it was a love born of gratitude. He had heard that gratitude is often a precursor to resentment, but that wasn't how it was for him. He doubted that he would have survived without her encouragement and support. Only very occasionally did he feel a twinge of discontent, an urge to shake her when his more challenging remarks were met with an anodyne response.

She was as homely and as shabby as their kitchen. She was plump, with frizzy greying hair and spectacles, and moved ponderously. She also had a Birmingham accent, which he'd always found risible. She hadn't been a looker even when they'd first met, 15 years before. But she was a woman, 10 years his junior, and back then there were few opportunities to talk to the opposite sex.

He began washing the dishes, and she stood beside him drying them. Cosy domesticity. Something he had scorned, in the years before his downfall. Now, he resolved never to take it for granted.

'How shall we spend the rest of the day, then?' she said as he peeled off his rubber gloves.

'After I've posted the letter I thought I'd spend an hour on the allotment, unless you want me to help with the shopping.'

'No need. Haven't got much to get. And then?'

'How about a pub lunch - *The George* maybe?'

'Sounds good to me. But don't eat too much: we're going for a meal with the Taylors at six, remember.'

'Hadn't forgotten.' He dried his hands on the tea towel. 'Right; I'll go and get the letter.'

He went into the living room. Gabrielle, mindful of their living in a small terrace and remembering her grandmother, called it 'the parlour', though in fact it wasn't just a place in which to relax. It contained an ancient writing desk on which a computer sat incongruously. He'd toyed with the idea of converting the spare bedroom into a study, but decided against it, not wishing to shut himself away. He'd enough of being shut away. So the parlour was multi-functional: he would sit at the desk writing while Gabrielle read, or she would take a turn at the desk while he read or listened to music through headphones. Sometimes they both watched TV, but rarely: most programmes seemed to be reality-shows with the whooping, screaming studio audiences apparently deemed necessary to sustain the viewer's interest, and that which passed for drama consisted of soaps and crime serials. So, when neither was engaged in their own pursuits, they usually sat together on the sagging settee, holding hands and talking.

The A5 envelope on the desk was unsealed. He pulled out the sheets of paper and leafed through them, wondering whether to check once more for any editing that might be needed. No, it was just a letter, not a work of literature, not yet, anyway. It was hand-written: although he was a proficient two-finger typist he found that using the computer inhibited the free-flow of thoughts required to write a narrative.

He replaced the paper and was about to seal the envelope when he remembered the photograph. It was, in fact, that small snapshot which had given him the idea of the form that his correspondence would take. His collection of photographs was one of the few possessions he had that remained from his previous life, his mother having rescued them from his flat soon after he'd been forced to leave it.

He'd made a copy of the photograph, not wishing to send the original. Although in his mind's eye images of his early life were vivid, and the times of his youth and early adulthood seemed to take on a greater clarity with each passing year, he wasn't sure he could trust his memory. He was aware that what one remembers isn't always what one had witnessed. His perception of his past as a neat arrangement of things that happened sequentially was probably erroneous; it was more likely a mishmash of events that he'd put together in a scheme of his own devising. Sometimes he wished he'd kept a diary. But at least the camera didn't lie (or it used not to, in the days before digital photography) and the monochrome snapshots proved that some things were indeed exactly as he remembered. Or was it that he remembered them clearly only because he had the photographs?

He thrust the photograph into the envelope, sealed and addressed it, and returned to the kitchen.

'Just off to the post box, then,' he said, waving the envelope.

'Have you got the right stamp on it?'

'First Class.'

'Yes, but it's a bulky envelope. You might need one of those special stamps.'

'Shit.'

He was still on occasions caught out by the changes that occurred since he last had charge of his own destiny. He had learned to cope with most of the technological developments – personal computers, mobile phones, call centres, digitalisation. And he was coming to terms with societal changes – acceptance of gays, multiculturalism, the ubiquity of popular culture, the strange way that young people spoke these days. No, it was the little things that still caught him out: only the other day he'd dialled (dialled? no, punched in the number) 192 and was exasperated by the 'number unobtainable' tone. And still, on sitting down with a pint in a pub, he automatically reached for a cigarette.

'You'd better get going, then, if you're going to the Post Office before the allotment.'

'Right. I'm on my way.'

It had been a wet, cold spring, but today was one of those rare warm April days that lifted his spirits, lightened his step and made him feel nineteen again, just for a moment. Ellesmere was set in deep countryside far from the grasping tentacles of urban Britain and, apart from the Tesco superstore, was largely untouched by the ghastly excrescences that had blighted many once-homely town centres. But it was saved from rural parochialism by visiting tourists taking a break from their navigation of the canal. Derek was growing to like the place. As he walked through the pretty but un-prettified town centre which was still blessed with some independent shops - though many were fighting a losing battle against the competition from Tesco - he nodded to a few people with whom he had become acquainted in the two years he had been there.

Back in the old bachelor days, his life had been filled with people. His old friends from university, of course, and then colleagues: many of these had become friends, and then he'd met the friends of friends, some of whom had become lovers – and then he'd met *their* friends. Now, he hardly knew anyone, apart from Giles and Davina Taylor. Sometimes he had to admit to himself that he was a bit – well, not lonely exactly, but lacking the stimulation that an active social life provides.

It was Gabrielle (who had been able to retire early when her widowed mother had died leaving her a small inheritance) who had suggested they move away from the Midlands and all the painful associations that the area held for him. He'd had reservations, at first. But he realised that his friends of 30 years before were unlikely ever to wish to see him again, and that indeed he had little desire to see them. So he had nothing to lose by moving. He'd reassured himself by constantly singing the words of Gerry Rafferty's 'Baker Street' – *One day he'll settle down in some quiet little town and forget about everything.* And though he hadn't forgotten everything, he had settled down. Helped by

11

Gabrielle, he'd begun to make some sort of life for himself, and there were people he had met whose company he thought he might come to enjoy.

The Taylors were such people. Gabrielle had persuaded him to join her at the local Book Group which met every Wednesday evening. Its membership was, as he'd anticipated, dominated by women of a certain age whose lurid taste in literature belied their respectable appearance. The quality of their literary criticism was dire, but the Taylors, both retired university lecturers, provided both thoughtful analysis and ironic comments on the contributions of the other members. Derek and Gabrielle had begun to meet them occasionally in the pub, and tonight was to be their first visit to their house for a meal.

His fellow allotment-holders provided a different sort of companionship based on shared concerns for fertilisers, pests, diseases and late frosts. Derek had referred to them as 'old boys' until he'd realised he was of similar age to most of them. The twenty-year hiatus in his life had robbed him of the chance to acclimatise to the gradual onset of late middle age, having lost contact with those former friends of his generation who would have accompanied him on that journey.

He had sometimes worried that Gabrielle might resent the absence of the company of long-standing mutual friends. Those few of hers with whom she remained in contact rarely visited, and when they did, most treated him with ill-disguised wariness. Gabrielle had told him that she didn't care what they thought of him, that in any case clinging on to friends of one's youth was often merely a matter of nostalgia for the past, and that reunions with them often revealed how little they had left in common. So that was all right, then.

He entered the post office, joined the inevitable queue, and after finally being served, dropped the envelope in the post box with only the very slightest hesitation. Making his way to the allotments his thoughts were focused on whether he could risk planting out his runner beans.

Chapter 2

Dear Marcus,

I could, I suppose, start my story in 1985 or thereabouts: that's probably what you expect. But I want to tell you about some of the things that happened to me before that. After all, you don't really know me at all, do you Marcus? You don't want to believe all that's been written about me. But I'm not going to make excuses. I'm not one of those who believe that we have no free will, that we are all the prisoners of our environment, let alone the playthings of some manipulative supreme being. But the experiences of our youth must have some influence on the way we react to situations in later life. You're probably too young to appreciate that. But you will one day, Marcus; you will.

You've probably glanced at the photograph already. Have another look at it. I'm the young lad (pretty little boy, wasn't I?), and the woman sitting beside me is my mother. I think it was taken in 1945 or maybe 1946, so I would have been two or three. On the original photograph (this is a copy) was written - *With all our love, Derek and Norah*. It was probably sent to my father, who was serving in Germany. He must have brought it back with him when he was demobbed in 1947.

The photograph was taken outside my grandparents' house, where my mother and I lived until my father returned. I can remember it all very clearly. We're sitting outside the front door. The house was detached, not large, but spacious by the standards of the time. Grandpa had it built in the 1930s when his business was prospering. The inside is etched on my memory: I could make a reasonable shot of drawing a plan of its layout even now. The house was furnished in a way that would doubtless amuse you, Marcus: linoleum-covered floors with carpets that stopped short of the edges of the rooms, bulky arm-chairs placed each side of the fireplace, a grandfather clock, a sturdy dining-room table always covered with a cloth, a walnut-veneered wireless (that's what they called the radio) standing on a French-dresser along with Granny's collection of china crockery, and each room lit by a single 100 watt bulb suspended from the ceiling. Those bulbs gave out a harsh, unforgiving glare despite the fringed lampshades which encased them. A three year old wouldn't, of course, have noticed that everything was shabby, but it doubtless was, for this was at end of the war. The whole country was shabby then, so I since learned.

Other things in the house and its outbuildings would be beyond your comprehension, Marcus, like the long leather strap that hung from a hook by the deep square kitchen sink, just above the wooden draining-board. Actually it may have been called a strop, for that was its purpose: Grandpa used to strop his cut-throat razor on it before shaving. He always shaved in the kitchen. He may have been comfortably-off, but he wasn't what you'd probably call 'posh'. He was of humble origins, left school at eleven, and started out as a carpenter. That would have been back in the 1880s. He was a Victorian. Did you cover that period of English history at school, Marcus? Probably not. I bet you know a lot more about Hitler and Stalin, don't you?

I digress. Let me tell you some more about the house. Outside the kitchen door was a substantial brick out-house. Grandpa's store of coal (open fires, no central

15

heating) occupied about half the space. But on the other side were a copper and a mangle. Does anyone of your generation have the slightest inkling what these were, I wonder? Let me tell you. The copper was a large vat. Every Monday morning Granny would load this with the week's washing (yes, washing was done only once a week, back then) and boil it up. I imagine there must have been some sort of coal- or coke-fired grate under the copper, but the detail escapes my memory. But I *can* remember her red face as she poked at the washing with a long wooden pole, rather as though she were stirring a cooking pot. It must have been a considerable effort for her, because she was what was then called a cripple. I can't remember a time when she wasn't hunched over a walking stick. It was arthritis in the hips, I think.

So using the mangle most have been agony for her. 'Mangle' - it sounds a bit like an instrument of torture, doesn't it? She had to pull the wet washing out from the copper using a giant pair of wooden tongs, dump it all on a nearby wooden table, then pass each item through the mangle by turning a handle´ at the side. How she used to puff and pant when she turned that handle! I can remember the dirty suds being squeezed out by the rollers, and the heavily-creased items of clothing and linen being put in a wicker clothes basket. I imagine that rinsing must have taken place at some stage of the process, but I can't recall it. Have I said enough to give you some indication of what a mangle was, Marcus? If I've not made it clear, you could always Google it, I suppose.

I'm trying to give you some idea of the sort of world into which I was born. It's now fast disappearing from living memory. The age of austerity, it's been called. I don't think of it like that, of course, because I was a child then and didn't know anything better. But I do remember how Mum and Dad used to refer wistfully to 'before the war' as though it were some sort of golden age, but then the time of one's youth is always a golden age, isn't it?

At the risk of boring you (and I know how short the attention span of young people can be) I want to mention one more room in the house. Not a room, but a closet – a WC, in fact. Not the one upstairs; this one was outside – no, not a privy at the bottom of the garden; it was integral to the house, but access to it was from the yard. Every detail of that closet is seared on my brain. I spent a lot of time locked in it, you see.

I know what you're probably thinking – that this is going to be a story about child abuse. It isn't; at least, not in the sense that the term is currently used. I wasn't beaten or starved or made to participate in adult orgies. My Grandparents had my welfare at heart at all times, I'm sure. The problem was that they were Baptists. Very strict Baptists.

We live in a secular age, Marcus, and I imagine you're an agnostic, though you probably put 'C of E' on documents where you're asked to state your religion. You might be a convinced atheist, of course, and I hope you are: it would be an indication that you think for yourself. But, just in case you are a paid-up member of one or other of God's Squads, please bear with me if what follows is uncomfortable reading for you.

Back then, many people were believers in a Christian God. Not like today, where apparently most just have a vague feeling that there might be something or someone up there. No: then they went for the full works – immaculate conception, virgin birth, son of God, miracles, crucifixion, rising again on the third day. If you were C of E then most likely these things didn't impinge too much on the way you lived from day to day. But if you were a Catholic or a Nonconformist they permeated your very being. Of the two, the Catholics probably had the better deal – if you transgressed then you confessed, said a few Hail Marys, and were forgiven. Not for the Nonconformists, though: you had to atone for your sins in a much more uncomfortable way, and of the Nonconformists it was the Baptists who decreed the worst discomfort.

It was a bleak, cheerless upbringing, Marcus, although of course I didn't realise it at the time, having nothing with which to compare it. No alcohol in the house, of course. Very few books, apart from the Bible and various other religious tracts. No fairy stories, no picture books apart from an illustrated edition of the parables. Grace said by Grandpa before every meal, which was then eaten in silence. The wireless turned on only for the news on the Home Service (I didn't know the Light Programme existed until Dad came home). No other children round to play. No playing outside at all on Sunday. And all the time the constant exhortations to be good. *You must be a good little boy, Derek. God is watching you all the time. If you're bad, you will be punished.*

And it seemed that I *was* a bad little boy. I did things like knocking my plate off the table while grace was in progress. And interrupting Grandpa when he was talking to Granny, to ask if I could go out to play. And getting mud all over my shoes that day I strayed over his carefully-tended vegetable patch. It was after that incident that I was first introduced to the confines of the outside toilet – probably for only 10 minutes or so, but they didn't say how long I'd be kept there, and I was terrified.

Thereafter I tried so hard to be good, but the more I tried, the more things seemed to go wrong. Granny recited prayers to me and I was expected to learn them and repeat them back, but I was so nervous that I stumbled over the words, and on one occasion I was rendered totally mute. Grandpa said I was being wilfully disobedient (I didn't know what he meant by 'wilfully'), and later that evening, for the first time, my imprisonment took place in the dark. You might wonder what my mother's role was in all this – well, whatever she thought, she raised no objection that I can remember, not in my presence anyway. A long time afterwards, when I was a teenager, Dad told me that in his absence she'd once again become in thrall to her parents.

Good old Dad. When he came home the toilet confinements ended. He wasn't a Baptist, you see. How it was that Mum had been allowed to marry him I'll never know. But he was a strong, intelligent, determined man in his own quiet way, and I imagine he was more than an intellectual match for Grandpa, who, if I'm honest, was probably an ignorant old bigot. Grandpa died when I was ten, so I was unable to have an adult's eye view of him, and dad never spoke ill of him, probably out of loyalty to mum.

A year after Dad's return from Germany he managed to secure the tenancy of a council house on the outskirts of the village, to which he, Mum and I moved in 1948. From then on I was happy at home and would have been content to stay there, with Mum, all day. But the move coincided with my fifth birthday, and that September I had to start school.

Which is another story. Are you still with me, Marcus? I hope so, because the next episode should arrive in a few days. Until then, I'll let you return to the 21st century.

Derek Bailey

Chapter 3

Milton Keynes, Saturday 28 April

It was there, on the floor by the front door. It was easy to spot amongst the junk-mail. He'd been expecting its arrival for over a week. Now that it had come, his curiosity had evaporated; in fact he felt apprehensive. He still wasn't sure that he wanted to receive it. His mother certainly didn't want him to: she'd made that abundantly clear. But there was nothing she could do to stop it now.

'Any mail for me?' Sophie shouted from the kitchen.

'It looks like junk.'

He reached for the envelope, folded it, stowed it in the back pocket of his jeans, then scooped up the remaining rubbish and carried it to the kitchen. He dumped it on the breakfast bar in front of Sophie where she sat eating a croissant. It was Saturday. It was only at weekends that the couple had time to breakfast together. The price they had to pay for keeping their jobs was to arrive ever earlier and stay ever later at their respective offices. Information Technology was no longer the safe haven that it had once been, and the mortgage on their modern but cramped town house was eye-watering.

Sophie shuffled through the mail, dismissed it as crap, and asked why he'd bothered to give it to her. She was probably feeling hung-over. They'd gone to the *Zanzibar* the previous night. Marcus didn't really like clubbing. In any case he was beginning to think that Friday evenings might be better spent at home recovering from the week's exertions. But he didn't want to suggest it.

'What you doing this morning?' he asked.

'Shopping, what else? Aren't you coming with me? Sainsbury's bloody murder on a Saturday morning, innit?'

'There's something I've got to prepare for a meeting on Monday. It'll take me a few hours. And there's the housework to do, of course.'

'Shit, Marcus; like, can't you do it this afternoon? Or tomorrow?'

'I want to get it out the way. It'll be hanging over me, otherwise, and spoil the weekend.'

'What about *my* weekend?'

Marcus bit his tongue. He didn't want an argument now. That would delay her departure. He wanted her out of the house.

She finished her croissant, drained her coffee cup, and stood up.

'S'pose I'd better get dressed and go, then, if you can't be arsed to help me.'

She marched to the door, still clad in the old tee-shirt and pants that she wore in bed. Marcus noted that she was getting even skinnier. But he was lucky to have her, he supposed. They'd been living together for two years. He hoped that some time in the future they'd get married. But recently his mother had begun to warn him against that. She'd told him it was because of the insecurity of their employment. 'With the dire state that the economy's in, Marcus,' she'd said 'it wouldn't be wise to get too financially entangled with each other, would it?'

He busied himself in the kitchen, waiting for her departure. After ten minutes she re-emerged, carefully made up, wearing a low-cut top and skinny jeans. She looked almost fit, dressed like that.

'See you later, then.'
'Right'

Up in the spare bedroom that served as a study, Marcus pulled the envelope from his back pocket, unfolded it, and placed it on the desk in front of the computer. The address was hand-written. He didn't recognise the writing, but then there was no reason why he should. He sat, staring at it.

Did he really want to open it? The shredder was under the desk - so easy to destroy it, irretrievably, right now. Mum would be pleased if he did. She'd told him very little of what had happened, even when he'd become old enough to understand. Only when Gordon came along had things begun to improve, and some things explained. He'd learned to like his stepfather, not just for being the dad he'd never had, but for the way he'd made Mum easier to live with.

Undecided what to do, he stood up, went to the window and gazed out. The back garden, like all on the estate of modern town houses, was little more than a yard, and half of it was covered with paving slabs. The remainder was a threadbare lawn which he impatiently attacked with a strimmer whenever Sophie suggested that he should. But some of the neighbours were more horticulturally inclined. Their shrubs had provided a display of blossom in April, and their newly planted small trees were coming into leaf. Marcus couldn't name any of them: he cared little for the natural world and was usually unaffected by the change of seasons. He hadn't noticed that it was being a cold wet spring until people at work started moaning about it. But, he was suddenly aware, today was warm and sunny. He felt a lightening of the spirit. *I'm young, aren't I? And well qualified. Yes, I can cope with anything.*

And he could cope with the past, couldn't he? He would read the letter, satisfy his curiosity, and then destroy the contents. He would tell mum that what was written was rubbish, not worth bothering with. Then he would put it all behind him and shred without opening any further letters that might arrive.

He sat down at his desk, ripped open the envelope and pulled out several sheets of paper, all covered in neat handwriting, closely spaced. There was something else – a photograph, a small one, about 7cm square, black and white. He peered at it.

It was of a child and a woman, taken outside, sitting on brick steps which led up to a door. It was obviously taken a long time ago: the woman, though youngish, looked old-fashioned: she wore a flower-patterned dress which covered her knees, and had a sort of flat-on-top, curly-at-the-sides hairstyle. The child, a boy, wore a neat coat which was buttoned up to the collar and gave the appearance of being double breasted. He wore white socks which came half-way up his calves, and shoes with centre straps and buckles at the side. What were their ages? Hard to tell, given the weird fashions, but Marcus thought the woman might be in her late twenties. She wasn't bad looking. The boy could be anything between three and five. He looked like he'd been specially groomed for the photograph. He had thick dark wavy hair which had been carefully parted at the side. He was holding the woman's hand.

He unfolded the sheets of paper. There was no address at the top, just a date: April 27. It was like he'd been sent a report. Pity it wasn't word-processed: he wasn't used to long hand-written documents. He turned to the last page. At the bottom was a signature – *Derek Bailey*. Well, yes: he knew who it was from.

He turned back to the first page and began to read.

What is all this? After reading four paragraphs Marcus was irritated by the way frequent use was being made of his first name, as though he was one of Bailey's old friends. Worse than that, it was patronising. And now Bailey seemed intent on giving him a history lesson; who needs that? Marcus hated history. What was the point of it? Bailey was probably one of those wrinklies who lived in the past and made no attempt to get with the modern world. His letter certainly gave that impression. Marcus wasn't sure that he could be bothered to finish it. He had better things to do, hadn't he?

But had he? Sometimes he felt a bit lost at the weekends. Friday and Saturday nights were okay he supposed, at a club or in a bar with Sophie. But, once he'd finished the housework, the daytime hours dragged. He couldn't spend much time on Facebook, and certainly not on the other websites he visited, with Sophie around. He hadn't any hobbies except photography; work took precedence. And he hadn't made any real friends in the town – oh, there were those that he and Sophie met up with at the club, but they were just casual acquaintances. Not like the guys on his course at Uni, whose company he still missed. Did Sophie feel the same about her mates, he wondered? They'd always been part of a group. Now they weren't. Was that, he wondered, why they'd started bickering recently?

He looked at the letter. *I might as well carry on reading this rubbish.*

When he'd finished the letter, he was mystified, what with all that stuff about religion. Marcus didn't like being mystified: he inhabited a world which dealt in facts, facts that could be memorised, understood, analysed and preferably digitised. His reading was restricted to magazines that informed him about the latest developments in computing and digital photography. The small bookshelf in the lounge held only manuals and reference books. The last time he'd read a novel was when he was in Year 11 just before taking his GCSEs. At school he'd hated being confronted with prose that served no purpose, prose that seemed to him to be designed to confuse rather than explain. And he'd hated those few of his fellow pupils, girls mainly, who seemed able to extract hidden and inexplicable messages from the works of fiction that they read.

A work of fiction – that was what Bailey's letter reminded him of. It was full of long words and complicated sentences – the sort of thing that arts graduates would read and then praise for its style and its themes and nuances, whatever *they* were. The sort of stuff you heard on those literary programmes on Radio 4. Why didn't Bailey just come out and say what he had to say? Was he playing some sort of game? Why go into all that historical rubbish about, what was it, the age of austerity? And who cares about what religious beliefs his grandparents had?

Suddenly angry, he crumpled up the letter and photograph and stuffed them into the wastepaper bin. He wanted nothing more to do with them, and he'd destroy any further letters from Bailey as soon as they arrived. He glanced at his watch. Sophie would be back soon. Could they, he wondered, afford to go to the local pub for lunch as well as out to the club this evening? A few shandies would calm him down. And a lunchtime drink might put Sophie in a better mood.

Chapter 4

Milton Keynes, Tuesday 1 May

He was home at a reasonable time, for once. Jenkins, his boss, had told him to leave at five, saying that he'd stay on and deal with the outstanding work. This had made Marcus uneasy – if Jenkins felt the need to demonstrate his own indispensability then it didn't bode well for the future of the department. After the cut-backs in April there were only six staff left in it, and Marcus was the most junior. And there were rumours that the council was considering outsourcing some of its services to private companies, and Information Technology might well be one of these. Sophie worked in the private sector, but even with her derisory pay her position was by no means secure.

She wouldn't be home for at least an hour. The arrangement was that whoever got home first should cook the supper. He opened the door of the freezer cabinet – three pizzas, four Sainsbury's ready meals for two, and a chicken tikka bhuna. He didn't fancy any of those. Maybe he could make an omelette? He investigated the contents of the fridge – only two eggs. It looked like it would have to be pasta. Sophie wasn't too keen on pasta.

He had plenty of time before he needed to start preparing it. He went up to the bedroom, took off his suit and pulled on a tee-shirt and jeans. He glanced at himself in the mirror: there was something not quite right, he didn't look like other young men who wore jeans. He couldn't put his finger on why this should be; it wasn't as if he were fat or anything.

He went into the study and turned on his computer: he had time to finish setting up the spreadsheet on which he intended to monitor the precise details of their income and expenditure. It was an easy process and his mind kept drifting back to the nagging worry about potential redundancy. Spending cuts and unemployment – these were things that had never concerned him before. Perhaps he ought to pay more attention to politics. He hadn't bothered to vote in the last election; they all seemed alike to him.

The telephone beside his desk trilled and he jumped. The digital read-out on the handset revealed the caller to be his mother. Oh God, he'd forgotten to call her at the weekend. He knew what this was about.

'Hello, Mum.'

'You didn't phone at the weekend.'

'No, sorry. I forgot. Had quite a lot to do.'

'Well, have you heard?'

'Heard what?'

'From Bailey, of course. You know I've been on tenterhooks. You might show a bit more consideration, Marcus, you know how upsetting I find–'

'Yes, I've heard. Had a letter on Saturday; it was–'

'On *Saturday*? And you didn't think to call me?'

'I didn't phone you because the letter was just a load of rubbish. He didn't mention you, or Dad. It was boring, just a long account of his childhood, that's all. I've thrown it away. If he writes again I'll shred it without opening it.'

Silence, then –

'So you needn't have put me through all this. Why you agreed to let him write to you I'll never know.'

'Mum, we've been through all that. I was thinking he might apologise or–'

'*Apologise*? A man like that? And do you really think an apology would go any way towards–'

'Well, he'd taken the trouble to track me down, hadn't he?'

'Yes, and I still don't understand how he managed to do it.'

Marcus sighed. For someone only just turned 50 his mother had a closed mind when it came to the Internet. He'd explained several times how simple it was to trace people using Facebook or *192.com*, but she never seemed to take it in. Sometimes he thought she was being deliberately thick.

'Mum, I've told you how easy it can be, especially with a name like Marcus Sidelski. Can't be many of those around.'

'Oh, I suppose you're blaming me, are you?'

'No, of course I'm not. Look Mum, I've got to go. Sophie'll be back soon and it's my turn to cook the supper.'

His mother sniffed. It wasn't an on-the-verge-of-tears sniff. It was one of those haughty, dismissive sniffs that he remembered his grandmother using when offended.

'I'll ring you later in the week, Mum. Goodbye.'

The line went dead.

Marcus felt annoyed, not just with his mother, but with himself, for the conversation had resurrected the ambivalent feelings he had about his surname. He'd hated his surname from his time at primary school, because it was peculiar and his classmates teased him. They all had the same surname as their mothers; why didn't he? Her explanation that Sidelski had been his father's name and that he should be proud of it only added to his confusion. Later, when he became more aware of marital conventions, he'd asked her why *she* wasn't called Sidelski. 'I'll tell you when you're a bit older, Marcus,' she'd replied, adding that he wasn't really old enough to understand but that it was nothing to worry about.

But he *had* worried about it. He'd always known his Dad was dead, but when, later, he was told that Dad had died before he was born he found it very confusing. She should have been straighter with him, much sooner, instead of leaving it to his stepfather Gordon to tell him. And now she was blaming him for ... well, he was quite justified in feeling angry, wasn't he?

He pulled off his spectacles and rubbed his eyes. He caught himself in the act, and stopped. Sophie was always on at him to get out of the habit; she said it made him look like he was about to burst into tears. But he'd done it for as long as he could remember, starting at primary school when the teasing had started. If they weren't teasing him about his name then they were teasing him about his specs. He hadn't realised at the time that they were very cheap specs. When he realised that they were he'd blamed his mother for not buying ones that were more up-to-date. Now, he wore the most fashionable frames he could afford, slim and black around narrow rectangular lenses. But somehow they didn't look quite right on him. He couldn't work out why this was. There was nothing wrong with the shape of his face, was there?

The front door slammed. *Sophie.* He fumbled with the mouse in his attempt to turn off the computer but then realised she wasn't to know what time he'd got in.

'Hello,' he shouted from the study door.

'You're in, then.'

'Yes, just. I'm getting changed.' He turned back to the computer, blanked the screen and hurried into the bedroom. Just in time: she'd started to mount the stairs.

'All right?' he asked, as she entered.

'No. Shit day. They're piling more and more on me.'

She didn't look at him while speaking. She rarely did. When was it that he'd first noticed this? And when did he first notice that she never asked how *his* day had been? He watched her as she opened the door of the built-in wardrobe. She wore a smart black suit as required by the company. He quite liked her in that suit – the knee-length skirt showed off her legs, which were good, and the jacket disguised the fact that she didn't have a bottom. He hadn't been aware of her lack of a bottom when he first met her at uni: it was one of his flatmates who had alerted him to it.

She stripped off her skirt, jacket and shirt. No disguising the lack of arse now. Nor the flat chest. He remembered the first time he'd seen her naked, in the bed-sitter she'd occupied at uni. Her skinniness didn't matter too much then. But, he suddenly noticed, she was getting even thinner – almost emaciated.

'What yer getting us for a meal, then?'

'Pasta, I thought.'

'Christ, Marcus, you know I don't like pasta. There's plenty of other stuff in the freezer. What's wrong with a curry?'

'I don't fancy curry tonight.'

'Well then, there's some pizzas, and some of them ready meals. Anything but fuckin' pasta.' She bent to the task of pulling on her jeans.

Marcus hurried downstairs en-route to the freezer. At least a pizza could be heated from frozen.

Her mood had improved once they'd finished eating. The remains of the bottle of red wine left over from Sunday had helped. Marcus let her finish it: he didn't really like wine, and made do with a small bottle of cider. As usual they'd eaten in the lounge, sitting on the settee, trays balanced on knees, the TV on but the sound muted. He walked in from the kitchen and handed her a mug of Nescafe. He sat down in the chair opposite her.

'Have you got much to do, then?'

'I said they were piling more on me, didn't I? Take at least an hour.'

'D'you need to use the study?'

'Nah. I'll use me laptop down here. Have you got stuff to do?'

'A bit.' He decided against confessing that the Department's work was drying up; he couldn't face an interrogation about his prospects tonight. 'Then I might send a few mails.'

'To your uni mates, I suppose?'

'Well, yes. On Facebook.'

'Don't know why you bother. They never reply, do they?'

'Jason and Mike do, sometimes.'

'Those two losers. They would, wouldn't they? Only saddos like them have to try and keep in contact. Anyway, I dunno why you keep pretending we had an awesome time at uni. It wasn't that great. Glad to be out of it, me.'

Marcus flinched. Worse than being reminded that university was not the liberating time that he'd anticipated was the implication that he was one of the losers and saddos.

'Well, *we* met there, didn't we?' he said.

For the first time that evening she made eye-contact.

'We could have met anywhere. People like us seek each other out, don't we? Just like lookers do. Everyone finds their own level.'

Marcus didn't really understand her last remark. Okay, he wasn't the best-looking guy, but he wasn't that bad, and he had brains. So did she; that was why they got together at uni, wasn't it? And it wasn't that bad a time. Some of his mates were quite ... well, lively, and witty, not the bunch of geeks that the arts and humanities students made them out to be. And Sophie – well, she wasn't unattractive by any means.

She'd turned her attention to her laptop. He studied her. Hair glossy, quite a nice skin. Pity about her mouth though – it was sort of twisted, and she would keep chewing the inside of her cheek. Nose a bit bulbous, maybe. Spectacles, which hid her best feature, her eyes: very dark, almost black. Thick eyebrows. But she wasn't that bad. She'd been very friendly, right from Freshers' Week. Not just with him, of course, but the others didn't seem to like her much. So in the end she latched on to him. Was it, he wondered, because he –

The telephone rang. Sophie, occupied with her laptop, ignored it. Marcus removed it from its base, noting too late that it was once again his mother calling. He was usually quick off the mark and took calls from her on the study handset. Now he'd have to carry it into the kitchen: he didn't like Sophie being present when he was talking to Mum.

He pressed the receive button as soon as he was alone.

'Hello again, Mum.'

'Marcus. I've been worrying ever since we last spoke. Please re-assure me. You're *absolutely certain* that you'll destroy any further letters from Bailey before opening them?'

'I said so, didn't I?'

'Easy to say on the spur of the moment. Did you mean it?'

'Yes. I know his handwriting now. Anything that arrives with that writing on the envelope will go straight in the shredder.'

'And you were telling the truth when you said his last letter didn't mention me, or your Dad?'

'I told you; it was all about his childhood.'

Silence. Then –

'All right. Sorry to fuss. Goodnight, Marcus.'

'Goodnight, Mum.'

He pressed the off button, and turned. Oh God, he'd left the kitchen door ajar. And Sophie was standing in the passage.

'What are you doing there?'

'What d'you mean? Just bringing out me mug, aren't I? What are you looking so guilty about?'

'Guilty? Don't know what you mean.'

'That was your mother on the phone, wasn't it? You always disappear when it's her.'

'Not always. Didn't want to disturb you, that's all. You'd started working.'

He stepped past her, went into the lounge and sat down. From the kitchen came the sound of running water. S*he's only swilling her mug under the tap. No chance of her doing the plates, I bet. It would only take her a few minutes.*

His forecast was correct. Sophie came in, sat down and reached for her laptop. Marcus picked up the *Daily Mail*. When he was at university he'd tried the *Daily Telegraph*, but there was far too much arty stuff in it. The *Mail* was much better for busy young professionals. It gave a good concise summary of the news, written in a common-sense way. Marcus was all in favour of common sense.

'What was all that about putting an envelope in the shredder?'

Marcus started. 'Eh?'

'What were you going on about when you told your mother you'd put an envelope in the shredder? What envelope?' Sophie addressed him without taking her eyes from the laptop screen.

'Were you listening?'

33

'Listening? To you talking to your mother? Got better things to do. Couldn't help hearing, that's all.'

Marcus groped for an explanation. He couldn't think of one.

'And whose childhood was it you were talking about?'

Marcus felt himself redden. He'd never told Sophie the details of his upbringing; she always made clear her impatience with people who went on about the past, and she was equally unforthcoming about her own early years. All he'd told her was that his father had died before he was born and that his mother had later married Gordon whom he looked on as his dad. There hadn't seemed any point in divulging any more, especially after Sophie had made apparent her dislike for his mother. 'Didn't think your folks would be so snooty' had been her comment after her first meeting with Mum and Gordon.

So there was no way he was going to attempt an explanation about the letter from Bailey. He decided attack was the best means of defence.

'It's family stuff. You're not interested in my family. It's just something that I promised Mum I'd do for her. Not important. Not really any of your business.'

'Oh, fuck off, Marcus.'

'Okay, I will.' He launched himself from his chair, headed for the stairs, stopped.

'I'm just going to send a few mails, Soph. I'll be down in about 30 minutes'

'Whatever.'

Chapter 5

31 May

Hello again, Marcus. Have you been waiting eagerly for this, I wonder? Or were you bored beyond measure by my first instalment? Perhaps you didn't even read it; had second thoughts, maybe, and threw it away as soon as you realised who'd sent it. Whether or not you're still with me, I shall continue writing. For me, it's a form of catharsis.

My last episode ended with me and my parents living in a council house (what you would probably call 'social housing') at the edge of the village, about half a mile away from my grandparents. The village was located in a leafy area of the Home Counties. It's probably a small town now, for it had, and still has, a railway station only 50 minutes journey time from London. I would imagine that the houses in that small estate are now all owner-occupied – indeed, Dad purchased his in the 1980s. He had no time for Mrs Thatcher but he took advantage of her largesse on that occasion. I can remember that house clearly, especially the kitchen, where we spent most of our time in winter, because the coke-fuelled stove kept it warm. I remember the kitchen well – patterned curtains, a gas oven ignited by a wand on a hose, cupboards with glass-doors that slid in grooves, a formica topped table, plastic-seated stools.

I don't think I mentioned that dad was a clerical officer with the County Council. Such species probably no longer exist. The job wasn't well paid, hence the council house. My grandfather refused to help Mum and Dad financially because he was incensed that they chose not to raise me as a Baptist. We saw very little of my grandparents, despite their close proximity.

This instalment is all about my time at primary school. It was a Church of England school. I wasn't sent there through choice; it was the only primary school in the village. So, having escaped from indoctrination by Nonconformists I came to be immersed in the dogma and rituals of the Established Church. Not quite frying-pan into fire, but pretty close.

Let me recount what happened on my first day at school. I'm sure it was like nothing that your generation has ever experienced, Marcus, growing up as you have in an age of educational enlightenment. I'll tell it as though I were writing a story, so forgive the literary embellishments. I can't write as a child would think.

Mum walked me to school, of course. She escorted me into the infants' classroom and delivered me into the care of Miss Daniels, an untidy, mouse-like woman with lifeless hair, tendrils of which escaped her loose bun and dangled greasily around her neck. I remember she had a large mole on the side of her nose. The room seemed vast. It had high windows under which bulky radiators served as shelves for rows of bottles of milk. Small tables with chairs on each of the four sides were being occupied by children, some of them staring round wide-eyed, others sniffing, a few sobbing. One had refused to sit down and was screaming, clutching desperately at her mother's skirt.

'They'll all soon settle down,' Miss Daniels said to Mum as she escorted me to one of the tables, 'and Derek's going to be a very good boy aren't you? Say goodbye to mummy, Derek, you'll be seeing her again soon.'

Mum kissed me goodbye and with an 'I'll see you very soon, Derek,' hurried from the room. I felt an instant lurch of loneliness and panic. Miss Daniels smiled at me and said 'Some of your friends are here Derek: you sit and talk to them for a minute,' and I recognised, sitting at the table, Carol Rance and Robert Seymour, both from the estate. They aren't really my friends, I wanted to protest, but my attention was distracted by the farewells taking place at some of the other tables, Miss Daniels moving urgently from one valedictory scene to another, gently ushering mothers from the room while at the same time making comforting noises of reassurance to those left in her charge.

The morning was spent playing with lumps of plasticine, interrupted for a while by the distribution of the bottles of milk I'd noticed on the radiators, and on occasion by the escorting of some of the children to the toilets outside in the playground. Miss Daniels continued trying to quell the tears and sniffs of those of her charges who had not been mollified by plasticine and milk, all the time casting anxious looks at the door to the right of the blackboard which led to an adjacent classroom. At times during the morning ill-tempered adult male shouts had been heard through the door, but I was more concerned with my own woes to pay much attention to anything outside the room in which I was confined.

Towards the end of the morning, however, the door opened, and the evident source of the shouting entered. He was short, stocky, and had a ginger beard.

'Now, Miss Daniels,' said the man in a strange accent which only years later I came to realise was Yorkshire, 'Has everyone settled down?'

'Children, please stand up,' said Miss Daniels. This was an unknown ritual and we took our time to comply:

she had to approach several of the infants to urge them to their feet. 'This is Mr Harley, our headmaster. He wants to talk to you for a minute.'

Mr Harley adopted the speechmaking pose, fingers in waistcoat pockets, that was to become so familiar to me over the next six years.

'Now children,' he said. 'You have come to school to learn, and your teachers will do all they can to help you. Always obey your teachers, always work hard and behave well, and you will have a happy time here. If on the other hand you are disobedient or lazy or badly behaved, you will find yourself in my office,' (he gestured to the door to the left of the blackboard) 'and you won't like that. Do you understand me? You are going to be good children, aren't you?'

'Say "yes Mr Harley" children,' exhorted Miss Daniels, and we obliged in a ragged, muted, sing-song chorus. The headmaster nodded approvingly, turned, and walked back to his classroom.

Soon it was lunchtime. We were shepherded into the assembly hall, set out with long tables at which sat more children than I had ever seen in one place. A sour smell rose from metal containers laid out on a trestle table behind which stood a pink-overalled teacher. Miss Daniels led us to the containers and handed each of us in turn a heavy plate onto which the pink overall slopped the meal, and ushered us to the long tables where we were enjoined to eat it. I can't remember what the meal was, but I do recall that it was horrible. I couldn't eat it, and neither could many of my classmates. The pudding wasn't much better – I think it might have been semolina with a blob of jam in the middle.

The older children sat at the tables around us obviously had better appetites. When all the plates on a table had been emptied, the children were dismissed, having first carried their plates back to the serving area. But we remained seated.

Mr Harley entered and approached our table.

'Children,' he said quietly, his low tone more menacing than his shout, 'as this is your first day I will be kind to you, but in future I shall expect you to eat up your dinners. Many children less fortunate than you would be only too pleased to eat what you have left. Take them back to their classroom, Miss Daniels.'

The afternoon, in which we graduated to crayoning pictures on large sheets of brown paper, dragged on. I was becoming increasingly desperate to see my mother. Occasional sniffles of distress still punctuated the silence.

Suddenly, an enraged bellow from the next-door classroom: 'Right, my lad, that's it! You've been asking for it all day! It's the office for you, and don't say you've not been warned!' The door opened, and Mr Harley emerged, dragging behind him a boy whom he pulled across the front of the blackboard and into the office behind the left-hand door. The total silence in the classroom was then punctuated by six muffled hefty thwacks, followed first by cries, then by sobs. The door opened: the lad, still sobbing, ran back across the front of the blackboard, chased by Mr Harley wielding a bamboo cane, lashing at the boy's legs as he ran. In his distress the boy was unable to find the handle to the door to his classroom, enabling the headmaster to deliver two more blows to his backside before finally hauling him inside.

Miss Daniels fiddled with her straying wisps of hair. 'Get on with your drawing, children' she urged tremulously. Thirty-five pairs of hands tried shakily to oblige. Maybe some of my classmates would in later years forget their terror and say that discipline never did *them* any harm?

39

You think I'm exaggerating, perhaps, Marcus? I can assure you I'm not. That's how it was, and it was probably the same in most primary schools, back in the 40s. However, I have more to tell –

It wasn't long before I became aware that there was a difference between me and many of my classmates. I was the son of a white-collar worker and had been brought up to be clean and polite. Most of us in the village were no doubt characterised by a post-war patched-and-darned shabbiness, but some of the children in my class were poor to a degree that I'd never seen before. They had snot running out of their noses, some of them smelled, and they weren't very polite. Mum explained patiently that some of the people in the village were very poor but that it wasn't their fault, that I should realise how lucky I was, and that I must remember to be nice to them.

I tried to be nice, but I found that it wasn't appreciated, and was certainly not reciprocated. Indeed some of the older pupils seemed to hate me for some reason and threatened to bash me up in the playground. My fear of them diminished only gradually as, with the passing of the years, I progressed up the school and my tormentors left no doubt to continue, after a short violent induction of their own, their reign of terror at the secondary modern school in the manufacturing town some miles away.

I was encouraged in my school work by Mum and Dad. They were eager that I should make the best of the chances that they had never had. The years spent living with my grandparents had inculcated into me the belief that God rewarded those who led a quiet, sober life and punished those who were lazy and who strayed from the straight and narrow. So I already had worries about the potential wrath of the Almighty. These intensified when, after progressing from the infant classes, our teacher for daily Religious Instruction was Mr Harley. He spent most of the time dwelling on God's anger and jealousy, providing bloodthirsty examples from the Old Testament. From the hour of RI it was a seamless progression to the fiery furnace of his arithmetic lessons in which the cane usually made its first appearance of the day.

I dreaded arithmetic: in my own time and at my own pace I could usually arrive at the correct answers, but the quick-fire cerebral gymnastics required of the mental arithmetic tests left me floundering. I was more comfortable with spelling, sentence construction and eventually simple grammar, and when I got to Junior Three I found I was looking forward to English lessons. I enjoyed writing essays ('composition' it was called) and from then I came to be regarded as one of the brighter pupils, a label which served to shield me from the worst of Mr Harley's excesses.

He was a bully. His severest punishments were often reserved for minor infringements of the rules or for mere slowness to learn. On the other hand more blatant transgressions seemed to be ignored, as when Robert Seymour, in the silence of a class exercise, had let fly a prolonged rumbustious rolling fart that echoed in the high ceiling and reverberated round the four corners of the room, the expression on his face denoting evident relish and enjoyment. Perhaps farting wasn't against the rules? And never once during my time at the school had any of the many incidents of vicious playground bullying ever been punished corporally. I began to think that it wasn't right, it wasn't fair.

But perhaps it was fear of him that made me work hard – or perhaps I was naturally conscientious? Whichever, six years at the school resulted in my passing the Eleven-plus. In fact at the time I had no clear idea of what passing the Eleven-plus really meant. I remembered sitting the examination, but no mention had been made by Mr Harley or by any other teacher as to why I was doing so. It was just another of those things that happened at school, like learning the alphabet or saying one's 12-times table, which one did not think to question, or even if one had considered questioning, would not have dared.

Richard Ingham and John Jeffries also passed. Mr Harley announced our success one morning to the whole class, and then allowed us to go home to tell our parents, tempering his munificence by threatening us with dire consequences if we were not back in time for afternoon classes. My mother was delighted, of course. She said she was so pleased that I wouldn't have to go to Jasmine Street Secondary with all those rough boys. She cooked me a makeshift meal and then insisted on taking me to the telephone box on the next street to call Dad at work. It took a long time for the call to be put through. As a result, I was late back to school. I arrived just as the class rose to acknowledge Mr Harley's entrance, but my attempt to slip into my place unnoticed failed.

'Stay standing, Bailey,' barked Harley. 'So, you think now that you're going to Grammar School you're too grand to ignore my instructions? Why are you late back when I made it quite clear that you were allowed to be absent only until the end of the dinner hour?'

'My mother made me phone my Dad to tell him I'd passed, sir.'

'And you think that good enough reason, boy? Well, do you?'

'No sir, sorry sir.'

'Well, I think you need to be taught that even grammar school boys' (the last words said with a sneer) 'don't get away with disobedience. Come out to the front.'

I shuffled to the front of the class, there to receive one of Harley's more merciful punishments, a single stroke of the cane to the palm of each hand, delivered without the usual ferocity, perhaps in belated recognition of the special nature of the day. Yet as I returned to my desk, the usual shame at having been publicly humiliated was absent, and my fear of Harley, though still there, was leavened by a feeling new to me, that of hatred.

After school was over I walked home as usual with Donald and Tim, two boys from the estate. They were chattering, but I wasn't listening. I was thinking about what it would be like at the grammar school, whether there'd be any bullying, and whether Dad might be persuaded to buy me a bike as a reward for passing so I could cycle there instead of going by bus.

Then Donald poked me in the ribs.

'Too posh to talk to us now that you're a grammar school boy, are you?' he said.

I was mortified. I started to say that no, I was thinking of what to say to dad, but then I realised that to mention the matter of the bicycle would further inflame their envy. Then I got angry, very angry. I did something I'd never done before, throughout the whole time at the school – I hit him, hard. Donald was a weedy boy and he fell over. So I kicked him. I got into a lot of trouble about that, as you can imagine. Mum and Dad had to go to the school to see Mr Harley. Surprisingly, I didn't get the cane, but my remaining months at primary school were even less comfortable than the six preceding years.

And there I shall leave it, Marcus. I hope it's been of some interest, and that it may have whetted your appetite for the next instalment. I have to say that I enjoyed writing it. As you can imagine, I've had a lot of time over the past twenty years to hone my writing skills; there wasn't much else to do. But that's another story.

Derek.

Chapter 6

Once again he'd left work early. Jenkins had let them all go early. This should have intensified his worries about redundancy, but today Marcus had other things on his mind. In fact, he was glad that he'd get home before Sophie. He had something to hide.

The previous evening Sophie had been parking their battered Mondeo just as he got to the house. It was rare for their arrival to coincide. He hadn't waited for her to get out, but went to open the front door. Inside, there was only one item of mail on the mat, a brown A5 envelope with the by-now familiar writing on it. In his hurry to pick it up he'd dislodged his spectacles, and charged blindly up the stairs to the study where he shoved the envelope under the pile of magazines stacked on the shelf behind the VDU screen.

He had been placed in a quandary. To leave the envelope in the study risked Sophie finding it, because he'd known she intended to use the desk-top pc that evening. There was no reason why she should choose to interfere with his photography magazines, but she did have periodic attempts to move his stuff about to make room for hers. He'd wondered about shredding it there and then, but the noise would have alerted her, and she always insisted on checking items before he shredded them lest he dispose of something of importance to her. Thus he'd spent a fraught evening in front of the TV while Sophie sat upstairs, her face only a few inches from the offending article. He thought he'd have to wait till the weekend before having a chance to be rid of it.

But now, thanks to Jenkins, he would be able to enjoy the night free from worry. Humming tunelessly, he walked up the short path to the front door, opened it (no mail at all today) and mounted the stairs, willing himself to move slowly and deliberately: there was no need to panic, was there?

There it was, just where he'd put it, under the magazines. He switched on the shredder and was just about to insert the envelope when he noticed that it wasn't sealed properly. *Oh my God, has Sophie opened it?* He examined it – no, it hadn't been opened; just one side not stuck down. Well, he might as well open it completely, the contents would be easier to shred if he took them out.

He extracted the sheets of paper. He couldn't help reading the first few lines. And then the next paragraph. And then the next ...

He pushed up his spectacles and rubbed his eyes. Some of what Bailey had written he didn't understand. But the account of his time at school ... well, it had got to him, somehow; he wasn't sure why. He would quite like to read it again, and the bit about farting in class was quite funny.

He was tempted to keep the letter, maybe tuck it into his file of bank statements. But it was risky, even though Sophie had her own bank account. Then, he remembered his promise to his mother. He turned on the shredder and pushed the sheets of paper through it. Well, he'd kept half his promise, hadn't he?

Chapter 7

Marcus deposited the last of the carrier-bags on the kitchen floor.

'Want any help putting it all away?' he asked.

'No. Can do it quicker myself.' Sophie was stowing the shopping in the cabinets. Marcus wished she would let him do it: she always put things in the wrong place.

'Anything else I can do?'

'Yeah. Unload the dishwasher.'

Marcus bent to his task. Saturday morning, again. They'd left the club early the previous evening. None of their friends had been there. He knew why: the week before he'd overheard Max talking about the party he was throwing at his place. Marcus had waited for an invitation but it hadn't been forthcoming. He assumed Sophie had overheard as well, but she'd said nothing. Neither had he.

So they were home by 11 and in bed by 11.30. They'd had sex, a rare occurrence. Perhaps, thought Marcus, that was why he was no longer bothered about the snub from Max, and why Sophie was in a better mood than usual. Or maybe it was because, for once on a Saturday, she wasn't hung-over

'D'you want anything to eat?' she asked, face buried in one of the cabinets.

'No. I'm not hungry yet.'

'Well, you can get your own, can't you?'

'Course I can. Why? What are *you* going to do?'

She shoved at a packet of muesli that was resisting her attempt to close the cabinet door, gave up, and turned to face him.

'I'm going over to see Em. Haven't been for ages.'

Emma was her elder sister who lived on a sink estate on the outskirts of Daventry. Long abandoned by her partner, she was raising two kids on Child Allowance, Housing Benefit and Job Seeker's Allowance. Marcus didn't like her. He knew that Sophie knew he didn't like her. Hence her defensive tone when she announced her intention to visit her.

'Right. What time d'you reckon you'll be back?'

'I dunno; oh, about six probably.'

'Right.' He paused. *Now's the right time.*

'Soph ...'

'What?'

'What say we give the club a miss tonight?'

'Why?'

The response was mild. Emboldened, Marcus ploughed on.

'It's just that I really fancy a curry. Shall I order one? And I could get a video for after. Let's just relax - chill out, I mean.'

A moment's silence, then 'Yeah, why not?'

Result! Marcus mentally punched the air.

Alone in the study, he logged on. Facebook. Plenty of postings, but not for him. Nothing from Jason or Mike. Why didn't they ever reply? Some chat between his Cyber-Friends, but mostly chat between them and *their* Friends. All about their Friday nights. Lots of photos, too. Everyone evidently drunk, having a good time. Guys red faced, red-eyed, sweating. Girls with boobs on display, short skirts, some showing their pants.

Downcast, he sought refuge in his Profile page. He had 21 Friends listed. Some of them he'd never met; they were Friends of Friends who had accepted his invitation to be his Friend as well, though subsequently they'd never responded to his pokes. He clicked on one, a really fit babe; her name was Nina. She had 147 Friends. Jason had 97, Mike had 80. Marcus had the least. He considered poking Jason – *no, he won't respond if he couldn't be bothered to reply to the last message. Poke Nina, maybe? No, she'd probably block me. Don't want that – she's worth following, just as an observer.*

Sophie didn't know about his secret voyeurism, at least he didn't think she did. She didn't do Facebook; she said it was dangerous. One of her colleagues had posted a joke about her boss, and the boss had read it and she'd been demoted – what an old saddo he must be, checking up on his staff like that. Facebook was for the young. Anyone over 40 who used it must be a bit of a perve.

But what about Bailey? Would he use it? Given his past he just might. He typed Derek Bailey into the search panel. Scores of them, probably hundreds if he were to scroll down. He couldn't be bothered to go through them all. He might be on Friends Reunited though; that was for wrinklies, wasn't it? But Marcus wasn't a member. Might be worth joining, some time. He knew that Bailey could be found by Googling his name; he'd done that some years ago - on Wikipedia there was a reference to the events of 1989, but it hadn't told him anything he didn't know already.

He'd logged onto Facebook so as to forget about Bailey, but there seemed to be no escaping from him. He wasn't thinking so much about Bailey himself, but what he'd written about his primary school days. It had made Marcus start thinking about his own time at his first school, something he'd largely blanked out. He could recall being at the grammar school very well, too well – but primary school? Not a lot; just the teasing about his name and his specs. But wait – yes, there had been some other sort of hassle: something had

49

happened which meant that his mother had to come to the school – he could remember her worried face even now; and she'd taken him home, but why? Had he been in trouble? Had something been done to him? Something that Bailey had written had triggered a memory, a memory so fleeting that it couldn't be grasped, like a vivid dream that on waking immediately slips away. And now he'd destroyed the letter he couldn't revisit it.

Enough of this. To hell with Bailey, and Facebook. He'd wanted Sophie to leave the house, to give him space to do his own thing undisturbed. But as so often happened, now he was alone he didn't know how to fill the time. Google some of the porno sites, perhaps? No, mustn't. He ought to get a new computer, because all websites he'd visited would remain forever on his hard drive, and no software had yet been devised that could successfully delete them. But Sophie would never agree to him upgrading: she kept going on about how short of money they were. She wouldn't even let him buy an i-Phone: his colleagues at work all mocked his out-dated mobile.

He logged off, then sat, drumming his fingers on the desk top. Nothing for it but to go down town early to HMV, get the DVD for the evening's entertainment. He ran downstairs and reached the sitting room before he realised that Sophie had gone and wasn't available to give him a lift. Marcus couldn't drive.

The curry hadn't been a success. It had been delivered half an hour late. Then Sophie's Chicken Madras had been too hot ('If I'd wanted a fuckin' vindaloo I'd have ordered one') and the naan bread was too salty. Shovelling the uneaten remains into the kitchen-waste container, Marcus was berating himself for not having told her before the meal that he hadn't been to get the

DVD. He had hoped that the Madras would go some way to lifting her from the foul mood that she was in when she'd returned home. She was always like that after a visit to her sister.

Marcus wasn't allowed to criticise Emma or her life-style, but there was no evidence of sibling affection between the two, and Sophie didn't hide the fact that her infrequent visits were made out of a sense of duty. 'I'm all she's got, aren't I? Since mum died and that bastard left her. So I've gotta see her sometimes. You go and see your bloody mother often enough, don't you? And *she's* got a husband, *and* she's not short of dosh' – these were the sort of sentiments usually expressed by Sophie prior to a trip to Daventry. But on returning from her visits she was always tight-lipped and glowering, and Marcus had learned not to ask the reason why.

And now, he thought, putting the plates and cutlery in the dishwasher, I've got to tell her there's no DVD to watch. The prospect of the evening to come was profoundly depressing. Maybe she'd agree to walk to the local pub? She couldn't drive anywhere, not after all the lager she'd consumed in an attempt to make the curry more palatable. Marcus insisted that Sophie adhered strictly to the drink-drive laws (a taxi was another expense incurred on their usual weekend visits to the club), for he was a firm believer in abiding by the law. The crowd at the club seemed to find this amusing.

He joined Sophie, who was sitting on the settee. She'd gone on to wine, he noticed. She was staring into space and ignored him as he sat down in the armchair opposite her.

'How was Em, then?' he ventured.

'How d'you *think* she was? Cooped up in a grotty flat with two kids and chavs for neighbours? I mean, what sort of question's that?'

51

'Okay, Okay.'

Silence for several minutes.

'Soph.'

'What?'

'I wondered ... I mean, d'you fancy going down the Plough?'

'The Plough? On a Saturday night? You've gotta be joking! It'll be full of old saddos eating. I'd sooner get wasted here. Anyway, I thought we were watching a DVD. What did you get?'

'I didn't get one. You left without telling me. So I couldn't get into town.'

'What's wrong with the bus?'

'But Soph, it takes ages on the bus; anyway– '

'You had all afternoon!' She swivelled round to face him. 'You *wanker*. What we gonna do now? Spend all evening staring at each other?'

'Well, there might be something on the box.'

She picked up the TV guide and hurled it at him. 'Go on then, find something. You always say it's all crap, don't you? Anyway, I don't want to watch TV. Why don't you go and play with your computer? That's what you wanna do really, isn't it? Spend time poking your Facebook Friends. Friends! You haven't *got* any friends. Oh for Chrissake stop rubbing your eyes, you pathetic little nerd. You're boring, *boring*. Take you away from your computer and your camera and you're nothing. And ...'

Marcus, his fists still clenched over his eyes, stopped listening. A deep, slow anger began to well up within him. *The cow. The bitch. The slag – yes, a slag, that's what she'd been at uni. Why do I put up with all this? It's always been the same. No one gives me a chance to explain things. Everyone interrupts me all the time.* His anger grew into an all-consuming rage.

'... and I bet you look at porn sites, don't you? I've seen your photography magazines, I know the sort of thing that turns you on. Can't get it in real life, can you? Can't cope with *anything* in real life. And you think you're so twenty-first century, don't you, with your skinny jeans and your gelled hair. All the guys at the club think you're a nerd. I've heard 'em talking. D'you know what they say? They say– '

'Shut up. *Shut up!*' He sprang out of his chair and lunged towards her.

The slap, delivered to her face with full force, provided an orgasmic relief. Almost as satisfying was her look of terror as she slumped backwards. But remorse followed immediately when, in the seconds before her hands covered her face, he heard her scream and saw the blood trickling from her nose. *God, what have I done? What have I done?*

'Why did you do it, Marcus?' He could hear his mother speaking. 'Darling, you *must* try and control your temper.'

Chapter 8

Hello Marcus, are you still with me? First of all, <u>don't open the enclosed packet</u>, not until I tell you to. I'm aware that your generation are easily bored without visual or aural stimuli, so the contents might serve to enhance your interest when you get tired of the written word.

If you managed to finish reading my last letter you will remember I passed the Eleven Plus and was set to go to grammar school. It may be that you attended one too, for I think they still exist in the town where I assume you grew up. Don't worry, I'm not about to engage in a polemic either for or against selection. Perhaps you will draw your own conclusions about where I stand from the story I'm going to tell.

I'm going to weave the first part of my story around the events that happened on one particular day, a fairly ordinary day, but one which stands out in my memory as being representative of the era. It was when I was in the 3rd Form (Year 9 to you) so it would have been 1956 or 1957 and I would have been about 14. Once again, I'll tell it as a story. So, picture me Marcus, sitting at a desk at the back of a class of some 30 adolescents.

'Look at his legs, look at his legs!' my mate Billy spluttered. I was already rocking with silent laughter and it took just one glance at Mr Bartram's spindly shanks, splayed under his desk at the front of the class to make me burst into an explosion of half suppressed mirth. Coppy Bartram raised his head and narrowed his eyes under their shaggy brows. 'Is there something amusing about this exercise, Bailey?' he enquired wearily, 'if so, perhaps you'd care to share it with the rest of us. Well, boy? We're all waiting.'

'No sir.' I managed a sniggering reply.

'And to which of my questions is that the answer, Bailey?' Coppy asked in his slightly tremulous voice, 'No there's nothing amusing about this exercise, or no you don't wish to share your amusement?'

'No to both sir, I was sneezing sir.'

This response produced an ironic cheer from my mates. It also, I was gratified to hear, brought giggles from Jackie Barlow, Vonnie Meadows and Judy Simpson, the prettiest and most flirtatious girls in my year. Even Liz Morgan, blessed with the most developed figure of all, but normally aloof and a resolute non-participant in lunchtime horseplay, allowed herself a smile.

'In that case, Bailey,' Coppy intoned, 'I suggest you make use of your handkerchief, if you carry such a thing, and then concentrate on completing the exercise. And while you do so, boy, would you oblige me by placing the logarithmic calculations at the side of the paper; an instruction with which you always seem either unable or unwilling to comply?'

Coppy wasn't a disciplinarian, but it was advisable not to test him too far. There was always the possibility that he might dish out a detention, and detentions for insubordination usually resulted in a visit to the headmaster's office followed by a painful exit a few minutes afterwards.

We all continued working at the exercise, but my attention kept being diverted by the sight of Jackie Barlow's knees peeking from under her blue gingham school dress and by her shapely calves, set off by white ankle socks. All my mates enthused about girls with big

55

tits, but these held no special charm for me. Legs, however, seemed to hint at pleasures still to come, pleasures about which I had a theoretical knowledge thanks to Mr Cotton's biology lessons, but which as yet I felt no urgent need to investigate. Jackie noticed me staring at her knees and pulled down the hem of her skirt. I felt myself blushing and reverted to my maths exercise.

Eventually Coppy said 'Right! Time's up. Pass your papers down to the front.' This instruction prompted the usual outbreak of minor disorder in the back rows, culminating in a squeal from Vonnie: Steve Johnson had seized the opportunity to twang her bra strap.

'Silence!' Coppy's quaver was more pronounced at higher volumes. 'What's the matter with you, girl?'

'I think she's been sponned, sir,' I volunteered. Unfortunately the reference (it was a word used in 'The Goon Show', but I won't attempt to explain this) appeared to be lost on Coppy, and, exasperated, he rounded on me. 'I've had just about enough of your stupidity and vulgarity, Bailey. Go outside and wait for me there.'

I rose and walked to the door, adopting an exaggerated bent-kneed Teddy Boy shuffle which brought appreciative cheers from my mates. On reaching the door I turned to give them a V-sign before departing. Outside in the lobby, standing by the rows of coat pegs, I peered in the cracked mirror by the lockers and combed my hair, glossy with Brylcream, into the Elvis quiff that was the envy of my year. My hair was my secret pride and joy, though I wished both the school and my parents would permit a duck's-arse at the back. I checked my collar to ensure it was still folded back to look like a cutaway, and re-rolled my wide school tie into a cylinder, the nearest approximation I could get to a Slim-Jim. Unfortunately nothing could disguise the 18-inch bottoms of my grey flannel trousers. I so wished that Mum would taper them into the near-drainpipes like those that Fred Pearce sported. Reasonably satisfied with my appearance, I stood hands in pockets awaiting Coppy's arrival, worried about the possibility of a detention, but basking in the feeling that I was one of the lads.

That was just a little vignette, Marcus, but I hope enough to give you some idea of how it was for adolescents at Grammar School back then. All very tame and innocent, wasn't it, compared to what I hear happens in schools today? You should know: I calculate that you must have left school only about eight years ago.

I'm wondering, Marcus, if you've noticed how different the adolescent Derek Bailey was from the timorous lad you last met at primary school? Had the change gradually developed over four years?

No, it hadn't. In fact my first few years at the Grammar school served to increase my timidity and insecurity. Thankfully, however, there was little bullying. And nor did I suffer unduly at the hands of the teachers. But the customs of the school were alien to me - the communal showering after games and P.E., the requirement to wear one's cap when walking to and from school, the segregation of the sexes when unsupervised (boys at the top end of the playing field, girls at the bottom), the division of the pupils into four Houses, the encouragement to join lunchtime clubs and societies. Many of my fellow pupils had very posh accents, particularly those girls who lived in the large villas on the outskirts of the town. Fewer in number were those from the nearby manufacturing town (I'll call it 'Disham') and the council estates that had been tagged on to the surrounding villages. For some reason most of them seemed to be relegated to the 'B'' stream. For the first time in my life I became first conscious and then ashamed of my accent and background. Do these social distinctions still hold in schools, Marcus? Or do all young people now adopt the language and mannerisms of the working class?

I was one of the weakest in the class academically. And I was also hopeless at sport. In football, relegated along with the other duds to the full-back position, I spent most of the game shivering in my pristine kit. My weediness and lack of physical co-ordination meant that I was unable to participate in playground rough-and-tumbles.

So, I'd entered the second form a worried, insecure little boy, still in awe of the articulate majority but unable to connect with the Disham boys, some of whom by that time had begun to behave rebelliously in the lessons of the less authoritarian teachers. I made no distinction between teachers: my deference to those in authority, learned at primary school and fostered by my parents, ensured that all had my respect.

So what was it that changed me? Stop reading now, Marcus: it's time to open the packet. In it is a compact disc. It has only one track on it (yes, I've mastered the art of copying tracks from CDs, something you probably already regard as outdated, for I believe your generation download music from the internet – am I right?). But bear with me and play the track before you read on.

I don't know if you're into music, Marcus, and if you are, what sort of stuff you like. But no doubt what you've heard means nothing to you: it's ancient history now. When I first heard it, sitting in the living room with Mum and Dad, the words meant nothing to *me*. 'One, two, three o'clock, four o'clock *rock*, five, six, seven o'clock eight o'clock *rock...*' What was it all about? What got to me was the urgent rhythm, the strange slapping sound that defined it, and the insistent monotone of the saxophone in the middle part of the song. It hit me in the solar plexus with the force of Sugar Ray Robinson.

It wasn't just me who had been affected. The next day at school my classmates were all enthusing about the sound they'd heard. In the weeks following, rock'n'roll became an obsession. For me, listening to 'Two Way Family Favourites' in the kitchen on Sunday morning while Mum prepared lunch became compulsive: just occasionally Jean Metcalfe or Cliff Michelmore slipped in a rock'n'roll record, and then, one Sunday, I first heard *Heartbreak Hotel*.

That record didn't punch me in the guts in the way that Haley's had. But it had had an extraordinary effect on some of the girls at school. Up until then, rock'n'roll had been a boys' enthusiasm, but overnight the girls became Elvis devotees, his photograph adorning their satchels and geometry sets and his name scrawled over their exercise books. Then, when *Hound Dog* was released, the boys were won over and the whole social nexus of the class changed. No longer were the pupils differentiated by home background or academic ability, but by whether they were hep or square. Jackie Barlow and Judy Simpson moderated their private-school accents, affected the 'Later alligator' and 'Daddy-oh' catchphrases gleaned from fan magazines, and gravitated towards Vonnie Meadows and her pony-tailed associates. I forged a growing friendship with the boys from Disham.

Most of my teachers expressed contempt for the music. At first I couldn't understand the depth of their loathing. The headmaster made it clear that any attempt to adopt the fashions and attitudes associated with rock'n'roll would not be tolerated: I remember he sent Fred home for the sin of wearing florescent socks. It was then that it occurred to me that the staff might actually be frightened of the effect that the music was having on their charges. This of course served only to make the music and fashions even more attractive. 'Up the Teds!' became our catchphrase, though our contact with these flamboyant peacocks was limited to seeing them parade, draped and drainpiped, along Disham High Street on a Saturday morning.

By the time I reached the fourth form, rock had begun to lose its raw edge and the songs reflected teenage angst: Chuck Berry sang of High School and teachers' dirty looks and deliverance from the days of old, and the keening vocals of the Everlys were easy to emulate in the classroom singsongs in which both boys and girls joined. The music served as an accompaniment to our sexual awakening.

Do you think you can see where I was going, Marcus? Don't be too sure! Because for me, the obsession with rock'n'roll was tempered by an interest in politics. It had been sparked off by the Hungarian uprising and the Suez crisis. I started reading Dad's *Daily Herald* which was strongly opposed to the Anglo-French invasion of Egypt. I began to wonder why the school was not encouraging pupils to knit blankets for the Egyptians as it had for the Hungarian refugees. I started to feel angry at the injustice of it all.

I decided to attend the next meeting of the school Debating Society when the motion for debate was 'This house believes that the West should have taken action to prevent the Russian invasion of Hungary'. The library was crowded; many staff were there, and half way through the debate the headmaster entered, smiling benignly. At the end of the set-piece speeches when the debate was thrown open to the floor, I raised my hand, shaking with nerves and was called on to speak by the head boy. Not very articulately, I said that if it was okay for the west to take action against Russia in Hungary then it was okay for the Russians to take action against Britain in Egypt, and as we'd been knitting blankets for Hungarian refugees we ought also to be doing something for the Egyptians who'd been bombed out of their homes.

A total silence greeted my contribution, followed by desultory clapping from one or two of the sixth-formers which was then swamped by prolonged booing and jeering from the majority of those assembled. The headmaster, glowering, raised his hand for silence, and staring at me, said he was appalled that a pupil of this ancient school should be so unpatriotic as to advocate actions that would give comfort and support to our enemies, and would Bailey now leave the debating chamber immediately. I made to leave, head down, red with humiliation and anger, an anger that exploded as I reached the door. Blind to what I was doing I turned and screamed at the headmaster 'You're a bloody old snob!'

Well, you can imagine the price I paid for that outburst. He laid it on hard, eight instead of the usual six. The news of what I'd done spread round the school in hours, and I was a real Jack the Lad amongst my mates, not because of my political stance (they had no interest in current affairs), but because of what I'd said to the Head.

There you are then, Marcus. I wonder what you made of all that? I'm not going to try provide you with some sort of pseudo-psychological explanation for my actions. I've had sufficient counselling sessions over recent years to teach me that such analysis is usually worthless.

I'm tired now, Marcus, as you can see from the deterioration in my handwriting. I had intended to continue with an account of what happened to me in the fifth and sixth forms, but that will have to wait. I hope you'll still be with me.

Derek

Chapter 9

Milton Keynes, Tuesday 8 May

He was again late home, deliberately so. He'd called in at a cafe after leaving work and spent two hours there, drinking alone. He couldn't face another evening of waiting for her car to draw up outside the house, waiting until after seven, by which time it was obvious she wasn't coming home. When she'd left on Saturday night, her face already showing a bruise, she spoke not a word, despite his apologies. She was carrying only a small suitcase and her laptop bag. He took some comfort from this – it seemed she wasn't planning a long absence.

Sunday had passed without a phone call, text message, or email. Monday, a Bank Holiday, found him in a stupor of worry. First thing this morning he'd phoned her office, to be told by a suspicious sounding supervisor that she'd phoned in sick a few moments before. Eventually, this afternoon, he'd received a text - *'At Em's. Not sure when back.'* He might have known.

He turned into the street: there was no car in the parking space. Another evening by himself, worrying. Worrying about his fate. If she left him, how would he cope? Just three nights without another person in the house had been hell: he'd been unable to settle to anything, unable to eat, unable to sleep. Worst of all, he'd dreaded a knock at the door, a visit from the police. Domestic violence it was called, he believed. It was a serious crime, these days. And Sophie was a woman of her times.

He pushed open the front door with some difficulty; there was the usual log-jam of junk-mail. As he kicked it away, his foot made contact with a small package. He picked it up – Bailey's handwriting. Despite all the trauma of the past few days, he hadn't forgotten about Bailey. He couldn't explain it to himself, but Bailey seemed somehow to be involved with his predicament.

He tore open the package. Inside were sheets of paper covered in the usual neat script, and a narrow packet, wrapped in more brown paper and secured by Sellotape along all its edges. On both sides, in large upper-case letters, was the legend – DO NOT OPEN YET.

Marcus was grateful to Bailey for providing something that might occupy his mind for an hour or so. He ran upstairs to his study (somehow it seemed wrong to commune with Bailey in the living room) and began reading.

When he reached the part where Bailey asked him to open the packet, Marcus was relieved. He removed his glasses and rubbed his eyes. With each page Bailey's handwriting was becoming more ragged. His story was quite interesting in a way, especially the bit when he was in the Maths class. It hadn't occurred to Marcus that Bailey's generation had been rebellious at school, nor that boys of that era had been interested in girls. Knee-length dresses and ankle socks! How would Bailey have reacted to the girls at Marcus's school, with their perfume and make-up and knicker-skimming skirts? Marcus had found them intimidating. And as for twanging a girl's bra-strap; well, that sort of thing would have resulted in a slap round the face, or even worse, unless of course you were shagging the girl anyway, which he never had been.

He ripped open the package and extracted the CD. Bailey hadn't labelled it. He turned on his computer, inserted the disk into the D drive and turned on the speakers.

An alien sound blasted at him. Marcus wasn't musical and secretly had never been grabbed by rap and hip-hop and all the other sounds that so obsessed his contemporaries, though he pretended to be. But he was aware that what he was hearing was old men's music. In fact, he thought he'd heard it before, recently, on some radio programme, something to do with popular cultural history. But it was just a noise to him. When the track finished he felt disappointed.

He turned back to Bailey's letter.

Well, the last part of the letter was pretty boring – all that stuff about politics. What were the Suez and Hungary things anyway? Marcus couldn't remember doing them in history. Strange that Bailey should have got so excited about it all. What had he meant by the headmaster laying it on hard, eight instead of six? Not beating at Grammar school, surely? Hadn't that been abolished a hundred years ago?

He put the letter on the shelf behind his computer. Some time he'd find a place to store it. No hurry, now that Sophie wasn't here. Realising this, his solitude flooded over him. How was he going to spend the rest of his evening?

Chapter 10

Sophie drove more slowly than usual as she negotiated the mini-roundabouts, chicanes and sleeping policemen that were a feature of roads in the estate. It wasn't that she was apprehensive about her return; no, when Sophie made up her mind to do something she did it without further thought, no messing. She just wanted to be sure that Marcus would be in when she arrived. If he came home after her, he'd be forewarned of her presence by the car. She didn't want that: she needed to have the advantage of surprise. If Marcus were given the chance to marshal his thoughts he'd just drone on repetitively – Christ, he bored the arses off people, the way he droned on – and blank out what she was trying to say. And she had a lot to say. Things were going to be very different from now on.

When she'd stormed out last Saturday, bruised and still bleeding slightly, but angry, not frightened, she had no clear idea of what to do or where to go. She had acquaintances and colleagues who lived in the town, but none was the sort of mate with whom she might seek refuge, and anyway, who'd be in on a Saturday night? Well, there was Ben Sidley, of course, her supervisor, who'd obviously like to get into her knickers. He was an old man, 40 at least, a divorcee, not bad looking, but he never made his intentions explicit. If someone wanted to shag you, why not come out and say it? At least that gave you the chance to say yes, or piss off.

There'd been no alternative but to go to Em's. She had no intention of staying there so long, but that was how it turned out. It was chaos in the flat, of course. Em, after a few choice obscenities directed at Marcus, soon seemed to forget that Sophie was a refugee and carried on moaning about her own problems. The kids were uncontrollable as usual. Em's situation, Sophie realised, was the fate that might have awaited her had she not made it to uni. The mayhem in the flat even led her to appreciate the order that Marcus sought to impose on their own domestic arrangements: usually she accused him of having an obsession with tidiness bordering on anal-retentiveness.

It was getting dark as she pulled the car into the parking area, and there were no lights in the front windows. Christ, wasn't he home yet? Or had he gone out? Or even gone to stay with his fuckin' mother? Wouldn't put it past him. Just because his mother had provided the deposit on the house Marcus seemed to think he had to keep in contact with the snobby bitch. That just wasn't cool for someone in his twenties.

She pushed open the front door. It wasn't total darkness; a glimmer on the landing indicated that the light in the study was on. *Yeah, of course; he'll be at the computer. Facebook, I bet.* She dropped her bag in the passage, slammed shut the door, and stood waiting. The light on the landing intensified as the study door opened.

'Soph? Is that you?'

'Who else were you expecting?'

He appeared in silhouette at the top of the stairs.

'Soph, where have you been? Your mobile's been off. I sent loads of texts but you didn't reply. I've been stuck here all week on my own. Look, I'm sorry about last Saturday. It was, like, you were getting at me and I–'

'Marcus! Just shut up! *Shut up!*'

He lumbered down the stairs. Sophie turned on the passage light and turned to face him. He lunged towards her: she side-stepped and stood behind her bag.

'Sophie, I–'

'Christ, haven't you got the message? I said *shut up*. That means *don't talk*. I'm going upstairs to unpack. Make me a cup of coffee. And turn some fuckin' lights on down here.'

Upstairs, she flung her case on the marital bed and began emptying it. Marcus didn't know it yet, but he'd be sleeping downstairs tonight, and for quite a few nights after, until they got things sorted. Their second bedroom had been converted into the study. Well, it would have to revert to its proper purpose in order to accommodate Marcus. He'd have to use the camp bed, and the computer would have to be shifted downstairs. The only reason he had it in his study was to have an excuse to go on-line in private.

She stuffed her dirty underwear into the laundry basket. From downstairs came the sound of Marcus tinkering about in the kitchen. It wasn't easy to obtain solitude in modern houses – the soundproofing was crap. There wasn't much privacy from the neighbours, either. On many nights Sophie's sleep was disturbed by the noise of the couple next door having it away, and they went at it for ages. It didn't seem to bother Marcus. But she found it doubly disturbing, for the woman next door – Jane was it? – obviously gained greater enjoyment from the act than Sophie ever had; well, since she'd been with Marcus anyway.

Right. Time to face Marcus. She'd come straight out with it, right from the start; no meaningless introductory chit-chat. She took a deep breath and went downstairs.

'Here's your coffee, Soph. Shall we go into the lounge?'

'No. We'll drink it in here. Sit down.'

Marcus glanced at her quizzically, but sat at the breakfast bar; Sophie took a seat at the opposite end.

'Soph, let me explain. I–'

'*No.* I don't want to hear. It's what's gonna happen from now on, that's what I want to talk about.'

'Look, I won't hit you again, if that's what –'

'You'd better not even think about it. I tell you, if I ever see you with that look on your face again I'll be out the door, for good. I might do that anyway; it depends on lots of other things.'

'What look on my face? I don't understand.'

'The look you always get when people disagree with you, or stop listening to you, or start cracking jokes. I've seen it so many times. You clam up and start rubbing your eyes, and then you get this expression on your face – it's like tensed up, twitchy. And you start clenching your fists, like you want to hit them. You did that once at uni, didn't you? You hit Toby Goldman. I heard all about it.'

'But he was –'

'I've seen you look at *me* like that, lots of times recently. You did it on Saturday night. But I never thought you'd land one on me, you bastard. It's the last time you ever will. So I'm telling you, if I ever see that look on your face, I'm off. And if I go, I'll want half of everything, right? And that includes the house. I don't reckon even your mother will bail you out a second time. So you'll be in the shit, won't you?'

'But–'

'*No.* Listen. If there's gonna be any chance of me staying here, things have got to change. *You've* got to change. Oh for fuck's sake, *stop rubbing your eyes.*'

To Sophie's surprise, he did, immediately. 'What sort of change?' he said into the middle distance.

'Okay. We'll start with the little things, right? This house. It's too bloody tidy. It's like living in a show house. The way you put my stuff away all the time so I can't find things – God, that pisses me off. What's wrong with a bit of mess? It makes a place homely. If you want to tidy things, clear your junk out of the study.'

'But– '

'Next thing. Stop spending so much time on your fuckin' computer. You're obsessed with it. Why not watch TV now and again? That's what normal people do.'

'But most of it's rubbish.'

'So what? It'll do you good to watch a bit of crap. It'll give you something to talk about with people at work. I bet they talk about TV, don't they? And another thing, when you're at work, go to the canteen for lunch.'

'But why?'

'So you can get to know people, you dickhead. Like, they must think you're a real nerd turning up every day with your little box of sandwiches. Anyway, didn't you say some of the guys go to the pub at lunch? Join 'em now and again!'

'But that crowd ... well, I don't think they like me much. You see, whenever I– '

'Fuck, Marcus, some of the guys at my place don't like *me*, and I don't care for most of *them*. But you've gotta make the effort. You know what you are? You're socially isolated, that's what. And it means I am as well.'

A look of blank amazement froze his expression. He started to remove his glasses, evidently thought better of it, and replaced them.

Sophie pressed on. 'Look, have you thought how much easier it would be for both of us if only you'd learn to drive? I mean, 24 and can't drive! That's why you're isolated. If you could drive you could go out in the evening, couldn't you?'

'What, without you, you mean?'

'Yes! Without me! Like, we're not an old married couple, are we?'

'What would *you* do, then?'

'Me? Well, I could always get a taxi, do my own thing, go clubbing maybe, meet up with the gang there. Might be better if I went by myself, 'cos you don't get on with 'em, do you?'

His bemused expression changed to one of anguish. There was a ten second interval of spectacle removal and eye rubbing. Sophie decided against intervening. Perhaps it was time to break off, give him time to take in what she'd said. She stood up.

'Look Marcus, I haven't finished yet, but I'm bloody starving. Have you got anything in?'

'Pizza in the freezer.'

'Okay. I'll microwave it. Carry on talking after we've eaten, okay?'

He was silent for a moment, then –

'But where would I go? In the evenings, I mean?'

'I'm not bloody organising your social life for you. C'mon, let's eat. Talk about it later.'

During the meal Sophie found herself making conversation, or at least making remarks. It wasn't something she'd intended to do. But she found Marcus's silence uncomfortable, accompanied as it was by his look of pained bafflement. Normally she would have welcomed the fact that he wasn't talking because he always spoke with his mouth full. His table manners (not that they often ate at the table) were really gross.

But she needed him to participate in the discussion yet to come, if only to confirm his agreement to her terms. So she found herself trying to engage with him. She made comments about her time with Emma but this elicited no response other than the occasional grunt. She explained how she'd told her office she was off sick, and asked whether her manager had phoned to ask about her. Marcus answered only by shaking his head. The rest of the evening was evidently going to be hard work, but she would persist: she had to. There was no other way forward, not yet anyway. She hadn't the money to buy a place of her own, and there was no way she was going to rent.

'Okay,' she said, after the pizza had been eaten. 'You load the dishwasher, I'll make coffee. Let's have it in the living room.'

Mutely, he complied. The kitchen was small, and in carrying out their separate tasks they occasionally brushed against each other. Was she imagining it, or did he recoil slightly at the contact? Shit, that was something new. He usually showed no awareness of the conventions regarding personal space. It was one of his problems.

She carried the mugs of coffee through to the living room and took her usual seat on the settee. Marcus followed and sat in the armchair opposite.

'No, come and sit next to me,' she found herself saying.

'But I always sit here.'

'Well, break the habit. That's something I want to talk about: habits, I mean. And I want this to be, like, you know, a conversation. If you sit over there it'll be more like a fuckin' debate.'

He sat down next to her. About six inches separated them. Sophie realised she was staring at the blank TV screen. She glanced sideways: so was he.

72

'Listen, Marcus. What I said about learning to drive. I'm sure you'd feel happier if you could.'

'But I can't. I know I'd never learn. Lack of hand-eye co-ordination. You know that.'

'Yeah, so you say. But you've never tried. You're gonna have to, Marcus. It's one of my conditions.'

'It was the same at school, you see. I was no good at games involving a ball.'

Sophie held back in time from saying she didn't give a fuck about what happened to him at school, and pressed on.

'But you're gonna give it a go, aren't you? Start taking lessons. At a driving school, I mean. Don't expect me to teach you.'

She thought she detected a slight nod of his head. She hoped it signified acquiescence, but there was no telling with Marcus. His body language was sometimes hard to interpret.

He turned his face towards her. 'Did you like it at school?' he asked.

'Driving school, you mean?'

'No. School; when you were a kid.'

Sophie felt the seething exasperation that she always experienced when Marcus abruptly changed the subject. Had his mind been elsewhere throughout the conversation? Or was it a ploy to distract her from her purpose? She fought back the urge to shout at him.

'We're not talking about school. Haven't you got it yet? I'm trying to tell you things you've got to do if I'm gonna stay here. Look, we haven't got any real friends, have we? Not as a couple. It makes me feel well lonely. The crowd down the club ... look; one of the reasons they often don't include us is because ... it's because you look a bit like, weird, y'know?'

'I can't help the way I look.'

73

'But you can! You *can*! Those skinny jeans! They're really rank!'

'But they're fashionable.'

'Yeah, sure, if you've got the legs and arse to wear 'em. You haven't. Your legs are too short and your arse is too big. You look a real wuss in 'em. Get some straights, not too close fitting. And start wearing your shirt outside your belt. And another thing – stop spiking your hair with gel. Your face is too fat for that. Let your hair grow a bit.'

'You've never said all this before.'

'I've thought it, though. Look, nothing's gonna turn you into a babe-magnet, but at least the guys might stop dissing you. And that'll make things a lot better for me.'

Throughout this exchange Marcus had been staring at her, expressionless. His responses indicated that he understood what she'd said, but had he taken it on board? Her strategy this evening had been all wrong, she realised. She'd started with the trivial stuff, hoping to soften him up for the more important things like his behaviour and the new sleeping arrangements. She should have remembered that sometimes he seemed unable to grasp more than one idea at a time. And she felt exhausted. Discussing personal things with Marcus was like repeatedly punching a sponge – until he lost it, of course. She couldn't cope with him losing it this evening.

She made up her mind. The new sleeping arrangements would have to wait until tomorrow. It wasn't as if he was likely to want a shag.

'Will you think about what I've said, then?' she asked.

'Yes,' he said, abstractedly. Then – 'Soph, were you teased at all at school?'

Chapter 11

Shropshire, Wednesday 9 May

'Fancy a drink at *The George*, you two?' said Giles, as the front door closed on the two couples. 'Could do with an ale after that.'

Derek and Gabrielle glanced at each other. It was after 9.30, and Gabrielle didn't care for late evening drinking in crowded pubs. But the Book Club meeting had been particularly tedious, and Derek felt the need for refreshment. And it would be churlish to decline an offer from the Taylors, whose company they were beginning to enjoy.

'Just a quick one, then,' he said. 'Is that okay by you, Gab? *The George* won't be too packed on a Tuesday.'

'Yes, why not?' she replied.

'Oh, good,' said Davina.

They set off towards the town centre, Derek and Giles together in front, Gabrielle and Davina a few paces behind. They began a post-mortem on the meeting they'd just left.

'It's not really about books, any longer, is it?' said Davina. 'It's just a competition about who can impress most as a hostess, and whose kids are making the most money.'

'That's right,' said Gabrielle. 'I reckon we spent about half an hour of that session discussing the book. The rest was just chit-chat and gossip.'

'Not surprising,' said Giles, over his shoulder. 'I don't think most of them grasped half of what the book was about. Julian Barnes isn't that difficult, is he? And

I chose his latest specifically because I though it would appeal to them. It's about ageing, after all.'

'I reckon that was the problem,' said Davina. 'Most of them are in denial about their age: look how they tart themselves up. They don't want to be reminded that they're getting past it.'

'Won't be a problem at the next meeting,' said Derek. 'Geoffrey Archer, for God's sake!'

'Well, at least it's got a plot,' said Davina, mimicking the languorous tones of Lynda Partington, whose choice *Sins of the Fathers* had been.

'Do we really want to keep on going?' said Gabrielle. 'All those pointed remarks about it being someone else's turn to host the meetings. They've got no chance with us. Can you imagine that lot in our parlour, squashed up on our tatty furniture? How about you two hosting it?'

'No way,' said Davina. 'I think we ought to suggest hiring a hall, or meeting in pub, and even better, hiring a tutor, someone to keep them in order.'

'If we did that the membership would be reduced to us four,' said Derek.

'That would be fine by us, wouldn't it, Giles?' said Davina.

They all grinned. Each had become aware that a point had been reached in their friendship where it was starting to become something more than casual: there was the potential for greater intimacy, the sharing of hopes, dreams, and fears. And, Derek realised, the sharing of their histories. Over dinner last week the Taylors had recounted how they'd met at Glastonbury. Derek had managed to steer the conversation to the topic of the music of the 70s, but he knew that there would come a time when the inevitable question would be asked – how had he and Gabrielle met? It was a hurdle he'd always known they might eventually have to face.

As Derek had predicted, *The George* was half empty. It was crowded from Thursday through to Sunday when many of the tables were reserved for dining, but for the remainder of the week it reverted to what it had been for the past two centuries – a drinking den for locals, though food was still served for those who wanted it.

Derek loved the place. It reminded him of the pubs of his youth. It had not suffered the sort of 'improvement' which so often resulted in a single cavernous space served by a bar more appropriate to a hotel lounge and where drinkers were scarcely tolerated if they weren't dining. It had four small rooms with genuine beams, each furnished with an eclectic assortment of wheel-back chairs, benches and tables, and three of the rooms had open log fires in the winter months. There was no piped music. One of the rooms, though not labelled as such, functioned as a public bar, where locals in overalls or work-stained jeans congregated at 5.30 for a few pints before leaving, some to return later, scrubbed up, with wives or girlfriends. The clientele in the other rooms were a mix of all classes and age groups, though teenagers were mercifully absent. To reach the bar required the negotiation of a route through the phalanx of middle-aged men standing at it, pints in hand, in the way that middle-aged men in pubs always used to do. All that was missing was the fug of cigarette smoke.

They sat in one of the small lower rooms. Sitting opposite their friends, Derek was again aware of how shabby he felt when in their company. Giles was 64, slim, and although slightly stooped, always dressed in a selection of pastel shirts, cravats, and linen jackets. He had white hair which flopped over his forehead which

77

gave him the air of an overgrown schoolboy, until he spoilt the effect by putting on his half-moon reading glasses. Davina, of similar vintage, was still an attractive woman with strong features, large brown eyes and straight hair dyed a flattering auburn. She had a figure that allowed her to wear close-fitting shirts and tight tailored jeans. She had a relaxed loping stride, and when she stood still, she adopted the pose of a model, one hip jutting, one leg in front of the other.

Compared to her, the comfortable Gabrielle looked distinctly dowdy, thought Derek: why didn't she make a bit more of an effort, have her hair styled perhaps, and change her lipstick from that bright red? He immediately felt ashamed of his disloyalty. It was as well, he thought, glancing again at Davina, that they were all of an age where the very idea of illicit liaisons was risible. That didn't mean that he no longer felt desire. What would it be like, he wondered, when his eye would no longer be caught by the curve of a thigh, the pertness of a bum, the swell of a breast? Would it come as a relief, when the restless hunger was finally extinguished? He hoped so. It was already difficult to bear, the fact that the spirit was so often willing when the flesh was occasionally incapable and his wife usually unresponsive.

'I suppose we've been being a bit unfair,' Giles was saying. 'We shouldn't disparage those whose taste in literature doesn't reach our lofty heights. It's good that people read anything, these days. Most of them have a very limited attention span. We even found that with our undergraduates, didn't we, Davina? God knows how school-teachers cope these days. How did you two find it?'

'Oh, we didn't have that problem,' said Gabrielle hurriedly. 'We were in adult education.'

'Oh, yes, of course you were,' said Giles. 'In Birmingham, didn't you say? What was the college?'

Derek swallowed his beer hurriedly. 'Who's for another?'

'Just a half for me,' said Giles.

'And me, please,' said Davina.

'Just a tonic water, please,' said Gabrielle.

As Derek made his way to the bar he heard Giles resume his interrogation – 'What was the college, then, Gabrielle? Did it offer full-time courses?'

Derek hurried out of earshot, not wishing to hear Gabrielle's response. *For God's sake stick to the script, Gabby.* Gabrielle was a quick thinker, but the story they'd rehearsed was a bit short on detail and wouldn't stand close examination. But she would, at least, remain calm under pressure. Derek knew that he would fluff his lines. Best that he was out of the way.

Returning to the table with the drinks, he was relieved to find that the conversation had turned to an assassination of the characters of David Cameron and George Osborne. As he sat down he glanced at Gabrielle: her slight smile and nod indicated that her account of their experiences of teaching adult literacy had been sufficient to divert attention from the name of the institution in which those experiences had take place.

'You got away with it, then,' said Derek immediately after they'd said their goodbyes to the Taylors and begun walking home. 'No close questioning?'

'No. I got their attention by making up stories about the students; you know, their deprived background, how primary education had failed them, the sort of things that would grab Giles. You know how he's burdened by his social conscience.'

'He had quite a privileged upbringing, I reckon. We must ask him about it some day.'

'But he'd respond by asking you about yours, wouldn't he?'

'I can handle that. It's my middle years that would cause a problem.'

'Derek, have you ever thought ...'

'Go on.'

'Have you ever thought that we might get so close to them that we ... well, that we might be honest with them? Tell them everything? It would be such a relief.'

'No way, Gab! I reckon even Giles might look askance at that, even with his social conscience.'

Gabrielle sighed. 'You're probably right.'

The remainder of their walk home was conducted in silence.

Once inside, Gabrielle said she fancied a long soak and an early night.

'You go ahead, Gab. I'm going to start my next letter to Marcus. I always find writing easier late in the evening.'

'Where are you up to now?

'Sixth Form.'

'Aren't you dragging it out a bit? Remember what we were talking about in the pub; you know, young people's short attention span. He might be getting bored with it.'

'He might. But, to tell the truth, Gab, I'm enjoying the process of writing. Catharsis, and all that.'

She ruffled his hair. 'Try not to wake me when you come to bed. Goodnight, sweetie.'

He extracted some sheets of paper from the pile behind the computer and unscrewed his fountain pen. He'd already planned this instalment, but Gabrielle's comment about Marcus's possible boredom had given him cause for thought: was he perhaps being a bit self-indulgent? For all he knew, Marcus might only have read the first letter and decided that the life story of an old geezer wasn't worth following, despite his link to the old geezer's past. Perhaps it was time to reveal his email address, to give Marcus the opportunity to respond should he so wish? It was, after all, Derek's long-term objective that they should communicate.

No, not yet. There was more that Marcus needed to know before they reached that stage. But perhaps Gabrielle was right – he was making the story too long. Too much history of the late 20th century, too much social comment. He would try to restrict himself to those events that shaped his personality.

Chapter 12

I'm sorry for the deterioration in my handwriting towards the end of my last letter, Marcus, but I had a lot to say. Perhaps it was too much for you to take in at one sitting – if you read it at all, of course. I feel rather like a radio broadcaster pouring his soul into the microphone, not knowing if anyone is actually tuned in. But I have to work through all this. Only when I reach a certain point (and you will know when that is) shall I feel able to provide you with the means of communicating with me, should you so wish. That may be some weeks away. So I shall press on, in the hope that you're still with me. If it's any comfort, this episode will be shorter than the last.

You will have found the photograph, I assume. I will come to its significance a bit later. Let me take up my story from where I left it – a lad in the 3rd form at grammar school, relishing the camaraderie of my mates and beginning to lust after girls, or birds as we called them then. I was all set to be led down the primrose path. By the time I reached the 4th form I'd become the class joker, if not the leader of the pack then certainly one whose company was always sought. And, though I blush to write it, I was becoming conscious of the fact that I wasn't bad looking, and that girls seemed to like me.

At the age of 15 girls are so much more mature than boys. The attractive, lively ones in my class were more interested in the 6th form boys or the lads they met at the local youth club than their peers, so I was not regarded as a serious contender for their favours. Except on coach trips.

Ah, coach trips! All aboard to be taken to the theatre in London, or to areas of geographical interest, or even to visit stately homes. Fun and games on the back seat, crammed in with Jackie Barlow, Vonnie Meadows, Judy Simpson, Billy Grove and Fred Pearce – all innocent fun on the way out, what my Dad would have called 'a bit of slap and tickle'. But on the way home, when it was dark, then began the pairing off. Snogging, to start with (yes, we called it snogging then; the term fell out of favour for decades, but it seems to have returned), but I soon graduated to inexpert breast-fumblings, first over the blouse, then under the blouse but over the bra, then that memorable day when Judy Simpson, with no prompting from me, reached behind her back and undid her bra strap.

Did your generation experience the joys of gradually surmounting each successive hurdle, Marcus? From what one gleans from the media it sometimes seems that you've all been engaged in full frontal fornication since the onset of puberty. Not so with us, not Grammar School boys. I'm pretty sure all my mates were virgins. But no doubt they were all prodigious masturbators – I certainly was.

Then, when I reached the 5th form, Judy Simpson failed to return to school after the Christmas holiday. No explanation was provided by our teachers, but the news soon leaked out: she was pregnant. Pregnant! By one of the Disham Teds, apparently. I can't begin to explain the enormity of such an event in 1959, that it should have happened to a Grammar School girl, who was probably only 15 at the time of conception.

The shock waves spread through the school. The event had a salutary effect on the girls in my class; dalliances on coach trips were strictly off limits; even suggestive teenage banter became *ultra vires*. And it served to remind me of the message drummed into me by my Grandparents – that pleasures have always to be paid for, that sin will inevitably incur atonement. Chastened, I turned my attention to my studies: GCE 'O' Levels were approaching. In fact I only just scraped sufficient GCE passes to make it to the 6th form. I'll explain why later.

I can remember very little about the 6th form. I studied hard and was made a prefect, but never felt part of the group who'd chosen to stay on at school rather than seek employment as Billy and Fred had done. Some of the others in the sixth form met up outside school, but it was a crowd made up largely of pairs, and to enter that charmed circle required the acquisition of a female companion. Most of the girls in the 6th form were far too posh for me, even if I'd had the inclination to approach them.

It was a strange time, those pre-Beatle early 1960s. Rock'n'roll had died. Most of my fellow-prefects affected an enthusiasm for Trad Jazz (ever heard of it, Marcus?) but it failed to move me. The Trad-dadders engaged in a peculiar loping form of jive, far beyond the aspiration of anyone with my co-ordination problems. In any case I'd never attempted any type of dancing.

So I just buckled down and got on with my studies. (English Literature, History and Geography, if you're interested. Such things as Media Studies and Psychology didn't exist then.) I even lost interest in current affairs. It was the age of Supermac and 'never had it so good'. Nothing seemed to be happening. As a result I achieved 'A' level grades sufficient to make it to university. But that's another story.

It's time to explain the photograph. It was taken one evening in my last term in the 5th form, in May or June

1959, the year of a glorious summer which lasted from April to September. That's me, in the middle at the front – yes, I'm giving the V sign (quite risqué in those days; I suppose your generation would just employ one finger). Billy Grove stands to my right, Fred Pearce is behind me. The names of the others don't matter. They were all in the 5th form with me. I can't remember the name of whoever it was took the snapshot, but he used my camera, a Box Brownie. It produced good contact prints.

We're standing in a meadow near the village where Billy Grove lived. Every evening throughout that summer, when we should have been revising for our 'O' Levels, we used to converge on that meadow. We all came by bicycle from our homes, arriving at about six and staying until dusk. I had the furthest to cycle, about eight miles. Dad had bought me a Raleigh the year before – it had straight handlebars and three-speed Sturmey-Archer gears. It was my pride and joy. However, it didn't have lights, which meant that the journey home was a bit nerve-racking, despite there being so few cars on the lanes.

The seven of us had started meeting up in Disham on Saturday mornings. We used to wander down the high street and ogle the back-combed bouffant-haired birds, parading in their white high-heeled shoes and stiff multi-petticoated skirts. Way beyond our reach, of course. I don't know whose idea it was to start gathering in that meadow in the evenings, but we'd become a gang of lads who took delight in each other's company, and it just happened.

And what did we do in that meadow, you may wonder? What was the big attraction that brought us there night after night? Girls? Woodbines and bottles of Pale Ale? The latest copy of *Health and Efficiency*? Sorry to disappoint you Marcus, but it was cricket.

Knock-about cricket, played with a tennis ball, using a tree trunk for stumps. Such, such were the joys.

It was a bit more than that, of course. That summer coincided with a last-gasp revival of rock'n'roll, fuelled by a programme on ITV called 'Oh Boy', and as we cycled the lanes, the overhanging beech trees fresh with new leaves and underlain by a profusion of bluebells, we sang the hits of the day – songs by Buddy Holly, Gene Vincent, Marty Wilde, Cliff Richard (yes, Cliff Richard! He was a scowling rebel, back then). We exulted in our youth. As Paul Simon later put it, *I'm feeling all right, I'm with my boys, I'm with my troops, yeah.*

So now you see why I only just scraped through my 'O' levels.

You're doubtless wondering what the significance of all this is. After all, nothing happened of any great moment: there was no life-changing event. It's only in retrospect I realise the importance of it all. I mentioned beech trees and bluebells. Truth to tell, I wasn't consciously aware of them at the time – what 16 year-old would be? But some twenty years later I revisited the place, alone, on a balmy summer evening just like those of 1959. It was then I appreciated the beauty of the scene, and it was the scent of the bluebells that evoked all the memories of that time. There is nothing so evocative as a smell. It was only then that I realised how happy I'd been.

So far I've avoided preaching at you, Marcus. I've been hoping that simply telling my story will help you understand the man I became. But let me now present you with a bit of home-spun wisdom – the moral of the tale, if you like.

It's this. As you go through life, things will happen to you when you'll think *Yes! This is a moment I'll savour for ever. This is when my life changes.* I'm referring to things like your first fuck, or graduating, or getting married, or having your first kid. But it ain't necessarily so, Marcus. Sometimes it's the little things, the mundane happenings, the quiet times, that, with age, you realise were the more important. Things like cycling along a country lane with your friends on a warm summer evening and playing cricket with them in a meadow fringed with trees and scented with bluebells. I hope you've had some moments like these, Marcus.

Until my next,
Derek

Chapter 13

Milton Keynes, Friday 11 May

'Marcus? *Marcus?*' Sophie yelled, standing in the passage.

No reply. She ran upstairs to the study: he wasn't in there. *Great*. He must be taking his driving lesson. She'd been on at him about it all over the previous weekend. He hadn't rejected the idea out of hand, but he'd done nothing about it. In the end she'd phoned the driving school herself, first thing on Monday morning, and booked a lesson for Friday evening, 6 pm. But this morning he'd refused to confirm that he'd attend. 'I might' had been all he would say.

So, she'd won another battle. Her other victory had been over the sleeping arrangements. He'd agreed to her demand almost meekly. He'd rescued the camp bed from the loft and had managed to position it next to the work-station without having to remove his desk-top pc. She'd wondered whether to challenge him about that, but decided against, just as she'd decided not to broach the matter of how he presented himself to the world, not yet, anyway. One or two steps at a time. Let him get used to the new arrangements first. And if his driving lessons proved successful, perhaps his other behaviour issues would be easier to modify. Also, she was relishing the relative calm that had characterised the past week and didn't want anything to disturb it. She'd forgotten how restful it could be, sleeping alone. Pity they had only one bathroom. Shared arrangements for shitting and showering necessitated a degree of intimacy that she no longer wanted.

She went down to the kitchen. It was, as usual, tidy to the point of seeming unused. She was seized with an urge to go around messing things up, but that would just result in frenzied tidying activity when Marcus got home. When was it that she first noticed his old-womanish traits and his other weird patterns of behaviour? Not at uni. Or maybe she *had* noticed then, but that they hadn't seemed too bad when there were other people around, when there were other distractions, when they weren't on their own together so much.

She opened a kitchen cupboard. It was in pristine order (he'd even labelled the shelves with the contents of each) and she immediately felt like screaming. Hastily she extracted the coffee jar, spooned coffee into a mug and switched on the kettle. The activity did nothing to distract her.

It had been his single-minded persistence that had led to her moving in with him at uni. He wasn't the most appealing guy on the course, but in truth the competition hadn't been up to much. The most attractive guys all seemed to be Arts and Humanities students, but she couldn't connect with them. Most of the time she didn't understand what the fuck they were talking about. And anyway, she wasn't fit enough for the likes of them, she knew that. Skinny, no tits, spectacles. That didn't stop her putting it about with second-raters, though. There'd been lots of one-night stands, but never any follow-up. She knew, for she had overheard a comment in a bar, that she was known as 'Sophie Blower, the sure-fire goer'.

She'd hardly noticed Marcus until the end of the second year when, suddenly, he'd started coming on strong – too strong, she realised in retrospect. His attempts to pull her were characterised by dogged determination and persistent haranguing. When she finally succumbed (out of weariness, mainly) he surprised her with his roughness. At first she thought he was acting the caveman, and quite liked it. But, once he'd moved in with her in their third year, it got a bit much – there was no finesse, no experimentation. Plenty of wham-bam but never a hint of thank you ma'am. But finals had been approaching and she hadn't the energy to suggest they split up.

She sat at the breakfast bar nursing her coffee. She never used the living room when alone. A living room should be a place to relax in. Theirs held all the comfort of a recently cleaned and disinfected institutional waiting room. And why did he insist on that glaring overhead light?

At uni she'd thought he was intelligent. He spoke intensely, articulately and at great length about his subject. He spoke at length about most things; sometimes she found it hard to get across her point of view. When she graduated with a 1st, she obtained a post with the I.T. company in Milton Keynes, and moved into a one-bedroomed rented flat near the town centre. Marcus managed only a 2.2: those sort of IT graduates were two a penny, so he'd stayed on in Luton taking a variety of casual jobs, visiting her occasionally and insisting that he would eventually find employment in Milton Keynes. She never thought that would happen. But it did: after two years he managed to land a post with the Local Authority. By that time she'd had enough of living by herself: she was, in fact, lonely, and it was hard to resist Marcus's insistence that they buy a house together. Property wasn't cheap in Milton Keynes, and the deposit was paid by his mother.

Soon, all the doubts she had about Marcus, prompted by his 2.2, had begun to reassert themselves. She realised she'd been fooled by his accent. In Dagenham the few people who spoke posh were also articulate, so she associated that sort of speech with intelligence. She hadn't realised that there were parts of the country where everyone sounded like that, places like that part of Warwickshire where Marcus had been raised. She discovered this when he first took her to a pub in the village where his mother lived.

She disliked his mother from the time she first met her. Meryl wasn't hostile, at first, but bloody condescending. She kept wittering on about the grammar school that Marcus had attended, what a wonderful education it had provided, how it was such a pity that the 11+ had been abolished in most areas. She'd probably learned from Marcus that Sophie had been to a comprehensive, and used this as an opportunity to discomfort her. Sophie hadn't been discomforted, just pissed off. She wasn't ashamed of her background. So she'd emphasised her Dagenham accent, with the result that Meryl had got more and more snooty. And the bitch would keep calling her 'Sophia', despite being corrected numerous times. From then on Sophie had deliberately adopted the argot of the streets, even at home. Marcus didn't seem to notice, indeed he'd started to copy her. He probably did it unconsciously.

She finished her coffee, and as an act of defiance rinsed her mug under the tap and put it away, still wet, in the cupboard. Marcus would have gone bananas if he'd seen that. Cleanliness was another of his obsessions. That was one thing he hadn't inherited from his mother – to Sophie's surprise her house was decidedly grubby with old fashioned furniture greasy from years of use, and stained threadbare carpets. The loo was disgusting. Weird, the ways of the wealthy. Perhaps Marcus was reacting against it, or maybe cleanliness had been drilled into him at that bloody school, which, she'd since learned, was not just a grammar, but a direct grant.

She found herself standing at the sink staring out of the window. Shit, how long had she been doing that? She wasn't usually one for prolonged introspection. She turned her attention to the breakfast bar on which rested a pile of mail that she'd collected from inside the front door when she entered. Junk, of course, but there were several clothes catalogues that she might glance at later. Something else, though. A brown envelope, addressed to Marcus. The address was handwritten. Strange. Neither of them ever received letters with a handwritten address. Who wrote letters these days, anyway?

She stood, holding the envelope, pondering. It wasn't bulky; it felt like it contained no more than a few sheets of paper. Who could be writing to Marcus? She was intrigued. She wasn't averse to reading his emails when he'd forgotten to delete them (nothing of interest there, just work stuff and the odd mail to fellow photographers), and she'd taken to checking his browsing history, which was more revealing. But to open a letter? Somehow that would be crossing a boundary. And yet ... Christ, why not? She could always say she'd opened it in error. But that wouldn't sound very convincing. She examined the envelope: just a simple adhesive seal, no Sellotape. It could be steamed open. Yeah, she could do that, then re-seal it with the Pritt-Stick that Marcus used to mount his photographs.

She glanced at her watch. 6.30. About half an hour before he got home. Better do the deed in the study. Wouldn't do to be caught in the kitchen with it should he come back early. She was half-way up the stairs before she remembered she hadn't steamed open the bloody envelope.

It took some opening, and then in the study she'd had to push back the camp bed so she could sit at the work-station. She pulled the papers from the envelope. Something small fell out, landing on the floor. She picked it up – a photograph, a very small photograph, black and white.

She examined it. Six guys, all grinning at the camera, one of them giving the V sign. They were standing in a field by the look of it; there were bicycles leaning against a hedge. How old were they? Hard to say – teenagers probably, but they were wearing naff clothes; baggy check shirts, tucked into what looked like jeans, but these were high-waisted, loose fitting round the hips and tapered to the ankles. And the hairstyles! Partings, greasy quiffs, short at the sides. She turned over the photo; on the back was written *1959*. Shit, they'd all be old men now.

The sheets of paper were covered in neat, joined-up handwriting, with loops and curly bits, the sort of handwriting some of her older teachers had used. There was no address on the front sheet, no date, no 'Dear Marcus'. She turned to the end page – at the bottom it was signed 'Derek'. Who the hell was Derek? She'd never heard Marcus mention anyone of that name. None of their generation was called Derek. It wasn't a name you heard these days.

She started reading. It began –'I'm sorry for the deterioration in my handwriting towards the end of my last letter, Marcus, but' – *Shit! So this isn't the first letter he's received from this guy. What's all this about? What's he hiding from me?* She started again.

When she'd finished, she wondered again what the hell it was all about. Why should this Derek, whoever he was, write to Marcus with a sentimental story of a time long past? Of what possible interest could it be to

Marcus? And how come Marcus knows this guy, anyway? He must be well into his sixties, old enough to be his bloody grandfather.

It would be strange enough if this were a one-off event. But it was evident there'd been another letter before this one – perhaps many letters. Marcus must have made quite an effort to keep them from her – but then recently he'd been getting home before her hadn't he? He was always the first to see the post. Christ, perhaps that was why he was so reluctant to take an evening driving lesson. The sneaky bastard. What was he trying to hide from her? It was most unlike him; Marcus didn't do secrets. He was too literal-minded for that.

But something was going on, here. Another thing to confront Marcus with. Or should she bide her time, see if she could intercept the next letter that this Derek guy had promised? Yeah, keep quiet about it for a while. But how could she intercept letters, given that Marcus was always home first? There was no way round that – or was there? Hang on – yes! There might be! The notion came to her, but not as an instant revelation: rather it emerged slowly as an accessory to another idea that had been lurking in the depths of her consciousness for a few weeks. Yes! If Marcus could have secrets, why shouldn't she?

She shoved the papers back in the envelope and got to work with the Pritt-stick. The photograph remained where she'd left it, on the desk but obscured by the VDU.

Chapter 14

Warwickshire, Friday 11 May

Gordon stood at the kitchen sink, waiting for the kettle to boil. Through the window he could see Meryl working in the garden. She was trowelling compost into the pots and urns on the edges of the paved terrace that extended across the width of the house. Beyond the terrace stretched a large garden, mainly down to lawn but with a few unkempt island beds, and beyond the lawn was an area of rough grass in which an apple and two pear trees grew – the orchard, Meryl called it.

It was a sunny day for once, and after coffee he would have to start mowing the lawn. This was a never-ending task during the summer months. He'd purchased a strimmer for the long grass in the orchard some years ago, but the stoop he was required to adopt to manoeuvre the bloody thing buggered up his back, and served to remind him that he was in his 50s, grossly overweight and short of breath. He didn't enjoy gardening, but felt obliged to give Meryl some companionship in the hobby that she loved.

The garden was too big for a couple in late-middle age, but then so was the house. It had been Meryl's mother's. Meryl had grown up there. When, 14 years ago, her mother had died, Meryl returned there to live, bringing Gordon and Marcus with her. The two women had been reconciled during the old lady's final illness, though by that time she was so ga-ga that she'd forgotten that she'd once accused her daughter of bringing shame on the family and told her never again to visit the house, or the village. Meryl now regarded the house as her birthright and refused to sell it. Gordon was sometimes amused, sometimes irritated, that since returning there she had begun to adopt the manner and attitudes of the country gentlefolk amongst whom she'd been raised, to the point of becoming a woman of consequence in the village – a leading light in the W.I. and a member of the parish council. She was on the way to becoming her mother's daughter.

Gordon had ambivalent feelings about the house. It was early Victorian, handsome enough, but draughty and devoid of modern conveniences. He'd like to improve it, at least replace the battered furniture and threadbare carpets. But these didn't worry Meryl; indeed she seemed to relish them. She said that modern houses and furnishings were tasteless.

He watched his wife as she moved from container to container, expertly wielding her trowel. The garden was always her place of refuge in times of stress, and she was, once again, stressed. She'd retained her slim figure - she managed to look elegant even in gardening clothes - but her face was careworn. She looked much older than her 51 years. Smoking hadn't helped her complexion, of course.

Marcus was the cause of her angst. He always had been. As her social worker Gordon had been well aware of her problems in coping with a child as a single parent, even without the dreadful circumstances that had preceded Marcus' birth. It had been easier for her once he'd married her (something that had done little to enhance his career), but Marcus had been a difficult child to raise. Gordon had done his best to provide the security that had been lacking. He hoped that as a stepfather he'd earned Marcus's liking and respect, if not his affection. Marcus had never demonstrated affection, but then he rarely showed any emotion except outbursts of irritation and anger.

The kettle boiled. Gordon tapped on the window and mimed the lifting of a cup to his lips. Meryl nodded and made her way towards the back door.

'Feeling better for the exercise?' Gordon enquired.

'A bit. What would really help would be if I could get a good night's sleep.'

'Well, sit down and drink your coffee. I'll come out afterwards and make a start on the lawn.'

She sat at the kitchen table and sipped at her cup. It had to be cup and saucer, of course, never a mug, not since they'd left Studley. Her posture was straight-backed, her head erect: the lessons in deportment she'd received at her private school were second nature to her. It was one of the things that had intrigued Gordon when he first met her, that, and her County accent. He'd never before encountered such characteristics in a single-parent client living in a rented flat.

She pulled a packet of Consulate from her gilet and lit one. She dragged at it furiously. She looked haggard and there were deep circles under her eyes. Gordon knew what was troubling her, but she'd not spoken of it for weeks. To introduce the topic might result in tears, but Gordon had come to the conclusion that anything would be better than for her (and him) to endure this pent-up anguish. He reached across the table and grasped her hand.

'Meryl, why don't you phone Marcus again? You're torturing yourself unnecessarily.'

'Why should I? If he hasn't phoned me it must mean he's got something to hide. And in any case, that Blower girl might answer the phone. I just can't stand listening to her. She's awful. What Marcus sees in her I'll never know. I wish he'd never gone to university, mixing with all that riff-raff.'

'Never mind Sophie now. It's not her that's worrying you, is it? Look, Meryl, Marcus promised he

97

wouldn't open any more letters from Bailey. He reassured you about that. Why don't you believe him?
Marcus isn't capable of lying. Just phone him for a
chat, can't you?'

Meryl ground out her cigarette half smoked. She
rubbed her eyes and then began scratching her head.
Gordon was alerted to the imminent storm. When she
started messing up her hair, the sleek blonde high-
lighted helmet that received so much attention every
week at the salon in Stratford, he knew that her fragile
self-control was about to snap.

'But why did he agree to let Bailey write to him in
the first place? I asked him not to. He knew it would
upset me. I know Bailey's game: he's trying to get
Marcus to .... And what about *me*? Doesn't the swine
think he's hurt me enough? To rake it all up again after
all these years – it's not fair! *It's not fair!*'

She covered her face with her hands. Gordon got up,
stood behind her and began massaging her shoulders.
He hoped that tears would bring some relief. At least
she was communicating, and he could now attempt
soothing reassurances, even though he'd said it all
before.

'Meryl. Listen. You know I think that Marcus won't
have read any more letters. But just let's suppose he
has. I know how distressing this would be for you, but
would it really upset Marcus that much? He never knew
Robert, after all. So he was never emotionally involved
with what happened. But all this is hypothetical.
Marcus won't have read any more letters. You have to
believe him, Meryl.'

'Not involved? Not involved?' Meryl shook off his
hands. 'How can you say that? Those years before I
married you, a child cooped up with an emotional
wreck like me in that ghastly flat, no playmates, no

father, no grandmother to speak of – no wonder he grew up so withdrawn. Of *course* he was involved.'

'But not with his father, was he? And I *know* how difficult his childhood was; I was your social worker, remember?'

She stood up. 'I'm going back to the garden.'

'No, Meryl, wait, please. Don't clam up on me. You know it does no good to keep things bottled up. Sit down, please, just for a few minutes.'

He reached out for her hand. She stood, statue-like, for what seemed like several minutes, then, with a shuddering sigh, sat down at the table. Gordon sat beside her, maintaining his grip on her hand. He was groping for a way to resume the conversation when, to his surprise, she spoke.

'I'm sorry,' she said. 'I shouldn't be so horrid to you. I know how good you've been with Marcus. He wasn't an easy child. You were wonderful to take him on.'

'Well, he was part of the package, wasn't he? Part of all the worldly goods that you endowed me.'

She gave a brief smile, and pulled back her shoulders. Her erect posture was a sign that she would be able to talk dispassionately.

'Did we go wrong with Marcus, d'you think?' she asked.

'What do you mean?'

'He's a strange person, isn't he? There, I've said it. Distant. Not able to make real friends. Strange obsessions. And those awful outbursts of temper. If Robert's death probably had little effect on him then it must mean the way he is must be due to the way we brought him up. What did we do wrong?'

'No one's a perfect parent. There were probably things we might have done better, but that's easy to say with hindsight. And in any case, I've always tended to

99

the nature side of the debate about nature versus nurture, despite being a social worker.'

'You mean it's in his genes? Well, thanks very much.'

Her last remark was made without bitterness. Gordon had broached that topic once before, but it was impossible to pursue it because she'd divulged very little about Robert's character. He'd mollified her by saying that there was nothing in her nature that anyone would object to inheriting. He did so again.

She lit another cigarette.

'I feel better now. And you're right, I ought to phone Marcus. I'll do it tomorrow, and just hope that bloody girl doesn't answer.'

'Good. And Meryl, don't mention Bailey. Just make it a social call. Ask him about his job. And why not ask him ask him how Sophie is, how she's getting on?'

'I'll think about it.' She got up. 'Right, I'm going back to the garden. Are you coming out?'

'Just as soon as I've washed up'.

She kissed him on the cheek then headed out to the garden, cigarette in hand.

There'd be no point in being totally honest, thought Gordon as he washed the cups; it would only upset her. But they *had* made mistakes with Marcus, in particular about his name.

The first mistake had been Meryl's. She'd registered the baby's name as Sidelski in Robert's memory. She said that this wouldn't be a problem for him: Studley, where she had moved after Robert's death, was far enough away from the village for no one there to register the significance of the name. Gordon forbore to say that it might be confusing for the lad, and the more so after they were married and Meryl took the name Whittaker.

But the second mistake had been his, although at the time it seemed a good idea. When they moved back to the village and Marcus passed the eleven-plus, Gordon persuaded Meryl that Marcus take his surname, Whittaker. Stratford Grammar was only a few miles from the village: the name Sidelski might be remembered by the parents of the boys there. Meryl disliked the idea, and only agreed when he said it could be an unofficial name only, and that on leaving school Marcus could decide for himself what his surname should be. The headmaster of the school had reluctantly agreed to the highly irregular proposal. But in retrospect Gordon wondered whether he'd been mistaken; whether the decision might have further added to Marcus's insecurity.

Then there had been the issue of what Marcus should be told, and when. He had to know sooner rather than later, lest he find out for himself. Privately, Gordon thought that Meryl should have told him when he was a young child, just as adopted children should be told of their origins at a young age in order that they grow up accepting the fact. But she hadn't. They'd agonised about this for years, Meryl always seeking to delay the fateful day, Gordon arguing for the sooner being the better. It was the only time a serious strain had been put on their marriage. In the end Gordon had to be forceful, something not in his nature, insisting that Marcus be told before he entered the turmoil of puberty. So one evening, a few weeks before his 13th birthday, they sat him down and told him the circumstances of his father's death. Gordon did most of the talking; Meryl was too fraught.

Marcus had taken it calmly. In fact there was no reaction at all: he didn't even ask questions. At the end he'd thanked Gordon politely for telling him, then disappeared upstairs to his room. Meryl was relieved

101

there'd been no outburst of anger; Gordon wasn't so sure. He was right to be concerned, for it was from that time that Marcus's problems began to become more pronounced. And the first thing he did on going to university was to abandon the name Whittaker and revert to being Sidelski. Although Gordon never admitted as much to Meryl, this had hurt.

Chapter 15

Milton Keynes, Saturday and Sunday 12 & 13 May

Sophie was swearing under her breath at other drivers, accelerating to close the gap between her and any car in front, then braking sharply at the last minute. Her face was set in a grim mask. Why the hurry, Marcus wondered? It was only their usual Saturday shopping trip to Sainsbury's. But he daren't ask her: any comment that implied criticism of her driving always resulted in an outraged response, and the last thing he wanted was for her to take her hands off the wheel or her eyes off the road, especially when negotiating the numerous roundabouts that they encountered on their way to the town centre.

It wasn't meant to be like this. When Milton Keynes was designed, each neighbourhood was supposed to be a village-like community each with its own church, school and shops. But competition from supermarkets meant that the few shops remaining were off licenses, newsagents and fast food outlets. Hence their journey to the town centre, and hence Marcus's dependence on buses when Sophie wasn't around. There were cycle-ways, but he had never been comfortable on a bike: balancing required too much concentration.

By the side of the road, newly-planted saplings and litter-strewn evergreen shrubs heralded the approach to Sainsbury's car park. Sophie swerved onto the slip road and juddered to a halt at the end of a queue of vehicles waiting to enter. It was always like this on a Saturday morning. Horns blared and headlights flashed. The queue inched forward. Marcus undid his seat belt in

103

preparation for the duty that had been assigned to him ever since their first visit to the superstore.

'You may as well get out now,' Sophie said.

'But it'll be ages before you get a parking space. It just means I have to hang about waiting for–'

'Oh for God's sake– '

'Okay, Okay'.

He jumped out of the car and made for the nearest trolley storage bay. It was easy to see – it was a glassed-in conservatory-like structure. But, although only 50 yards away as the crow flies, the journey to it was fraught with difficulty. No concessions had been made to pedestrians, who were required to make a convoluted zig-zag approach between cars parked in echelon formation and then run the gauntlet of vehicles competing aggressively for the few spaces that remained vacant. If only Sophie could be persuaded to drop him off at the same point on every visit, he was sure he could then work out a system to minimise the time spent and the distance travelled, but she would have none of it.

He reached the storage bay safely but was confronted with the next obstacle, one which required a challenging combination of manual dexterity and physical strength. He groped in his pocket for a pound coin, extracted it, and inserted it into the slot of the release mechanism that was designed to free the trolley from the chains that bound it to its fellows. That was the theory, anyway. But the tray containing the coin wouldn't push forward as it was supposed to. He always had this trouble. He pushed as hard as he could: no result. He banged the edge of the tray with the palm of his hand: no result apart from a sharp wrench of pain in his wrist. Everything was going wrong again.

A man standing behind him offered to help. He was shaven-headed and dressed in a hoodie and track-suit bottoms. With a delicacy that belied his appearance he gently manipulated the mechanism: the coin tray slid forward and the chain was released. But more humiliation followed: Marcus tugged at the trolley, but it stuck resolutely to the others. He tugged at it and was rewarded by another agonising spasm in his wrist. With ill disguised impatience, and with a muttered 'Fuckin 'ell', the hoodie grabbed the handle of the trolley and with no apparent effort pulled it free.

Marcus, his humiliation complete, tried to hurry away, eager to distance himself from witnesses to his ineptitude. But the trolley wheels refused to respond to attempts to steer it in the required direction. Sweating again, he manoeuvred it in jerking, crab-like movements towards the store entrance, pretending not to hear the blaring horns and foul-mouthed insults that came from the cars that were forced to avoid him.

He was relieved to find that Sophie wasn't waiting for him at the doors: evidently she was having trouble finding a parking space. He stood alone, trying to regain his composure. Not for the first time he wished he could obtain the solace that some people seemed to find in nicotine, but he didn't do cigarettes. He'd tried them on several occasions while at uni, but his attempts had always brought about paroxysms of coughing, much to his companions' amusement and Sophie's irritation.

His mood darkened as he waited for her. The previous evening had been the curtain-raiser for a weekend that was obviously going to be unpleasant. First, Sophie had quizzed him about his driving lesson – how had he got on? He'd grunted noncommittally: he *hadn't* got on. He didn't want to think about it, let alone discuss it. The experience had been mortifying: the driving instructor was barely able to conceal first his impatience then his evident contempt, his parting shot being an enquiry as to whether Mr Sidelski really wanted to learn to drive, and if not, might it not be best to cancel next week's lesson so as not to waste the time of both of them?

Sophie's next interrogation had been about the envelope placed on the breakfast bar. Who was writing to him, she'd demanded, and what was it about? He'd muttered that it was from a fellow photographer, and took the envelope up to the study where it still lay, unopened. When he returned downstairs Sophie had shot him a look of such malevolence that he cringed. For the remainder of the evening she hadn't spoken, beyond saying that she didn't want to eat, and no, she didn't want to go to the club, that she was feeling rough and was going to bed. Marcus hadn't dared read Bailey's letter even when he'd retired to his camp bed in the study, lest she make a surprise entrance and catch him in the act.

'Come on, then. What are you waiting for?'

He snapped to attention and followed her as she hurried into the store. He hated this next bit. He was obliged to follow her as she darted from aisle to aisle, not an easy task even when he had a trolley that behaved itself. Why couldn't she adopt a more methodical approach, plan her purchases so that he knew the sequence in which the items could be picked, enabling him to arrange them in the trolley in an orderly fashion? It would make things so much easier at the check-out. Today, when they finally reached the check-out she didn't engage in her usual banter with the senior citizen manning the till. Marcus envied her ability to chat to wrinklies when necessity demanded: he couldn't do banter.

As they made their way back to the car, Marcus still grappling with the trolley, they were greeted by Jane and Kevin, the young couple from next door, who were on their way in. Sophie barely acknowledged them: for some reason she seemed to dislike Jane, even though the extent of the couples' acquaintance was limited to each saying 'Hi!' to the other when they met outside their houses. Marcus had nurtured a hope that they might become friends, but when he'd suggested to Sophie that they invite them round for a meal she'd poured scorn on the notion, and accused Marcus of secretly fancying Jane. Marcus had been stunned: he hadn't thought of Jane in that way, but Sophie's remark had alerted him to how attractive Jane was; slim, blonde, and with the sort of bottom that he wished Sophie possessed. From then on Jane had become a focus for his erotic daydreams and night-time arousal as he listened, through the thin party wall, to her noisy appreciation of the service that Kevin provided. Marcus, laying rigid in bed, wondered what Sophie was thinking, but she always seemed to be asleep when the act was taking place. It had come as something of a relief when he'd been banished to the camp bed in the study.

He nodded and smiled at the couple, then set off in pursuit of Sophie. But he couldn't resist one backward glance at Jane's neat denimed backside, a vision spoiled by Kevin, at that very moment, placing a proprietary hand on it.

He spent the afternoon in his study, playing with his computer and not daring to open Bailey's letter while Sophie was around: she was in the lounge working on her lap-top. Scarcely a word had been exchanged since their return from the supermarket. When it got to six o'clock, hunger drove him to the kitchen, there to find

Sophie bent over the open fridge door. She extracted a packet of chicken breasts.

'What are we eating, then, Soph?'

'We? Well, *I'm* having a stir-fry. I don't know about you.'

'That's fine by me.'

'That's lucky, then, isn't it? Means only one of us will have to cook.' She pulled two chicken breasts from the packet and slammed them down onto the chopping board.

'I'll do it, if you like.'

'I do like. But I'll chop the chicken; you never slice it fine enough. You know where the bean sprouts and carrots are – oh, and don't forget the ginger. And don't put in too much soy sauce. While you're cooking I'll get a shower. It'll save time afterwards.'

So it seemed they were going out this evening – the club perhaps? Though grateful for the apparent thawing of her mood, Marcus was uneasy. There was something strange about her manner, no, not just her manner, but the way she was speaking. She seemed to have abandoned her street-jargon. And her speech modulation was different, somehow, more like an older person, like she used to speak in tutorials at uni, like how she probably spoke at work. Why?

His unease grew during the meal, during which she reverted to near silence. When, as he cleared away the plates, she chose to break it, it was with devastating affect.

'So what are *you* going to do with yourself this evening, then?' she said.

'Aren't we going to the club?'

'*I* might be going to the club. Haven't made up my mind what I'm doing yet. But whatever it is, it won't be with you. Like, I need some space. Need to get my head round things. Need to think out where we're

108

going, where *I'm* going. Sorry if that ... if that inconveniences you. I'm going to get ready.'

Marcus was left to load the dishwasher and ponder his future.

9.30pm. Sophie had been gone for an hour. She hadn't said goodbye; hadn't said when she'd be home. Marcus had read the letter from Bailey, but he couldn't concentrate on it. Bailey had referred to an enclosed photograph; Marcus had shaken the envelope, but nothing was lodged inside. He wasn't bothered. He'd lost interest in Bailey's doings. All he could think of was Sophie – where was she? What was she doing? And who was she doing it with? What had he done to make her behave this way? He'd gone along with all her demands, hadn't he? He'd even taken a driving lesson. What else was he supposed to do? How could he make amends if he didn't know what he'd done wrong?

Suddenly, the study with its narrow camp bed felt like a prison cell. He jumped up, ran downstairs into the kitchen, boiled a kettle for coffee, but stopped in the act of pouring the water into the mug. He didn't want coffee. He wandered into the living room, turned on the TV: the usual Saturday night rubbish: he turned it off. He glanced at the bookcase: nothing there that he wanted to read; in any case, he couldn't settle to read. He couldn't settle to anything.

He slumped in the armchair, took off his spectacles, rubbed his eyes. The dread of solitude rose up and smothered him. There wasn't anyone he could call.

2am. Sophie not back. Thrashing about in his camp bed, worrying. He'd sent her three texts, had phoned twice, but her mobile was turned off. The need to be with her, near her, overwhelmed him. He sprang up,

109

charged into the bedroom that he'd so recently shared with her, flung himself on the bed, buried his face in her pillow. It smelled of her, but was no comfort; it merely emphasised her absence. He curled into a foetal position.

A door slammed. He jumped up – *she's back!*

'Sophie!'

No reply. No footsteps. He moved to the landing: no light. Then, the muffled sound of feet stumbling up stairs, a shout of laughter, a high pitched giggle. It came from next door. Kevin and Jane, no doubt drunk after a night out. Marcus knew what would happen next. He returned to the bedroom and pressed his ear to the party wall. They started almost immediately. Marcus closed his eyes, visualising the scene. It excited him: he lay on the bed, began to unbuckle his belt ...

No! No! It wouldn't help: he'd feel ashamed and even lonelier afterwards, like he had the times he'd done it before, when Sophie was staying with Emma.

Fighting back panic he lumbered downstairs to the kitchen. No booze in the fridge, he knew that, but didn't Sophie have some brandy somewhere from the brief period she experimented with cooking? He hated spirits, but was seeking oblivion. He ransacked the kitchen cabinets, found a half bottle of Sainsbury's cooking brandy. It was nearly full. He carried it into the living room, slumped in the armchair and began drinking from the bottle.

He woke, and was disoriented. What was he doing here, in the sitting room, fully clothed? Then recollection came, accompanied by a thundering headache. *What's the time?* He peered at his watch. 8am. *She must be back now. She probably went straight up to her room.*

He heaved himself from the chair and staggered as he stood; the pain in his head renewed its attack with added vigour. He groped for his spectacles, put them on, shuffled to the door. At the foot of the stairs he stopped – *I'll take her up a cup of tea, show I've forgiven her for all the worry she's caused.*

It took a while to make the tea. His hand-to-eye co-ordination was shot to pieces. Half the water from the kettle missed the mug. Eventually it was done. Slowly and carefully he mounted the stairs: her bedroom door was open.

'Hi Soph, I've brought you a–'

The bed was empty, but the duvet was rumpled. Had she gone to the bathroom? He half turned, ready to call her, and then remembered – it was he who'd disordered the duvet. *Oh God, surely she's not still out?* He went to the window. No car in the drive.

Physical malaise suddenly overcame his mental anguish. He just made it to the bathroom and vomited into the toilet.

9am. He'd spent an hour slumped at the breakfast bar, head in hands, fighting back nausea, his mind a hamster on a wheel, frantically and fruitlessly covering the same ground over and over again. There was no one from whom he could seek reassurance. He'd considered trying Facebook, posting a message to the regulars at the club to ask if they'd seen her, but couldn't face the humiliation of having to ask, and, even worse, perhaps receiving a reply that she'd been there but had left early with some man. He'd thought of phoning Emma: maybe Sophie had spent the night there? Unlikely, given the way she was dressed when she left. But perhaps she'd gone on to Emma's later.

He reached for the phone, and as he did so it trilled: startled, he fumbled with the handset, didn't bother checking the caller's name – it *had* to be Sophie. Relief flooded through him.

'Soph? Where are you?'

'Marcus? It's me.'

Oh no. Oh please no.

'Marcus? Are you all right?'

'What? Oh, yes. I'm okay.'

'Are you sure? You sound strange.'

'I'm okay. What is it you want?'

'Well *that's* a nice thing to say to your mother. I haven't heard from you for over three weeks. Didn't it occur to you I might be worried?'

'Sorry. I've been a bit busy. You know, work and things.'

'And how *is* your job, Marcus? You never say much about it.'

'It's okay.'

'Well that doesn't tell me much, does it? Are you *sure* you're all right, Marcus?'

'Yes, yes. I said so, didn't I?'

Her sniff was audible down the line, then –

'And how's Sophia?'

'Sophie? She's okay.'

'Where is she?'

'Eh?'

'She's not there, is she?'

'No. She's gone to Sainsbury's.'

'Really? Then why were you asking where she was?'

'What d'you mean?'

'When you answered the phone. You thought it was her, didn't you? You asked her where she was.'

Can't handle this. Just get her off the line.

'She's a bit late back. Hang on, I think that's her now. I've gotta go, Mum. I'll phone you later maybe.'

'But Marcus–'

He clicked off the phone.

Why was she asking after Sophie? She's never done that before. Does she know something that I don't? Is it all part of a conspiracy, everyone keeping me in the dark? Why don't people tell me things? Why don't they listen to me? Even when I tell them interesting things they don't respond.

Another wave of nausea assailed him, accompanied by a churning in his bowels. He blundered his way to the foot of the stairs, but as he was about to mount them he heard a key turn in the front door. It was Sophie. But he hadn't time to greet her: nature wasn't just calling, it was screaming insistently.

Ten seconds later he was seated on the toilet, his face turned towards the washbasin. There was a bang on the door.

'How long are you going to be in there? I need a shower.'

'Just give me a few minutes.'

'Give me a shout when you're out.'

She joined him in the kitchen. When he'd emerged from the bathroom she'd pushed past him with a 'Hi' and locked the door behind her. Her shower took at least 15 minutes: he'd spent the time wondering how to approach her – tell her how worried he'd been, tell her how inconsiderate she'd been? No, that would provoke an outburst, or, worse, a silence. Maybe ask her where she'd been, or who she'd been with? That might seem like an interrogation. Ask her if she'd enjoyed herself? Yes, that would be cool. It was how people spoke, wasn't it, after a period apart?

But she spoke first.

'I stayed the night with Michelle. Needed some female company.'

'Who's Michelle?'

'A girl from work.'

'You've never mentioned her before.'

'She works in the human resources department. She's just split up with her fella. Thought she might like some company.'

'But Soph, why didn't you text me? I was worried. You could have been–'

'Had my phone off. Lots to talk about. Didn't want any interruptions. Sorry if you were worried.'

'Well, if you're going to do that again, could you–'

For the first time since she'd got home, she looked at him.

'Yes. I probably will be doing it again. But you'll know where I'll be, won't you? So there's no need to go on about it. I could murder a coffee. Do you want one?'

It was a peace offering of a sort, he supposed.

Chapter 16

Shropshire, Tuesday 15 May

Gabrielle had gone shopping and had arranged to meet Davina for a coffee. The two seemed to be getting on very well, and Derek was pleased about this. Gabby needed some company other than himself. As a couple, they got on well with the Taylors, but Derek hadn't yet reached the sort of rapport with Giles where he would be a comfortable drinking partner on his own. He'd observed that men seemed to be much more guarded in the early stages of friendship: women bonded more quickly, unless of course they took an instant dislike to each other, in which case they took pains to avoid each other.

Gabrielle's absence meant that he could concentrate on his next letter to Marcus. When he'd begun the one-sided correspondence it hadn't mattered if Gabrielle was around, sometimes coming into the room to peer over his shoulder and express interest in what he was writing. But now, for some reason he couldn't explain, he needed to be alone: more than that, he was discomforted by the idea of her reading the letters.

He sat, pen in hand. His first idea had been to describe life at university in the early 1960s, to put right any misconceptions that those of Marcus's generation had of that period. Derek had noticed that whenever the 60s were featured in TV documentaries, programmers resorted to the same footage to illustrate the culture of the time – a shot of a rock festival, girls in floaty dresses with flowers in their hair, bearded guys with flared trousers and headbands, all with dreamy dope-induced smiles as they waved their arms in the air and swayed around to an extended guitar solo.

But of course that sort of scene occurred only in the late 60s, and it lasted little more than a year. It was no more representative of the decade than flappers doing the Charleston were of the 1920s.

The reason for the inaccuracy was, he realised, that because for those now in charge of the media, the 1960s were ancient history. They weren't around to witness the flowering of the decade, nor its sad demise. Only Derek's generation could tell it like it was. Watching documentaries of the time made him feel sad – not with regret for his lost youth, but with the awareness that in not too many years (ten? twenty?) his generation would have gone, and there'd be no one left to recount what really happened. But by then, he supposed, no one would be interested.

In any case, his story was not that of a typical child of the 60s, if such a species ever existed. To be young at the time wasn't necessarily heaven. Not everyone had wild times at university or engaged in rampant hedonism in the years after.

He'd intended to contrast his time at university with the life that he imagined students led today, assuming that Marcus would find this of interest. The idea had been prompted by his revisiting Leeds the previous year, 50 years after his first year there. There'd been tremendous physical changes of course. Most of the back-to-back housing had been cleared, the industry had gone, and with it the smoke. He'd wandered round the university – some of the old Victorian buildings remained, squeezed between new steel-and-glass erections, and the area outside the Union building was largely unchanged. He had sat there for a while, watching the students. They'd looked so young – well, he would think that, wouldn't he? Listening to them, it occurred to him that they were living in a parallel universe to his – they had their own speech patterns, vocabulary and jokes, their own conventions and systems of etiquette. Many of them were thumbing their smart-phones or jabbering into them. No doubt they were gossiping, flirting, boasting and teasing just as he and his contemporaries had, but it was all being conducted in a patois he didn't understand. And they seemed so much more relaxed and easier with themselves and each other than his generation had been: they touched each other when talking, embraced on meeting and parting, exchanged kisses.

My God, that wasn't how his generation had been, not in 1961! He'd kept a photograph of the English Department taken that year. It could almost have been a scene from the 1950s; okay, there were a few sweaters and jeans on the lads, the odd bee-hive hairstyle on the girls, but many of the young men had short-back-and-sides and were dressed in blazers, ties and flannel trousers with the obligatory striped scarf hanging round their necks, and many of the young women had permanent waves and calf-length skirts and sensible shoes. And the sexes appeared not to be mixing, let alone touching, as though a gender-apartheid were in force. It represented the fag end of the post-war era, and it was all swept away in the three years while he was an undergraduate.

He'd also intended to tell Marcus about this, and his political involvement. He'd become very left-wing, of course, and a member of CND. A lot of students had, in those days, thinking they were likely to perish in a nuclear apocalypse. He'd attended one of the many end-of-the-world parties held the night before the Soviet fleet steered away from Cuba, but had soon left, intimidated by the girls who by that time had started to wear skirts at knee level, black stockings and knee-length boots.

117

Girls. Yes, it was girls he needed to tell Marcus about. And that last party after graduation, when he'd begun to suspect that he might have a serious problem.

He started to write.

Chapter 17

Well, Marcus, we've reached the 1960's. Don't worry, I'm not going to bore you with a panegyric about that decade. I know that we old farts bang on about it far too much. And in any case for me it wasn't – no, let me just tell the story.

I went to university in 1961. It was at Leeds, then a grimy industrial town, a hell of a culture shock for a soft southerner. I became politically involved, of course, but that's another thing I won't bore you with. I'm going to tell you about girls.

Girls. At that age, everything revolves round girls, doesn't it? It did for me, but not in the way you think. I harboured romantic notions about getting a steady girl. But to be honest, the female students terrified me – they made me feel like a little boy. In my first term I went to one of the Saturday night Union dances (they didn't become 'hops' until later), but it was all strict-tempo stuff, which I'd never learned to do. Dispirited, I resolved not to go again. I took refuge in my studies.

But in my second year I moved into a flat (squalid, of course), with three fellows on my course, Melvyn, Godfrey and Dick. I was surprised to be asked to join them; they were live wires and I was a loner. Dick had a girlfriend, Viv, who was a Geographer, but very attractive notwithstanding. For some reason she seemed to find me amusing. I got to be very fond of her.

Godfrey was from Liverpool. It was he who introduced us to the sound of that city. I remember him returning from a visit home triumphantly waving the 'Please Please Me' LP. My waning interest in popular music had been hastened by the Marxists' disparaging remarks about it, but I listened when Godfrey put the LP on the Dansette, and when it had finished I knew I was hooked again. Sorry, Marcus, I had resolved not to bore you with a paean to the swinging sixties. But the beat, the tunes and the half-way intelligent lyrics were the soundtrack to other events like the Profumo Affair and the assassination of Kennedy which seemed to signify the start of a period of profound change. (You probably have no idea what the Profumo Affair was, Marcus. These days we're used to politicians rutting like stags, but back then it was unheard of. That's not to say it didn't go on, but the media was deferential to our so-called betters.)

Sorry: this is supposed to be about girls, isn't it?

With the beat boom came new dance crazes (one was called *The Shake*, believe it or not) which meant one could hop about without any bodily contact with one's partner. For me, it was salvation of a sort. Until then, at parties, I was one of those saddos who stood getting drunk in the kitchen while most of my mates and their girls were jiving in the other room. I had never learned to jive.

Was this my initiation into the swinging sixties, you will be wondering? Was this when I finally overcame my reserve and began to make it with the girls? Are you anticipating seduction scenes? Well, Marcus, I began to enjoy parties, just for the joy of no longer being confined to kitchens but instead dancing with girls in the company of my mates. But seductions? Well, let me tell you about the last party I attended, just after finals.

The party was thrown by two of Godfrey's friends, Smudge and Ian in their flat near the university. They were both ravers. I was in awe of most of their crowd, especially, of course, the women. In particular Trudi,

Ian's current girlfriend, scared the shit out of me. She was what you would no doubt call 'hot' - and sexually voracious, by all accounts. When in her company I found it hard to keep my eyes off her, but was reduced to gibbering inarticulacy whenever she spoke to me.

I began the evening in the usual way, dancing with Viv. Dick liked to sink a few pints before he took to the floor. When he eventually came to claim her, I found that everyone had paired off and there was no one whom I could ask to dance. In any case most of the couples were smooching rather than bopping (smooching tended to start very early at Smudge's parties, a precursor to horizontal activity), and I wasn't comfortable with that. I made for the kitchen and the solace of booze, but was stopped at the door by Trudi, on her way out. She was shoeless and staggering slightly.

'Derek!' she said, and put her arm round me. 'Come an' have a dance with me!' Her speech was slurred.

'Where's Ian, then?'

'He's puking his guts up in the bog. He's no use to me in that state. Fancy a bop, me. C'mon.'

She pulled me into the scrum of shuffling couples and wrapped both arms round my shoulders. I made an attempt to adopt the strict-tempo dance posture, one hand clasping hers, the other decorously round her waist, but she was having none of it. She kept one arm round my neck; the other strayed down my back and her hand fluttered over my backside. She put her cheek against mine and then inserted her tongue in my ear. Her loins were grinding against mine.

Arousal? A bit. Fear? A lot. Fear not that Ian might emerge from the toilet and witness the scene, but rather fear that he might not. Fear that I was being led into a situation that I didn't know how handle; fear that I'd not be able to rise to the occasion.

121

I froze.

Trudi stepped back.

'What *is* it with you? Are you scared of me or something?'

'No, of course not. It's just–'

'Yes you are. It's not just me either, is it?'

'What d'you mean?'

'You're scared of all women, aren't you? You always back off, don't you? Everyone says so.'

Her voice was getting louder, her Lancashire accent more pronounced. Luckily. the slow number playing on the LP came to an end and was followed by a rocker. The couples around us started bopping, singing along to the track, thus sparing me the humiliation of them hearing what followed.

'It's all a con, isn't it, the way you look? So with it, aren't you, with your cord jacket and jeans and your Beatle hair-cut? You're such a pretty boy, aren't you? Tell you what I think; I think you're queer. Never had a woman, have you? Never even seen you with a girl. It's boys you fancy, isn't it?'

You probably can't appreciate, Marcus, what a heinous accusation this was in the days before gay liberation. It shook me to the core. My one aim was to put the maximum distance between myself and Trudi before more humiliation followed: I turned and made for the kitchen. She started to follow me, but I was saved by the emergence of Ian, who grabbed her and started dancing.

I can't remember much about the next few hours. It was spent in the kitchen (my old familiar refuge) as I sought oblivion by sinking as much booze as I could. When the party broke up, I staggered back to our flat with Godfrey and Melvyn (Dick was escorting Viv back to her digs). Once there, I began to feel distinctly ill and decided to forgo the usual post-party post-mortem and made for the bedroom. All I wanted was to sleep, to obliterate the ghastly possibility that Trudi's accusation might have substance.

But the ceiling began to spiral above me. I raised my head and placed one foot on the floor hoping to achieve some sort of equilibrium between the desire to sleep and the need to vomit. The latter demand gained the ascendancy, but I couldn't face the prospect of the descent of four flights of stairs to reach the outside privy. At all costs I mustn't puke in the bedroom: I shared it with the fastidious Melvyn. It had to be the sink in the living room. I managed to make it downstairs, charged past the coffee-drinking Melvyn and Godfrey, and reached the sink with a second to spare. A few moments later my relief was tempered by the realisation that the contents of my stomach now decorated the two days supply of unwashed plates and saucepans that remained in the sink.

The ever-sardonic Melvyn looked at me and raised his eyebrows.

'So, Derek,' he said wearily, 'this is the way your undergraduate days end; not with ejaculation but with evacuation.'

That was enough. There'd been countless times when I'd been irritated by Melvyn's elegantly-phrased put-downs, but I could never think of a witty riposte. This time, pissed as I was and bruised from my encounter with Trudi, words would not be enough. I grabbed a plate from the sink and, with all the force I could muster, smashed it into his face.

I was going to go on, Marcus, but I think I've said enough. Truth to tell, writing all this down has awakened feelings that are best perhaps left dormant. I'll leave you to make of it what you will.

Derek

Chapter 18

Milton Keynes, Thursday 17 May

Nobody in the cul-de-sac would be at home at 1.15 on a weekday. Sophie was fairly sure of that. Most of the occupants were young and were out at work all day. But she still felt apprehensive, on this her third lunchtime visit to the house in as many days, and she could still not think of a feasible story to tell Marcus should he ever be informed of her visit by some sneaky neighbour. So she insisted that Ben park a few streets away. To be seen repeatedly entering the house at this unusual hour would be bad enough: to arrive in a car with a strange man would be courting disaster.

Head down, she scuttled up the short path to the house, and after fumbling with her key for what seemed like minutes, she entered. She saw it immediately on the floor, the unmistakable brown envelope. Third time lucky. She now had a temporary respite from these excursions: that Derek guy would be unlikely to write twice in one week. She scooped up the envelope, turned and left, taking care not to slam the front door.

'Not another wasted journey, I hope?' said Ben as she got in the car.

'Not this time.'

'Good. I don't think we could keep on doing this on a regular basis. I may be your boss, but I have to be careful.'

'Yeah, I know.'

'That doesn't mean I don't want to go on seeing you, of course.'

'Good.'

'It'll have to be outside work time.'

'Yeah, I understand.'

He started the car and they set off back to the office, which was located on a business park on the other side of town. With her mission at last accomplished, Sophie could relax and enjoy the luxury of being driven in an Audi. She'd played her cards to perfection. The idea of their taking working lunch-times together had come to her after reading the letter. She needed a reason to take extended lunch breaks, her house being too far away to visit in the 45 minutes permitted by the company. And as she and Ben were both engaged on the same project, it had been just a question of the most appropriate time to make the suggestion. In the event, it had been easy, a natural thing to propose over breakfast after the night she'd spent in his flat. And she'd managed to phrase the proposal so that it could be interpreted not just as a reward for her favours but as a possible condition for their continuation. She'd seen in his face the battle being fought between concern for his position in the company and his evident desire to get between her legs again. Lust had won out.

He executed an unnecessarily ostentatious gear change and accelerated past a white van.

'So you'll come again next Saturday, then?' he asked.

'I'll see what I can do. I've got to be careful as well, you know.'

She needed to play it a bit cool. There would have to be more of these visits if she were to keep on intercepting those letters. If only the letters could be relied on to arrive regularly, but that was unlikely. She'd have to devise a new strategy to keep Ben compliant, but she couldn't think of one now. One of the problems was that she'd told him that she'd wanted to intercept an expensive purchase that she'd made without Marcus's knowledge, but this was an excuse that couldn't really be repeated. The other problem was that she didn't like Ben very much.

Saturday night had been strange. She'd felt somehow removed from what was happening, as though she were watching herself perform in a play. He was, as she'd expected, obviously gasping for it, but had the same difficulty in making his intentions explicit as he did in the office. She'd had to take the lead, and when it came to it he wasn't very good. A great disappointment, in fact. She thought someone of his age would have been more experienced, more adept. Perhaps that was why his wife had left him. He'd said a lot about his wife; called her a rampant feminist. He evidently hated feminists. Sophie was beginning to find that there was a lot that he hated – the government, rich people, chavs, immigrants, banks, trade unions, skivers, the council, the police. He reeked of discontent. It was reflected at work in his management style, one which involved niggling at his subordinates whilst complaining about his superiors. It hadn't bothered her unduly but now, in the three working days since they'd shagged, it had begun to grate on her. Was her liaison with him really worth it, just for the sake of intercepting those letters? She had to keep reminding herself that this was also her revenge on Marcus for his secrecy. And, she told herself, it was good to be with a man who looked presentable, despite his age, and one who might be useful in enhancing her career prospects.

'Usual procedure now, Sophie,' Ben said as he pulled into the company car park.

'Yeah, yeah, don't worry. Your reputation's safe with me.'

The usual procedure involved them keeping a careful professional distance between each other as they walked towards the entrance, Ben ostentatiously consulting his Blackberry while Sophie made sure the folder of papers she carried would be visible to any colleagues they might meet. It would have seemed unnatural not to have taken the lift together, and once on their floor Ben said loudly 'A productive session, Miss Blower. Thanks very much. We'll have this project wrapped up well ahead of schedule' and then made straight for his office.

Her colleagues kept their eyes on their computer screens as she crossed the floor to her work station. She'd had of course to explain to them the ostensible reason for her lengthy absences, and the explanation had done nothing to endear her to them. Ben Sidley was an unpopular boss, and she was dammed by association. She didn't really care: they were all older than her and most of them not very bright. She had no intention of remaining on the lowest rung of the company ladder for much longer, and if her colleagues thought she was sucking up to the boss for the sake of promotion, well, fuck 'em.

She switched on her pc, then extracted the letter from her folder. It was rare for a fellow-worker to visit her work station (such opportunities for social chit-chat were discouraged by the company) so there was little chance of her being disturbed. She was in the process of inserting a fingernail under the flap of the envelope when – *shit! I mustn't tear it! Christ, what do I do now?*

She'd forgotten it had to be steamed open and then re-sealed. There was nothing so antique as a kettle in any of the working areas. Beverages were dispensed from a machine located by the lift, and employees were expected to return to their posts with their plastic cups and take refreshment while continuing to work. Would the hot water taps in the toilet generate sufficient steam, she wondered? No, and in any case she might be interrupted.

Of course, old Ted! Ted the maintenance man, Ted whose cubby-hole was on a lower floor, so far from the beverage dispenser that he was allowed to brew up in his room. Sophie knew this, because she remembered his kettle boiling when she was being taken on an introductory tour of the premises on her first day at the company. She half rose from her seat, then subsided immediately. She couldn't leave her desk so soon after arriving. She returned the envelope to the folder and turned her attention to the screen. Or tried to.

A long, unproductive hour passed. At last, one of her colleagues stood and made his way to the beverage machine, prompting a gradual general exodus. Sophie waited until she judged the corridor outside to be a melee of those arriving at and departing from the point of sustenance, then sauntered out past the crowd by the lift and made her way to the top of the stairwell. No one paid her any attention. She clattered down two flights of stairs. Ted's door was open, and fortuitously he was at that moment filling his mug with boiling water. She made her request casually, and was told to 'Help yourself, love.' Ted was noted for his lack of interest in anything outside his maintenance duties and the breasts of the more well-endowed women in the company. Sophie, not blessed with those advantages, was spared his leering stares and any curiosity about her need for the services of his kettle.

Five minutes later she was back at her desk, the envelope unsealed. She extracted the sheets of paper, laid them in front of her screen, and with one hand toying with her mouse, began to read.

So, this guy was a wimp with a temper when he was at uni: what was so significant about that? He was now an old man, and there was something sordid about wrinklies writing about their attempted sexual exploits;

the guy probably got off on it. She shuddered at the thought.

It looked as though the correspondence was going to be just an excuse for him to tell his life story, and she couldn't be arsed to wade through any more. The curiosity she'd had about his connection to Marcus was evaporating. Marcus could keep his little secret, it was of no concern to her. And she'd be spared the hassle of further lunchtime visits to the house. But she'd continue to visit Ben on Saturdays, now and again. It would get her away from Marcus, and wouldn't do her prospects any harm.

She shoved the letter back in the envelope and thrust it in her bag before remembering that it would, that evening, have to be lying on the doormat in pristine condition for Marcus to find when he came home. She removed it: it was decidedly crumpled. After a few half-hearted attempts to smooth it out on her desk top she abandoned her efforts. What the fuck. Marcus probably wouldn't notice.

She replaced the envelope in her bag and turned her attention to the pc screen.

Chapter 19

Marcus was home even earlier. Jenkins had emerged from a day-long purdah in his office to announce that all the staff in the section could leave at 4.30. 'And that'll let you ride home on an almost empty bus, Marcus,' Jenkins had said with a smile. Marcus wasn't sure how to take Jenkins's smile. He often smiled at Marcus when he said things that weren't the slightest bit amusing. But then so did many of his colleagues, when they bothered to speak to him at all.

All day, rumours of forthcoming redundancies had been circulating the section. His colleagues seemed almost to relish the grim scenarios with which they might be faced. Sam Davies, leader of the office pack to whom the others (except young Mohammed) deferred, said that of course it would be a case of 'last in, first out', before adding gleefully that this would be tough on you, wouldn't it, Marcus, mate? Marcus hated it when Sam called him 'mate' and ignored the remark, though he was only too aware that what Sam said might be true. Sam had gone on to say that the union would threaten industrial action when it came to the crunch. Mohammed said in his usual quietly assertive way that Unison was a broken reed, and that in any case what would be the point of striking if the whole IT function were to be outsourced to a private company? Sam, who hated being challenged, had taken refuge in ranting loudly about spending cuts and those bastard toffs in the Coalition, sentiments with which his acolytes expressed agreement. On the bus home, Marcus had debated whether to tell Sophie about what was happening. But to do so might provoke a tirade about the iniquity of her having to be the sole wage-earner, so he decided to keep quiet until the worst happened, assuming that it would. The worst was just the sort of thing that *would* happen to him.

He pushed open the front door. There, on the mat, was the familiar A5 envelope. Bailey again. The events of the day had almost driven Bailey from his mind. All that stuff he wrote about his youth seemed totally irrelevant to the situation that he, Marcus, was in. And hadn't Sarah, the girl who occupied the work-station next to him, said that the mess the country was in was all the fault of those baby-boomers who'd had all the good times in the 1960s and were now living off the fat of their index-linked pensions? Marcus wasn't sure what a baby-boomer was, but if Sarah had been referring to wrinklies then Bailey would seem to fit the bill.

He picked up the envelope. It was a bit crumpled. Mangled in the post, Marcus supposed. But he may as well read it – Bailey's past might take his mind off his own present, and fill the time before Sophie came home.

He took the envelope up to his study/bedroom, opened it, and began to read. *Oh God, he's writing about 1960s.* Had Marcus been possessed of a sense of irony he might have found the coincidence amusing.

He threw the letter down on the desk top. So, Bailey hadn't enjoyed his time at University. So what? Not everyone could make it easily with girls: Marcus was only too aware of that. What was Bailey trying to tell him? Was he seeking sympathy? And that bit about thumping his flatmate – was he trying to impress? People thump people sometimes, don't they? It was no big deal. In fact it was boring.

131

Exasperated, he went down to the kitchen to make a coffee. The kitchen was untidy: the breakfast things hadn't been loaded in the washer, and there was a scattering of breadcrumbs over the table. Marcus had been trying hard to abide by Sophie's enjoinder that he should be more relaxed about domestic mess, but it made him feel twitchy. He itched to bring order to chaos. Sometimes it gave him sleepless nights. He thought about Bailey's reference to his own flat being squalid – yes, he could imagine that; so had been the place that he'd shared with his untidy flatmates when he'd been at university. Marcus had expended much energy clearing up after them. It was one of the reasons he'd hit Tony Goldman, after Tony had mocked him for it. Just like Bailey had hit *his* flatmate – *Christ!*

He forgot his coffee, and ran upstairs to read Bailey's letter again. Yes, why hadn't he spotted it? The parallels were obvious – Bailey was a failure with girls, wasn't one of the crowd, was inclined to lose his temper. Did Bailey know that he, Marcus, had similar issues? *No, nonsense.* How could he know? Unless ... had Bailey made contact with others who knew him? His former flatmates perhaps? Or even Sophie? Was it all part of a conspiracy? No, no, no. Totally illogical. Bailey knew nothing of him or his life. It was just a coincidence, surely?

He fed the letter and the envelope through the shredder. It did little to calm him. Though he'd almost completely discounted the conspiracy theory, the letter had spooked him: it was as though he had read his own life history written by one who had observed him unseen.

He couldn't settle. Activity was the only balm. Tidy the kitchen, maybe? No, Sophie insisted that breakfast debris be cleared along with that of their evening meal. But she held no domain over his study – yes, he could tidy that. It was a bit of a mess now that it had to accommodate a camp bed. He would start with the desk top. It was cluttered with general office detritus - documents, assorted pens, memory sticks - and a film of dust covered the surface.

He set to work. When it was clear, he reached for his aerosol duster and puffed it at the keyboard, the desk surface and the base of the VDU. More dust lurked behind it, so he pulled the VDU forward. Behind it was a small black and white photograph.

He examined it. Six guys, grinning at the camera. One of them was giving the V sign. They looked young – teenagers maybe – but they were dressed in weird clothes. Who the hell were they? How come the photo was on his desk? He glanced at the reverse side: on it was written *1959*.

It didn't come to him immediately. There was just a vague feeling that he'd discovered something that was familiar, like seeing a face in a crowd whom one seems to recognise but can't put into context. 1959? Did that date have any significance? Why should there be, in his house, a photograph taken over 50 years before? He could understand if it had been sent by Bailey, but there was no enclosure in today's letter, and he'd made no reference –

But wait - yes! Bailey *had* said he'd enclosed a photo! Not in today's letter, but in one he'd received weeks ago. What was it about? He dredged his memory. Finally it came to him – it was when Bailey had written about cycling out to some place to play cricket with his mates, when he should have been revising for his exams. But the photo hadn't been with that letter – he'd checked several times, not just in the envelope but on the desk.

Then how come ...?

There was only one possibility. Someone else must have opened the letter before he had. And there was only one person who could have done that. He was suffused first with anger, then with a sense of betrayal, then with renewed suspicions, which morphed into a near certainty, that there must be a conspiracy.

He must be careful. On no account should he confront Sophie with her crime. To do so would alert her to the fact that he suspected she might be in contact with Bailey. Vigilance was the way forward, if he were to discover the nature of Bailey's game.

He stored the photograph in his Domestic Finance folder, placed the folder in the filing cabinet, and sat down on his camp bed. He needed to devise a plan of campaign.

Chapter 20

Warwickshire, Thursday 24 May

It was raining, as usual. It had rained almost unceasingly all through April, and May was proving to be little better. It was inevitable, she thought, that the deluge had begun almost immediately after the imposition of a hosepipe ban, and inevitable that it was in this spring of all springs that gardening, her refuge in times of stress, had been largely denied to her.

She hunched against the wind, battling to control her umbrella as she walked home from the village hall, but the brolly and Barbour gave no protection to her skirt. Most of her fellow members of the Womens' Institute had been clad in jeans and hooded puffas, testament to the organisation's decline in dress standards that she so deplored. Meryl would no more have dressed that way to attend a WI meeting than she would have served tea in a mug primed with a teabag, something else that now seemed acceptable amongst the matrons of the village. The ritual of pouring tea from china pots into delicate cups had been abandoned when Debbie Cartwright had become chairwoman (or 'chair' as she insisted on being called), something to be expected from a woman who dressed like a tart and who, it was known, was carrying on with Jan Barlow's husband, possibly with Jan's acquiescence. The singing of 'Jerusalem' had long been consigned to history. Meryl was all the more determined not to let her own standards drop: this, at least, she felt she owed to her mother, who had been confident in her unchallenged place in the scheme of things.

She hadn't enjoyed the meeting. The sole item on the agenda had been to finalise the arrangements for the WI's contribution to the village's celebrations of the Diamond Jubilee. They'd been discussing this in meetings since the previous autumn, and until recently Meryl had been an enthusiastic and forceful participant, determined to ensure that the event would be conducted with the sort of decorum required of such a milestone in the nation's history, and indeed she'd won her battle with Debbie Cartwright over the proposed inclusion of a glamorous Granny competition.

But today she'd been distracted and unable to participate. She couldn't stop thinking about her unsatisfactory phone call to Marcus the previous Sunday. Something hadn't been right. Marcus was never the easiest of persons to chat to on the phone, but on Sunday he'd seemed distracted; on edge. And he'd said that Sophie was at Sainsbury's. Why? Shopping at Sainsbury's was something the couple always did together on Saturday mornings, a weekly event that Marcus, with his obsession for routine, would never forgo unless something was amiss. No doubt that bloody girl was to blame for the trouble, and trouble, Meryl believed, there certainly was.

She entered the house and deposited the dripping umbrella into the antique stand in the hall. There was the sound of the Dyson trundling about upstairs. Whenever she was out Gordon always took it upon himself to 'do a spot of tidying'. Recently he'd tentatively resumed his suggestions that some of the junk, as he called it, could be cleared out, something she fiercely resisted. For her, the house was a domestic archive in which everything had to be preserved.

The Dyson expired with its peculiar sighing moan, something that had annoyed her from the day that Gordon had proudly presented her with the replacement for her ancient hoover. Recently she was finding that the comfort that her marriage to Gordon had brought her was becoming an ever-thinner membrane stretched tightly over a drum of increasing irritation. She knew that the fault was all hers: Gordon was as kindly and thoughtful as he had always been. The dreadful possibilities raised by Bailey having contacted Marcus had resurrected all the neuroses buried within her, and she was, she knew, becoming difficult to live with.

'I'm home' she shouted.

Gordon trundled down the stairs, kissed her and began helping her off with her Barbour. Such gentlemanly assistance with divestment was something she'd taught him when they were first married, but now it was yet another source of irritation.

'Good meeting?' he asked.

'I suppose so.'

'Fancy a cup of coffee? Then we can sit down and you can tell me all about it.'

'Not coffee; not in the afternoon. I'd love a cup of Lapsang Souchong. And can we have it in the drawing room?'

'Of course.'

Once in the drawing room she began to relax, soothed by a cigarette and the familiar comfort of the shabby armchair in which she sat. Gordon entered clutching a tray, tripped over the fraying edge of the carpet, and almost fell. He managed to rescue himself and the contents of the tray, which he deposited on the battered occasional table in front of her.

'Aren't you having any tea?' she asked.

'Had a coffee just before you got in.' He sat down on the settee opposite her. 'Well, tell me about the meeting. All arrangements for the beanfeast agreed?'

She poured her tea.

137

'Yes, I suppose so.'

'To your satisfaction?'

'Yes, I suppose so.' She didn't want to talk about the meeting, mainly because she could remember so little of it.

'Meryl. How long is this going on?'

'How long is *what* going on?'

Gordon sighed. 'You know what I mean. This abstracted behaviour. You're not with me half the time. It's Marcus, isn't it? You're still worrying about that phone call, aren't you?'

The relaxation that she'd begun to feel evaporated. She dragged at her cigarette and ground it out, half smoked, in the pewter ashtray that she'd inherited from her father. Another counselling session was about to begin. She didn't think she could stand it. But to remain silent would only provoke an interrogation; a gentle interrogation but an interrogation nonetheless.

'Of course I'm worried. I told you, something was wrong, I know it. I can tell when Marcus is ... upset.'

'Look, Meryl, have you thought about going to see him? We can drive over at the weekend if you like. It'll take less than two hours. Then you can satisfy yourself that—'

'No! That girl will be there. She's the problem, I'm sure. Marcus will never say anything while she's present.'

'Well, it will have to be a weekend visit, won't it? Marcus works. So, how about inviting him down here next weekend?'

'Don't be *ridiculous*: how could he *possibly* do that? The train journey would take an age. He'd have to go to Birmingham and then out to Stratford and then we'd have to collect him, and take him back there on Sunday and the trains are terrible on Sundays, and anyway Marcus hates travelling by train, and—'

'Okay, okay! Just a suggestion. He really ought to have another go at learning to drive. How many 24 year olds can't drive, for God's sake?'

'Well, *I* couldn't at that age. And neither could Marcus's father – Robert never learned to drive at all: maybe that's ...' She stopped, horrified that she'd given Gordon an opportunity to revisit her past. She felt the dizzying onset of panic. The hand holding the saucer shook slightly. She put it down and lit another cigarette.

Gordon was looking at her quizzically. She knew what was coming next.

'Robert never learned to drive?' he said. 'You never told me that before.'

'It wasn't important.'

Gordon was silent for a moment, then got up, approached her and squatted in front of her. He took her hand.

'Meryl, listen. I know you hate talking about the past, but can't you at least tell me more about Robert? I could understand it when I first met you, it was all so recent, so raw, but after 25 years? Is his death really still so painful? And he was the father of your child, after all. You've never even spoken much about him to Marcus, yet you insist he bears Robert's name. Maybe if you had ... well, maybe–'

'Stop it, Gordon, please.' She jerked away her hand. 'I've tried to tell you countless times. Don't you understand? My time with Robert was so short. I have so few memories of him.'

Gordon rose stiffly. She tensed. Was he going to pursue the matter? Dread settled on her stomach like a hastily consumed meal.

'Okay, love. Sorry to upset you. I won't bother you about it any more.' He moved over to the French windows. 'Looks like the rain has stopped. I think I

139

might go for a bit of a walk before dinner. D'you fancy eating at the pub tonight?'

Meryl didn't relish the idea of eating surrounded by the raucous jollity of an evening in *The Bell*. But the thought of sitting opposite Gordon in the silence of their dining room, with so much between them that could not be spoken of, was even less appealing. She opted for the former.

'Good,' said Gordon. 'It'll do you good to get out. I'll phone and book a table before I go for my walk.'

It was strange, she thought, how the irritation engendered by one's partner evaporated as soon as one was left alone in the house. Meryl hated being alone. She was painfully aware that she had few inner resources other than a love of gardening. In her youth she'd been an avid reader, but novels had ceased to be of any comfort to her after the horror that had befallen her in her twenties; in fact they served to remind her that it was the source of her literary awakening which had led to the catastrophe that had so nearly ruined her life.

She got up and carried the cup, saucer and ashtray into the kitchen, emptied the cigarette ends into the pedal bin, rinsed the crockery under a running tap, then left it to drain. She stood, staring through the window at the sodden garden, wondering how to occupy herself. There was no housework to do: Gordon had seen to that. But she had to do something – perhaps undertake a mental inventory of all the stuff that Gordon called junk, to see if she could bear to part with some of it?

But she knew that few of the items were easily disposable. It wasn't really clutter that Gordon objected to. It was the bulky furniture dating back to the 1930s, the threadbare rugs of similar age, the oil paintings collected by her grandfather which still adorned hall, staircase and landing, the towering oak bookcases laden with bound volumes that no one ever read, the brass and china ornaments on mantle-shelves, sideboards and dressing tables – all the stuff she'd grown up with, stuff that reminded her of her father and her safe, secure childhood and adolescence, stuff that had once again cocooned her when she'd returned to the house after her mother's death, bringing Gordon and Marcus with her. And now, more than ever, she needed it around her; a bulwark against the intrusion of a more recent past.

She wandered back into the drawing room, slumped down in the armchair and reached for another cigarette. Only two left in the pack – perhaps it was as well they were going to *The Bell* that evening so she could replenish her stock.

Inhaling deeply, she wondered, as she had so many times before, whether her fate had been decided when she made such a mess of her 'A' Levels at her all-girls grammar school. If she'd managed to get good grades then she might have gone to university, have mixed with different sorts of people, met boys, lost her virginity, done all the things that she imagined most girls did at university in the 1970s, and, most important, have left the village. Instead, she'd undertaken a secretarial course at the local college in Leamington whilst still living at home, and then took a job at a solicitor's office in Stratford, where, after three years, it dawned on her that she was bored, unfulfilled and still a virgin at the age of 22. She'd been a pretty young woman and had a few boyfriends, mainly the sons of her parents' friends, but they all disappeared after the first few dates. This, she'd realised later, was because she had been prissy, introverted and demure to the point of frigidity.

Gradually resentment had begun to build within her for all that she had missed. Her mother started to irritate her, with her insistence on the need to keep up standards, this at a time when her father's health and business were beginning to fail. One night, after a day in which her mother had driven her to screaming pitch, it occurred to her that it was not too late. An acquaintance in the village, in her forties, had just gone to university as a mature student – why shouldn't she do the same? It would mean re-sitting her 'A' Levels, of course.

And so, in the teeth of affronted opposition from her mother, she'd again become a student at the college in Leamington. It was her liberation. She was only a few years older than her fellow students, and she began to act out the adolescence she'd never had. But she was always required to return home every evening at the time when things started to become interesting. It was one of her lecturers, an Adonis in his early forties who'd opened her eyes to the world. She'd begun to read voraciously; novels, journals, serious newspapers; she joined the Labour Party, demonstrated against the Falklands War. And it was he who persuaded her in her second year that she really ought to break away from the stifling confines of her village, and how about moving to Leamington, into his flat? Dizzy with expectation, she agreed. Her mother was outraged.

Three years later, armed with three reasonable 'A' Levels, she'd still been living with the lecturer, and no nearer to going to university. She was enjoying herself: the lecturer and his colleagues provided ample stimulation. And one of his colleagues was Robert Sidelski, the college librarian. And then ...

She stubbed out her cigarette angrily. If only her memory of those days could filter out all the things she regretted. She had heard it said that it was humankind's good fortune that memory is a sieve that lets all the unhappy bits through, but it wasn't like that for Meryl – the unhappy bits forced their way back up again, sullying the sparse recollections of Robert. Normally, when someone close is lost, the things that define them remain – their records, their books, their photographs, the places visited together, the songs they had sung. But she'd not been long enough with Robert to accumulate these things. The memories one has of the departed live on in the heads of those left behind, but this is a comfort only when others can share one's memories with others. But there was no one around who'd known him. She'd never met his family. Their mutual friends had long moved on. She was alone with his memory, and it was sometimes too much of a burden to carry.

The only thing she had of his was Marcus. That was why, of all the rooms in the house, Marcus's old bedroom was the most sacrosanct, untouched since he'd left for university. She scarcely dare acknowledge to herself her secret hope that one day he might come back and sleep there again.

Chapter 21

Shropshire, Friday 25 May

Gabrielle was away. She was on one of her occasional visits to Liz who lived in Birmingham. Liz was one of a few old friends with whom Gabrielle had kept in touch. Apparently she was totally accepting of Gabrielle's marriage to Derek, and by implication accepted, or even forgave, his past. Derek was grateful to her for that, and pleased that Gabrielle had someone with whom she could spend time having girl-talk.

She had left the house at 7 o'clock, when it was already raining. The rain had got heavier, driven by a strong easterly wind, enough to prevent Derek from having his morning jog. And a morning at the allotment was definitely out. He still hadn't sowed his runners, and his broad beans were only four inches high, stunted by the waterlogged soil and the lack of sunshine. Christ, what a spring.

He'd cooked breakfast, washed up, had a shower, read the paper, and was now at a loss for something to do. The day stretched ahead with no prospect of any company. Derek was edgy when by himself for any length of time. He was reminded of his early 20s when he'd lost his way and was without a steady job, when, penniless, he'd shied away from his former university friends and had become a near recluse. But in your 20s there's always hope for the future. When in your 60s, extended solitude is not just depressing, it's alarming.

Not that he was really alone, of course. Gabrielle would be home this evening. But whenever they were apart, despite his occasional irritation at her presence, he felt the onset of a lowering bleakness. With no one else around, there was only the overpowering awareness of himself. He always dreaded the possibility that Gabrielle, though ten years his junior, might pre-decease him, for him then to be faced with aimless days and frightened nights, and nothing to look forward to. Oh God, he hoped she would drive carefully.

He thought about writing to Marcus, but he knew he couldn't settle to it. His muse had deserted him: he wasn't sure which period of his life to describe next.

He sat in the kitchen, half listening to 'Woman's Hour' until the ranting of an unreconstructed feminist forced him to turn the radio off. It made him, suddenly, itch for male company – again, something he never sought when Gabrielle was around. He'd thought he'd had enough of male company to last a lifetime.

Then, the idea came to him. Giles. He and Giles had never met alone; Davina and Gabrielle were always present. But there was a growing rapport between the two of them. They saw eye-to-eye on most things – literature, politics, the decline in educational standards. They would have plenty to talk about, and without any obligation on his part to divulge his personal history. When blokes were together the conversation tended towards the factual, or the exchange of ideas and opinions. Women, on the other hand often spoke more of personal matters. He doubted that Davina would join them if Gabrielle were not present.

He picked up the phone.

'Giles? It's Derek. Okay, thanks, and you? Are you busy? Look, mate, I'm at a bit of a loose end; Gabby's away for the day. Fancy a lunchtime pint in *The George*?'

'Cheers,' Derek said, raising his glass. They were on their second pint.

145

'Cheers,' Giles said. 'Let's drink to the downfall of the Coalition.'

'Well, yes. But I reckon they'll go their full term. Mid-term council losses won't count for much when it comes to a General Election.'

'You're probably right,' Giles acknowledged, and took a swig from his glass.

They'd been discussing the Council elections which had taken place three weeks before and had resulted in substantial Labour gains. Not in north Shropshire of course, despite the canvassing contribution made by Giles, who dressed and spoke like a Tory grandee and might have appealed to some disillusioned Conservatives. He'd tried to get Derek involved in the campaign, but Derek hadn't the energy – nor the time, given the hours spent writing to Marcus. Nor, if he was honest with himself, did he have the inclination. Today's paper had been full of the financial crisis in the Eurozone, with dire prognostications for the future. It was the sort of thing on which he ought to have an opinion, but he was unsure what his stance should be. It was so much easier to take up a position in the 60s and 70s, and even more so in the days of Thatcher. But Blair's Third Way had muddied the waters of conventional politics. He sometimes found himself, to his shame, lapsing into the belief that there was little to choose between politicians.

Now the campaign was long over, Giles evidently felt it safe to push him further about his political commitment. 'Weren't you ever active in the Labour Party?' he asked.

'Wouldn't say really active,' said Derek. 'I was a member of the local branch when I lived in Rochdale, just for a couple of years.'

'I never knew you lived in Rochdale: when was that?'

'Oh, late 60s. I was lecturing – well, teaching, at the college there. It was my first post in further education. I had two years there, and after that I moved on to a college in Warwickshire.'

Giles took a swallow from his pint.

'You're a bit of a dark horse, Derek. You never told me you were in FE. I had the impression your whole career was in adult education.'

Derek felt a slight frisson of discomfort, then pulled himself together. Just keep the conversation impersonal, he told himself, and avoid adult education if possible.

'No, I spent 20 years in FE, And before that I even had a year trying to teach in schools, well, just one school in fact. That was enough for me.'

'Tough, eh?'

'You're not kidding. It was in a Secondary Modern in Leeds, my first post after getting my PGCE. It was before comprehensives had got going. I had ideological objections to teaching in a grammar school, and when you're young you try and live by your beliefs, don't you? At least, that's what some of us did then. It was the time when we were naive enough to believe that the revolution was at hand. You know - CND, Vietnam, Grosvenor Square and all that.'

'I should have thought that teaching in a sec mod would have increased your revolutionary fervour. Selection was an iniquitous system.'

Derek grinned inwardly and resisted the temptation to remind Giles of his public school education.

'Oh, sure. Yes, I was sympathetic to the plight of the kids, poor little buggers. Trouble was, they had no sympathy with me. They tore me to pieces. I had no idea how to handle them. So I resigned after a year.'

'And went straight into FE?'

'I wish! No, I spent the next two years doing casual work, trying to sort myself out. Actually for quite a bit of the time I was on the dole.'

'*Really*?' Giles's fascination for the lifestyles of the disadvantaged was immediately awakened. 'What was it like? It sounds interesting – tell me more.'

Derek hesitated. Gabrielle was the only person he'd ever told about his dark years. They didn't accord with his image as the self-assured cock-of-the-roost that he'd later cultivated during his time in Leamington. But to Giles he was just an ageing retired teacher with cultural interests, literary aspirations and left-wing leanings – there would be no harm in telling him, would there? It would help give him a bit more inverted social cachet in Giles's eyes.

So he started to relate the story. He told of his time working as a clerk in the Social Security office in Leeds, where his fellow employees regarded him with suspicion and where his supervisor, a bully of limited intelligence, had taken every opportunity to mock his southern accent and sneer at his university degree, finally goading him into the frenzied outburst of anger that had resulted in his instant dismissal. He told of his time washing dishes in the kitchen of the Queen's Hotel where the mind-numbing boredom of the job and sheer physical exhaustion had led him to resign after six months. He told of his time on the dole, eking out an existence in a squalid bed-sitter in Hunslet, of how when his entitlement to the dole expired he was forced to spend endless days alone indoors trying to survive on the meagre social security cheques which only a year before he'd been employed to write out. Giles responded to his story with sympathetic grunts and nods, with the occasional interjection of 'disgraceful!' or 'iniquitous!'

But he didn't tell Giles about the emotional depths to which he had sunk. He didn't mention the loss of contact with his university friends as they took the first steps on their career ladders and acquired cars, wives and mortgages, nor his gradual descent into complete social isolation and his loss of interest in the world around him as depression descended on him and he became an unkempt, unwashed and malodorous recluse.

'So, what gave you the idea of going into F.E. then?' Giles was nothing if not persistent.

'It was one of those things that was pure chance. I didn't know anything about F.E. – don't think I even knew of its existence. But I met up with one of my old university friends who put the idea into my head. So I put in a few applications, and got a post after my first interview – in Rochdale.'

'Strange, how the pattern of one's life is often determined by chance meetings,' Giles observed.

'Yes, you're right there.'

*

But it hadn't been a chance meeting. After two years of avoiding any contact with his university friends, he had been tracked down by Dick. Dick came with news and an ultimatum. The news was that he and Viv were to be married the following month. The ultimatum, delivered with his usual bluntness, was that unless Derek stopped feeling sorry for himself and got off his arse to attend the wedding, then he, Dick, and Viv as well, wanted nothing more to do with him and he could sit here and rot for all they'd care.

A few weeks later, wearing a suit that he'd purchased with money loaned by Dick, he had been reunited with his old friends who seemed to bear him no ill-will for his self-imposed purdah. At the reception, he sat on the veranda and watched the antics of Viv's younger sister and her friends on the grass below him. To Derek, who'd been exiled from youth culture for two years, they were akin to a swarm of exotic butterflies. The girls had long hair and fringes, and those not wearing the briefest of miniskirts were clad in long floating dresses that reached to the ground. The trousers of the boys were flared, their shirts patterned with flowers and their hair curled over their collars. One of the youngsters had emerged from the club house with a portable record player and a collection of LPs, to appreciative cries of 'Great, man!' Derek assumed that dancing was about to begin, but they all remained sprawled on the grass and listened in silence to a series of songs which sounded as though they were being sung by the Beatles, but not the Beatles that Derek remembered, certainly nothing that could be danced to. He began to listen as intently as the youngsters – *Tangerine trees and marmalade skies? Henry the horse? Meeting a man from the motor trade?* What the hell was all that about, he'd wondered? What had happened to the world in the past two years?

His reverie had been interrupted by the approach of Melvyn. They stuttered into awkward conversation - they'd not spoken since Derek had smashed the plate over his head three years previously - during which Derek learned that Melvyn had already obtained a promoted post at his school, and Melvyn was told of Derek's disastrous experience at the secondary modern.

'So you've no intention of returning to teaching?' Melvyn had asked.

'Dead certain. I can't relate to kids.'

'Had you considered working in a technical college?'

'A tech? But they're for training people for things like engineering and secretarial work, aren't they?'

'Not entirely. Some of them have started offering GCE courses for school leavers. And you could teach liberal studies to vocational students. All the students are there by choice. Not many discipline problems, I reckon.'

Derek had felt a flicker of interest and was about to ask Melvyn more, when a new sound came from the record player. It sounded like a classical piece – Bach, perhaps? He turned to watch the youngsters, who were all sitting in a circle: one of them appeared to be rolling a cigarette, watched with expectant interest by the others. But it wasn't Bach that was playing, there was a vocal – *They trip the light fandango, turn cartwheels on the floor* – sung by a husky, keening male voice. Derek was moved, but he didn't know why.

'Can't hear ourselves talk with all that racket,' Melvyn had said. 'Let's go inside. I'll tell you all I know about technical colleges.'

Derek had followed him towards the door, pausing once to look back at the group encircling the record player. There had been something in Derek that wished to be part of the scene – he'd been missing out on so much. But instead he'd turned and followed Melvyn.

*

'... did it, Derek?' Giles was speaking.

'Eh? Sorry?' Derek was far away in the summer of 1967.

'You were miles away then, weren't you? I was asking you if it took you long to settle back into teaching when you got to Rochdale.'

'It was a bit strange at first, all the students being over 16. Had to learn to stop treating them like kids.

151

Teaching GCE was a doddle. But Liberal Studies with vocational students could be a bit hairy – especially with the craft apprentices. Liberal Studies always seemed to be timetabled for the first hour after lunch, which the lads had spent in a pub, of course. Welders 4 after a few ales weren't exactly receptive to my attempts to expose them to culture. In the end I gave up and showed them films. It kept 'em quiet.'

Giles nodded thoughtfully, then began an exposition on his favourite topic, the way that modern education had failed the working classes. Derek listened with only half an ear, for he had just decided on the content of his next instalment to Marcus. It would be his time in Rochdale. He wouldn't bore Marcus with his bleak years in Leeds, and, tempting though it was, he would omit a description of his sudden exposure to flower power and *Sergeant Pepper.* Rochdale was a story it was necessary to tell, the final chapter before Derek's life began to impinge on the world which Marcus would recognise.

'Fancy another pint, Giles?'

Giles, his peroration interrupted, glanced at his watch.

'Good God, is that the time? Afraid not. I promised Davina I'd go to the garden centre with her this afternoon.' He stood up. 'But we must do this again, Derek. I've enjoyed it.'

'Yes, we must,' said Derek.

He hurried home, eager to put pen to paper. He needed to start the Rochdale instalment while the motivation was still there. He hadn't told Giles the half of it. Such was his shame over what had happened that January night in 1970, that he had glossed over the event even when telling Gabrielle about it. But with Marcus he must be totally honest: he owed it to the lad. Once the story of the incident had been told, he could move on. He wanted it out of the way, done and dusted.

Such was his eagerness to start that he went straight to the parlour without first making himself a coffee. He grabbed a sheaf of paper, unscrewed his fountain pen, and then sat. How the hell should he start this? With his experience teaching at the college? With his continuing unwanted chastity? His social life, such as it was? No, he'd go straight to that evening, sitting in that grim cafe along with Barney McGuiness and the two yobs that Barney had brought with him. Even now, after more than 40 years, the thought of Barney and his accomplices made him shudder. This was going to be difficult to write. He must try not to make excuses for what he'd done, just tell it how it was.

Chapter 22

Hello once again, Marcus.

I wondered whether to give you my email address with this letter. But on thinking about it, I think it's best left until my next. Before that, I'm going to tell you about something that happened in 1970 – I was 27 then, only a few years older than you are now. I hope it will help you to understand why I was the sort of young man I'd come to be.

I'm not going to bother telling you about my life in the three years after I graduated: suffice it to say it was not a happy time. But in 1968 I took a job teaching in a technical college in Rochdale. To describe what this involved would be tedious. It wasn't as academically rarefied as it sounds – far from it. But for me it was a lifebelt, my first steady job after three years of drifting, and I was reasonably settled. I shared a flat with a fellow-lecturer in a tower block in the city centre – oh, in case you're wondering, he was male. I still hadn't 'got it together' (as the saying then was) with chicks, as they'd come to be called, not in any meaningful way. And I was in my late 20s! Pathetic, eh?

My social life, such as it was, was confined to the odd drink with colleagues at weekends and with my fellow members of the local Labour Party on Thursday evenings after the branch meeting. It was my membership of the local branch that led to the events of the evening that I'm about to describe. What happened that evening represented the nadir of my self-esteem. Things began to improve after that.

At the Labour party branch I'd got to know a fellow called Barney McGuiness. He was draughtsman in a

154

small engineering company. When we first met he'd singled me out for attention and at first I was flattered. But I'd begun to feel uneasy in his company. He was a Trotskyite, a member of the Socialist Labour League and had begun to adopt the role of one whose mission was to lead me away from political naivety towards his particular enlightenment, and he conducted his tutorials in an increasingly hectoring manner. I'd begun to try to distance myself from him when at meetings or in the pub afterwards.

On the evening I'm going to describe he'd insisted on my meeting him in a café near the station. It was in a street of semi-derelict buildings and its interior reflected its location. The formica-topped tables were grimy; cardboard covered several broken window panes, two of the fluorescent tube lights were not working and a third was flickering its way to expiry. When I arrived, there were four other occupants, aged down-and-outs eking out their tea and clinging to the fuggy warmth of the place before being turned out, probably to go to the Salvation Army hostel. Had there not been a few vacant tables I would have walked out immediately on seeing them. You see, Marcus, I shrank from the odour of the disadvantaged, despite my sympathy with their plight.

I'd only been in the place a few minutes when Barney entered, accompanied by two young men whom he introduced as Terry and Chris. Apparently they were shop-floor workers in the engineering company where Barney worked. They both wore black imitation-leather jackets and greasy hair styled as though Teddy Boys were still in fashion. When they made their way to the counter to purchase tea, Barney hissed at me that I shouldn't mention anything about the Socialist Labour League in their presence; they wouldn't understand.

155

'Why are they here, then?' I asked. 'More to the point, why am *I* here? What's this all about?'

'Look on it as a sort of test,' said Barney. 'You've begun to disappoint me recently, Derek; you don't seem so committed. We're reaching a crisis of capitalism and the time's approaching when progressives may have to take direct action to precipitate its demise, starting at local level. I want to know if you're going to be in the vanguard of the struggle.'

The reference to the 'direct action' and 'local level' buried in the jargon made me feel uneasy. Barney had hinted before that his political activism extended beyond the confines of local branch meetings and this was somewhere that I had no inclination to follow.

'What about those two?' I said, nodding towards Terry and Chris who were being handed mugs of tea. 'What do you need them for?'

'They're here 'cos they can look after themselves. Useful to have around when you're in a spot of bother.'

'What sort of bother?'

As you can imagine, Marcus, I was getting nervous. This wasn't my scene at all. Barney didn't answer my question because Chris and Terry approached bearing mugs of tea.

Chris addressed me for the first time 'So you're a bloody liberal studies teacher. I went to the Tech some years back. A load of wankers, you lot.' He pushed a greasy hank of hair back from his acne-scarred forehead and took a swallow of tea.

Terry smirked. 'Fuckin' arseholes, those teachers, eh Chris? Cushy number they've got, spend all day just talking then have ten weeks holiday.'

I could think of nothing to say in response.

'Right,' said Barney. He lit a cigarette and took a drag. 'I'll tell you what this is about. You know the

156

National Front are active in the town?' (I should explain, Marcus, that the National Front was a racist organisation, precursor to the BNP)

'Are they? D'you mean they have a local branch?'

'Not yet, but they're fermenting trouble. Christ, look at all the attacks on the Pakistanis recently. I've found out that one of their organisers lives in Albert Street. His name's Ackroyd and every night he drinks in *The Weaver*, just a few streets from here.'

'Blimey. How did you find that out?'

'We make it our business to track down fascists.'

'We?'

'The League', Barney muttered, with a glance towards Chris and Terry. He needn't have worried: the pair were sniggering at one of the down-and-outs who'd just spilled his tea.

'What is it that you're going to do?' I asked.

'We're just going to put the frighteners on Ackroyd a bit, that's all.'

'Look, Barney,' I said, 'You know I'm against everything the NF stands for, but I don't go along with the sort of thing I think you're proposing.'

'You middle-class *wanker*', said Barney. There was real venom in his voice. 'Sometimes I think it's all just a game with you so-called intellectuals. You expect us workers to be grateful when you condescend to join the Party, then all you do is try to turn it into a bloody university debating society. Either you're with me or you're against me, comrade. Better make up your mind.'

'What do you need me for?' My apprehension was turning to dread.

'You can do the words. Give him a lecture on the error of his ways once Chris and Terry have persuaded him that he'd be well advised to listen.'

'What do you want me to say?'

157

'For Christ's sake, do you need me to write your script for you? You're the bloody lecturer. Make him realise he's a thick piece of shit instead of a member of the master race. Come on, drink up you two, it's time to go. Ackroyd will be leaving for the pub in 10 minutes. Creatures of habit, these fascists.'

I reluctantly got to my feet. Barney led the way out. Chris turned at the door and shouted at the proprietor that it was a crap cup of tea and a crap café and he ought to get rid of all the fuckin' dossers.

Barney led the way down towards the town, turning off into Albert Street, a terrace of dilapidated houses, some with their windows boarded up. It was a cold damp January evening. A murky orange light oozed out of two streetlamps. Half way down the road he turned into an alley that ran between two of the dwellings.

'In here. We can see his door from here. He walks this way to get to the pub. When he gets near us, grab him and drag him in here – make sure one of you puts your hand over his mouth. Don't want him rousing the fuckin' neighbourhood.'

My dread was turning to panic; my instinct was to run away but I felt as though I were gripped by the onset of an incapacitating disease. I saw to my horror that Chris was pulling on a knuckleduster.

I shrank back into the depths of the alley, shivering. I was trapped, helpless, and lurking under the terror was a sickening self-loathing. I despised myself for my reluctance over the past two years ever to challenge Barney, despite my awareness of his intellectual shortcomings. Not for the first time, Marcus, I cursed my deference. When, and why, had I ceased to defer to the wealthy, the powerful and the privileged, and instead had developed a cringing servility towards those who'd not had my advantages?

'He's coming,' Barney muttered. 'Ready, you two? Wait till he's right opposite us.'

I turned to face the other way. I heard the sudden scrabbling of feet on the setts of the street, a hoarse cry, instantly stifled into straining grunts which suddenly ended after a muffled thwack.

'Put the blindfold on him, quick,' said Barney; then, 'Here you are then Derek, come and have a look at a member of the master race.'

I looked. Bent almost double between Terry and Chris, each gripping an arm and the latter with his hand over the victim's mouth, a blindfolded figure was gasping for breath. I didn't know what I was expecting to see – a bullet-headed thug perhaps? Leather jacket, jeans and Doc Marten boots? Swastikas tattooed on his neck? But this fellow was slight, puny almost, clad in an old fashioned long gabardine overcoat.

'Right, listen, you bastard,' said Barney, 'Chris's going to take his hand off yer mouth, but you're gonna keep quiet, right? One yell out of you and Terry'll give you another one, only this time it'll be in yer bollocks. Understand?'

A nod of assent, accompanied by a whimper.

'Ackroyd, that's your name, in't it? Well?'

Another nod.

'And you're an NF organiser, aren't you? Trying to set up a branch in town, eh? Whose pay are you in? What bunch of rich bastards are bankrolling the NF locally?'

'No one,' Ackroyd's voice was soft and high pitched. 'No one's financing me or the NF. We're all volunteers.'

'Lying bastard.'

'It's true. Decent working folk want a stop to immigration. You try living in a street where none of

159

your neighbours speak English and stink of curry all the time. And they're taking all our jobs.'

I noticed that the accent had traces of the burr of rural Lancashire, unlike most of the young locals who had adopted the whining cadence of Manchester. Anyway, this fellow didn't seem to be that young – difficult to tell under the blindfold that covered half his face.

'Don't lecture me, you piece of shit.' Barney's voice was choked with hatred. 'I asked a question and you're going to answer. This is your last chance. Ready, Terry?'

'For Christ's sake!' Ackroyd's voice rose a further pitch, 'I'm telling the truth. No one's paying me. Who are you lot anyway?

Barney nodded at Terry. I knew what was coming but stood paralysed, the scene before me taking on a dreadful slow-motion clarity. Terry pulled back his right arm as far as it would go and then, with studied deliberation, aimed a blow at Ackroyd's genitals. He didn't scream, just gave a rasping gurgle, and slumped to the ground, clutching his balls and whimpering. Terry laughed. 'Nice one, mate,' said Chris.

'Pull him up, pull him up,' Barney urged. 'Stand up, you pathetic bastard. Perhaps you'll answer to my friend here. Go on, Derek, give him one of your short lectures on the evils of fascism and then ask him again who's paying him.'

I wanted to retch, and could only shake my head.

Barney turned on me. 'You're useless. I give you a chance to prove your solidarity, and you chicken out. Your stance has been noted, comrade.' He turned back to his victim. 'Last chance, Ackroyd.'

'I've told you the truth,' Ackroyd gasped, still grasping his genitals, 'If I knew I'd tell you, but I don't. Please–'

'Oh, it's please now, is it? Not so tough now the boot's on the other foot, are we?'

Suddenly, inexplicably, I was seized with an overpowering rage. I don't know whether you'll understand this, Marcus, but it was directed not at Ackroyd, but at Barney, and the other two, and all those little bastards who ruined my liberal studies lectures, and all those bosses and supervisors in my temporary jobs who hated me for my education, and girls, yes, all those girls who had humiliated me over the years. But it was Ackroyd who was there, available, ready to be my whipping boy.

So I hit him. Hard, in the face. It felt good. So I did it again. Chris tore off his knuckleduster, handed it to me. I put it on, and used it, just the once. There was a crunch of metal against bone. Ackroyd slumped to the ground again, and after a second's silence began to scream.

'That'll do,' said Barney, 'He won't be active for a few weeks. Let's go.'

He led the way out of the alley, but I hovered over the writhing body, wracked with indecision. My rage had left me as quickly as it had come. I was filled with remorse. Should I assist? Or go for help? Then I heard footsteps approaching down the street and someone shouted, 'What's going on?'

I bent over Ackroyd. 'I'm sorry, mate,' I whispered, 'I'm so sorry.' Then I turned and ran, ran as I'd not done since a schoolboy, down the street, heading for my flat, my one thought now to get home without encountering Barney.

There you are, Marcus. I've told only one other person about this. I'm still deeply ashamed of what I did. It haunts me even after 40 years, more even than when I – well, you know. It's helped to write it down, even at the risk that you'll be so disgusted that you'll destroy any future letters. But I think you need to know about it. My next letter will be much more cheerful, I promise.

  Derek

Chapter 23

Milton Keynes, Tuesday 29 May

It was, for once, a warm sunny evening, and, for once, Sophie arrived home before Marcus. She'd called up the stairs on entering, but there was no response from the study. She was relieved. She never had the house to herself these days. The pathetic little dick-head had given up his driving lessons, and his continual presence was beginning to suffocate her. He'd begun to act strangely – even more strangely than usual. He was taciturn, answered her only in monosyllables, said nothing about his working days, hadn't even asked her where she'd been after she'd spent last Saturday night at Ben Sidley's. He was spending less time up in his study on the computer. After dinner he would sit silently in the lounge, seemingly deep in thought, but whenever she stole a glance at him he would be staring fixedly at her, as though observing her every movement. It was unnerving. Several times she had almost shouted out 'What the fuck's the matter with you?', but held back. She wouldn't give him the satisfaction of knowing she was irritated.

She threw down her car keys on the breakfast bar, and they landed on a brown A5-size envelope. She glanced at it: the address was written in the familiar hand. Bloody Derek Bailey again. After reading the last letter Sophie no longer felt any curiosity, only annoyance that Marcus should waste his time with all that shit.

She was about to go upstairs to change when it occurred to her that it was strange that the envelope had been left in the kitchen, on full display for her to see.

Marcus must have come home and gone out again, otherwise it would have been on the doormat or secreted away in his study. This lack of concern for what he'd previously kept secret from her was yet another facet of his recent weird behaviour. Where was all this going, she wondered? Was he on the verge of some sort of crisis, a breakdown or something? Christ, he'd better not be. No way would she be cast in the role of his carer. A rented bed-sitter would be better than coping with that. And there was always Ben's place if she wanted temporary refuge.

She found she had picked up the envelope. She noticed it had been opened. More than just opened – several sheets of paper protruded from it. Shit, what was all this? Had something in the letter caused Marcus to thrust it aside and leave it there? Where the hell was he, anyway? Had he been spooked by something Bailey had written?

There was, of course, only one way to find out.

*

She dropped the sheets of paper on the breakfast bar and stood still, her mind uneasy. The description of what happened in the cafe, which had in any case been of only minor interest, had been forgotten. It was the final scene, the brutal attack, that had disturbed her. Not because it was any more horrific than things she knew were commonplace on the streets – similar acts were reported in the news every day – no, it was because this was the second time that Bailey had apparently resorted to violence. Smashing a plate down on a flatmate's head – well, that sort of thing happened sometimes, didn't it? But to viciously assault someone who was pinned down, helpless, and with a knuckleduster? Who was this guy? Why was he so concerned to tell Marcus all about it? And that last paragraph in the letter, the bit about something else haunting Bailey, something which he hinted that Marcus knew about. What was he to Marcus?

Then, another thought – was Marcus getting off on it? And, oh shit, Marcus had a violent streak in him, didn't he? A dreadful possibility presented itself to her – no, impossible; Marcus's dad had died before he was born. And Marcus had never spoken of any other male relatives, though come to think of it Bailey was old enough to be his grandfather. Surely not?

She shook herself. Marcus mustn't know that she'd read the letter. She set about inserting the handwritten sheets back in the envelope, remembering to leave them protruding, just as Marcus had left them. The mood he was in at present meant that he'd be quite likely to note anything amiss that he might ascribe to her: he was being so watchful. An unfamiliar emotion gripped her. It was fear.

Chapter 24

'There they are,' said Gabrielle. Giles and Davina were waving at them from across the pub garden. 'I bet they've had some trouble keeping a seat for us.'

'Not surprised it's crowded,' said Derek. 'First warm dry evening for weeks.'

He negotiated a way through the gaggle of youngsters who were standing, drinks in hand, waiting to pounce should a table become vacant. Gabrielle followed close behind.

'Sorry we're late,' Derek said. 'Overstayed my time at the allotment: had a lot of catching up to do. It'll probably rain tomorrow.'

'Ever the optimist, eh, Derek?' said Giles. 'I got your drinks in while I was at the bar. It's heaving in there. Pint and a half of bitter okay, I hope?'

'Just what the doctor ordered.'

Davina laughed. 'I haven't heard anyone say that for years, Derek. How are you, Gabby? Enjoy your trip to Birmingham? How was your friend?'

'Liz was fine. Yes, I enjoyed my day. Are you both okay?'

'Yes, we're good – oh God, did I really say that? I mean we're both well.'

Derek grinned. 'Must be your exposure to the chatter of the massed ranks of the under 30's, Davina. The fine weather certainly brings 'em out, doesn't it?'

He gestured to the surrounding tables. Many were occupied by young couples with children, some of whom were evidently reaching the tipping point of boredom, their fidgeting a precursor to either grizzling protestations or wild rampages round the garden. No doubt the families would soon depart, leaving the tables free to be occupied by the kids in their late teens and early twenties, who were already guffawing and shrieking.

'Yes, and it also brings out a lot of naked flesh,' said Davina. 'Hope you're enjoying the view, boys.'

Gabrielle giggled. Giles remained straight-faced. Derek had noticed before that Giles was uncomfortable when the conversation verged on the risqué. He wondered about the couple's relationship. Davina could be earthy, whereas Giles was much more cerebral – at least, that was the impression he liked to give. How did the two make out alone together, Derek wondered? The lives of others were of endless fascination for him.

True to form, Giles responded by remarking that it had been interesting to sit and listen to the conversations around them, not for their content, but for the mode of delivery.

'How do you mean, Giles?' asked Gabrielle.

'I'm not referring to their slang,' Giles said, 'Much of that I don't profess to understand. It's their cadences.'

'Here we go,' muttered Davina.

Giles ignored the interruption. 'Remember how a few years ago all young people seemed to end their sentences with an upward inflection as though they were asking a question? It now seems to be diminishing, thank God. But have you noticed how, recently, young women, and it is exclusively women that do it, adopt a peculiar low-pitched drawl which verges on a croak? And it's the more educated ones that have adopted it. You hear it on the radio. I wonder where that came from?'

167

'Giles obviously doesn't find it sexy.' Davina said this with a straight face.

Giles frowned slightly. 'Sorry. Was I being tedious?'

'No, mate,' said Derek. 'Interesting.'

'So, Gabby,' said Davina, 'no doubt Derek told you that our two old boys sneaked a crafty lunchtime pub session while you were away? Getting to be quite a pair of ravers, aren't they?'

'It was only two pints,' Giles protested. 'And we had an interesting discussion. Derek's description of his time on the dole in Leeds in the sixties was most enlightening. And I never knew that he spent so long teaching in further education.'

Gabrielle shot Derek a quizzical glance.

'A bit of a dark horse, aren't you Derek?' said Davina.

She treated him to her lopsided grin which Derek was beginning to find alluring: he smiled back at her. Though pleasing to find that he could still flirt with an attractive woman, his pleasure was tempered by the realisation that he was of an age when flirtation was unlikely ever again be the precursor to an amorous adventure. Glancing round at the surrounding tables he felt a pang of regret for lost youth.

'So aren't you going to tell us about it?' asked Davina.

'Tell about what?'

'Your time in FE, of course. Giles tells me you were in it for 20 years.'

'Not much to tell. I never climbed the promotion ladder: stayed a teacher of English Lit. I enjoyed it.'

'I've been meaning to ask you about that,' said Giles. 'Some of my English Literature colleagues at university were aspiring novelists, though as far as I know none of them was ever published. Had you ever thought of it - writing, I mean?'

'Now and again. Trouble is, I'd always compare my efforts with the literary giants that were my stock in trade. And I've come to realise I don't have much imagination.'

'Then why not write a novel based on your personal experiences?' said Davina. 'That seems to be a popular genre these days. And I'm sure that you had a lot of experiences, Derek. You could – '

'Oh, Derek thinks that's a cop out,' Gabrielle interrupted. 'Giles and Davina have finished their drinks, Derek; are you going to get them another?'

'Hang on a second,' said Giles. 'I'd like to pursue this. Why do you think it's a cop out, Derek?'

'It's not so much that. It's just that, well, one's personal history is fascinating to oneself, but probably of no interest to a reader, unless one's happened to have lived an extraordinary life, of course.'

'But you needn't turn your life into a novel,' said Davina. 'Why not just write your life story, tell it like it was, even if it's just for your own satisfaction?'

'Drinks, Derek!' urged Gabrielle.

'Just a sec, Gab. Davina's made an interesting point. In fact, one always writes with a reader in mind. For whom would I be writing my story? For my own age group? It might have some resonance for my contemporaries. That would be easy. But it's far more challenging to write for a younger reader. That's why I'm writing to ...' He tailed off.

'Yes? Go on, Derek. So you *are* writing your story? Who's the lucky recipient?' Davina again favoured him with her grin.

'Oh ... it's the ... grandson of an old colleague, and I haven't started writing yet. Probably never will. Right,

169

let me get the drinks in. Tonic water, yes, Gab? Same again for you two?'

He stood up and walked across the lawn. Gabrielle hurriedly asked her companions if they weren't fed up to the back teeth with all media hype about the Jubilee.

'Bloody hell, Derek,' said Gabrielle as they set off on the short walk home, 'You were sailing a bit close to the wind then, weren't you?'

'I know. Got a bit carried away. Literature is a topic where I feel I can hold my own with Giles. Only realised where I was heading when I nearly let slip about writing to Marcus.'

'It's not just Giles you want to impress, is it?'

'What do you mean?'

'Oh come on, sweetie. I've seen the way you look at Davina. You fancy her, don't you?'

'Fancy her? Are you serious? Christ, Gab, we're all in our 60s.'

'Speak for yourself. I've a year to go yet. And even I can see that Davina's a very attractive woman. I wouldn't blame you for trying.'

Derek stopped, grabbed Gabrielle by the shoulder and turned her to face him. 'Gabby, you don't really think I've got the hots for her, do you? I assure you–'

'I'm teasing, you silly old bugger!'

'Oh, right,' said Derek sheepishly. He pecked her cheek and they walked on.

'There's one thing disturbing me a bit, though,' said Gabrielle. 'That letter you've written to Marcus about your Rochdale incident. It's the first letter you haven't told me about, in detail, I mean. Have you told him things you haven't told me?'

'No, Gabby. It was just that I wrote it while you were away and posted it on my evening walk. Don't you trust me?'

170

'Course I do. I was just wondering, that's all.'

Derek forbore to comment that trust doesn't require full disclosure. That was the whole point of trust. And that was why, yesterday, he'd written his final letter to Marcus and had posted it without having told her.

*

Although he'd never admitted as such to Meryl, Gordon wasn't entirely comfortable living in the village. It was populated by the ageing remnants of the local toffs and, now outnumbering them by far, by the younger and wealthier representatives of the new entrepreneurial class, most of whom worked in Leamington or Coventry. Of the two groups, Gordon preferred the former. At least they were polite, if at times a little condescending. It was the brash newcomers who dominated the life of the village: their 4x4s blocked the lanes, their offspring swamped the primary school, and their loud self-confident braying tones were to be heard everywhere - in the church, in the village shop, on the parish council and, most gratingly, in the pub. Not that *The Bell* was a real pub any more: to Gordon's sorrow it had been transformed ten years before into an eating-house with a small bar attached, not the sort of place where you could call in for a quick pint, let alone settle down to a protracted boozing session with your mates, not that Gordon had any mates in the village. The only time you could sit and drink without being made to feel uncomfortable for not dining was on a warm summer evening when the pub garden came into its own.

Tonight was one such evening, a rare occurrence in this washout of a summer. So it was that they were seated at a bench at the edge of the garden, Gordon with a pint, Meryl with a glass of Chablis. From time to

171

time they waved at acquaintances occupying neighbouring tables. It struck Gordon that Meryl was the only female in his view who was wearing a dress; all the others were in trousers of one sort or another, mostly jeans, apart from some of the young ones who were wearing that strangely un-alluring combination of denim shorts over black tights. Perhaps none of them had the legs for dresses. Meryl, despite her age, still had. He was, even now, sometimes surprised that a fat, bald, asthmatic lump of a man such as he should be in the company of such an elegant woman.

'You're looking more relaxed than you've done for weeks,' he said.

'I feel much better for a day spent in the garden.'

'I can tell that: you've caught the sun. On your legs as well as your face.'

'We could all do with a few weeks of this; let's hope the weather holds for the Jubilee. What's happened to our summers?'

Gordon started to outline a pet theory of his, that the expectations the British had of endless alfresco living from May to September only began in the drought summer of 1976, but he was unable to develop his thesis because Meryl interrupted him. 'Don't look!' she hissed, 'Debbie Cartwright's just arrived with David Barlow. The brazen hussy!'

'They could just be having a friendly drink, Meryl. They *are* neighbours, after all.'

'Oh, come on. Everyone knows about Debbie and David. Jan Barlow certainly does. Why she tolerates it I'll never know.'

'For all you know she might be consoling herself with Jim Cartwright. Perhaps they're swingers.'

'That's an awful suggestion!' Meryl looked outraged, but then grinned suddenly. 'Do you really think that's possible? I wonder if they get together, you know, as a foursome?' She giggled, and for a moment Gordon saw the Meryl he used to know in the days before she returned to live in the village.

'It's good to hear you laughing, love.'

'Yes. Well. Look, Gordon, I feel a lot happier because I've come to a decision. You were right, we ought to go over to Milton Keynes and see Marcus.'

'Oh, I'm so glad! When did you decide that?'

'This afternoon, while I was gardening. I'll just have to grit my teeth and be polite to ... to *that girl*. Perhaps we could take Marcus out for a meal.'

'What, without Sophie? I don't think that's on. They live together, Meryl; they're partners. And it would make things difficult for Marcus, wouldn't it?'

'I suppose so. Oh God, I wish Marcus had never started going out with her.'

Gordon threw back his head and guffawed.

'What's so amusing?'

'You are, love. "Going out" – does anyone use that term these days?'

'You know very well what I mean.'

Gordon didn't think he did. He thought back to his adolescence, when 'going out' with someone meant regular dating (did the term derive from the Victorian 'walking out' he wondered?), and regular dating with a girl usually meant that the relationship was unconsummated. Sex, if a boy had it at all in the 1950s and early 60s, was a casual encounter with a 'scrubber'. He wondered what girls had called the male equivalent. Perhaps ...

'Come on, let's go,' Meryl had stood up.

'What's the hurry?'

'Let's go and phone Marcus, and fix a day for our visit.'

Gordon hastily drained his glass and followed his wife as she hurried out of the garden. 'Hello Debbie,

173

hello David!' he heard her say cheerfully as she passed the couple, 'Where are your other halves tonight?'

*

Marcus was sitting with his work colleagues at a table outside the *80s Bar* in the centre of town. The bar was in a pedestrian area, and the proprietor had seized the opportunity provided by the weather to provide additional tables, so that the seating area now extended beyond the limits prescribed by the town planners. But most of the tables were empty: the bar was never full until after 10pm when the youth of the town descended on it to down shots in quick succession before moving on, suitably inebriated, to one of the clubs.

All the staff from the department, apart from Jenkins, was there – Sam Davies, Sarah Beckinsale, Greg Chambers, Mark Butler and Mohammed Ashraf. Jenkins's presence would not have been welcome, for he had been the messenger who that morning had delivered the news that the work of the department was to be out-sourced to a private company, and that apart from himself the company would require the services of only three others. 'I'll be seeing you all individually tomorrow to tell you how you stand,' he'd said, 'but in the meantime you can all have the afternoon off.'

Sam had suggested that they all meet up that evening to get pissed. Marcus hadn't fancied that: he found Sam difficult enough to cope with at work. But Mohammed had persuaded him to attend, indicating that he found Sam equally hard to take, and that he, Mo, would welcome Marcus's presence at the bar. He'd offered to pick Marcus up and take him there. Marcus, aware that an evening in town might be preferable to having to tell Sophie the bad news when she got home, had accepted the offer.

174

'So, young Marcus,' said Sam, 'Looking forward to a life on the dole, are you? Being a house-husband? How's your lady going to cope with that?'

Greg and Mark sniggered.

'It might suit you, Marcus,' said Sarah. 'Make a new man of you.'

'New man?' said Sam. 'More like an old woman. You've got all the makings of one, mate.' He guffawed at his own wit, then drained the dregs from his bottle of Budweiser and belched.

'But he looks a cool dude this evening, doesn't he?' said Sarah. 'Nice jeans, Marcus: they really suit your neat little bum. And where did you get that shirt: M & S, was it?'

She stared at Marcus levelly. Was she mocking him, he wondered? No, there was no hint of a smile, though Sam, Greg and Mark seemed to find her remark amusing.

'I usually wear this sort of thing when I'm at home,' he said. 'and when I go to the club.'

'Oh, you go clubbing, do you mate?' said Sam. 'Quite a little raver, aren't you? I bet your lady has a job keeping all the chicks away from you.'

'Yeah, and with those shoes! They're a real turn-on,' said Greg.

'I don't usually wear these at the club,' said Marcus. 'These are my work shoes. I forgot to change into my loafers.'

Greg and Mark burst into raucous laughter: Sam and Sarah grinned. What was so funny, Marcus wondered? Loafers were okay, weren't they?

Throughout this exchange Mo had been silent, staring into his glass of orange-juice, but when the laughter had subsided he addressed Sam. 'Why should it necessarily be Marcus who'll be made redundant?' he said. 'It could be any three of us, including you.'

175

Sam scowled. 'Me? With all my years of experience? You've gotta be joking, Gunga Din.'

'Perhaps,' replied Mo, 'the company that's going to take on three of us will be looking for aptitude and intelligence. These qualities don't necessarily go with experience.'

There was an astonished silence round the table. At work, Sam had never been subject to such a put-down.

'Whose bloody round is it?' he said eventually.

'Mine,' said Mark. 'Same again for everyone? Sticking to your halves of shandy, I suppose, Marcus? Why don't you let yourself go? And why the fuck don't you drink from a bottle like normal people?'

He got up and walked towards the bar.

'Hang on,' said Sam hurriedly. 'I'll give you a hand.'

'Could it be,' said Mo, quietly, as if to himself, 'that Sam Davies is actually learning how to behave graciously?'

An hour later, Marcus was feeling ill. One by one the faces of his companions loomed at him through a haze, but he was unable to keep them in focus. They were talking too loudly. He couldn't be drunk, could he? He'd only had four shandies. They'd tasted a bit odd, though; perhaps the beer was off?

Suddenly, he needed to pee. He tried to stand up, but the world began to spin around him and he staggered, groped for the edge of the table, missed, and would have fallen had Mo not grabbed him. He was vaguely aware of jeers from the others.

'You're not well, Marcus.' Mo's voice reached him as though filtered through cotton wool. 'Come on, I'll take you home.'

Home. Yes, that would be a good place to be. In bed. He was glad of Mo's supporting arm as he was led away from the table. But it was a long way to Mo's car, and on the trek to the car-park he became conscious of a warm dampness seeping down his leg. He stopped. 'Pissed myself,' he whimpered.

'Don't worry. I'll get you home soon.'

'No!' Home, there to be further humiliated by Sophie's disgust, was no longer an inviting prospect. 'Can't go back there.'

'All right. Let's just get you to the car.'

'Can I stay at your place, Mo?'

'Yes, if you wish, Marcus. But hadn't you better phone your partner to let her know?'

'I'll text her.'

But by the time he was helped into Mo's flat he felt so ill that texting was a task too complex to undertake: all he wanted was to lose consciousness. Which he did, as soon as Mo had manoeuvred him onto the settee.

*

Sophie had heated up a ready-meal and had eaten it sitting in front of the TV. She'd then spent an hour working on her laptop. Now, her work completed, she realised it was 9pm and Marcus hadn't returned. Where the hell was he? He never went out alone in the evening. Not that his absence worried her; she was just pissed off that he hadn't bothered to let her know: another example of his recent strange behaviour.

The phone rang. That would be him. She picked up – 'Where the hell *are* you?'

'I *beg* your pardon?'

'Who's this calling?'

'This is Marcus's mother. I assume it's Sophia to whom I'm speaking.'

'No, Meryl, it's Sophie. It's always been Sophie, never Sophia. Geddit?' *Toffee-nosed bitch.*

A sniff. 'I'd like to talk to Marcus, if you wouldn't mind.'

'Well, you can't.'

'What on earth do you mean?'

'Because he isn't here, is he?'

'Where is he?'

'I dunno, do I?'

'You're not being very helpful, are you Sophia?'

'What d'you expect me to say?'

'The least you could do would be to ask if you could give him a message from me.'

'Okay then, what's the message?'

'I think, actually, I'd prefer to tell him myself. Just tell him I phoned, and ask him to ring me back. Good evening.'

The line went dead.

Enraged, Sophie slammed down the handset, so hard that it bounced out of the base. She left it on the floor, and stomped into the kitchen, cursing loudly, then returned to the living room. She didn't know why she did this, she just needed to do something, something active, something physical. That fuckin' woman always got to her. And now she'd have to sit around, seething, waiting for mummy's boy to come home. Why should she? She'd had enough of the Sidelskis for one evening, for a lifetime in fact.

It was time to make her move. She should have done it sooner; gone to a place of refuge while she figured out what to do next. Well, now she had one. It would do for a few weeks, or months if necessary.

She picked up the handset from the floor, punched in a number.

'Hi, Ben? It's Sophie. All right if I come round? Spend the night at yours?'

Chapter 25

Milton Keynes, Thursday 31 May

It was 11 am, and it was raining. Mo pulled up outside Marcus's house and turned off the engine. The sound of the swishing wipers was replaced by the insistent drumming of the rain on the roof.

'Will you be all right, Marcus?'

Marcus stared straight ahead and nodded.

'Would you like me to help you out? Or come in and get you a cup of tea, perhaps?'

A shake of the head.

'Marcus, please keep in touch. I'm concerned about you. And I might be able to help with you finding a new job – I do have many contacts in I.T.'

'Thanks.'

Mo felt the first twinge of exasperation. Since rising this morning Marcus had communicated only in monosyllables. The poor devil had a hangover, Mo supposed, but he might at least have offered thanks for the overnight refuge that Mo had provided, not to mention having to clear up his vomit. And after his meeting in Jenkins's office, Marcus had emerged without speaking a word, unlike Sam Davies who'd walked past with a volley of expletives, and Sarah Beckinsale who'd come out in tears, accusing Jenkins of gender discrimination.

He decided to try one more time.

'Marcus, I hope you don't think I hold it against you for being ill. It wasn't your fault. I strongly suspect that Davies and his cronies added something to your drinks.'

For the first time since starting the journey from the office, Marcus turned to face him.

'Then why didn't you warn me?'

'Because at the time the possibility hadn't occurred to me. It was only after you vomited that I began to suspect. Davies is a nasty piece of work. I'm glad he won't be working with me from now on.'

'Neither will I.'

'I know, Marcus, and I'm very sorry. Look –' He pulled a pocket notebook from his jacket, scribbled in it, and tore off the page – 'Here's my telephone number. Give me a call if you want to talk – and you're welcome to come and see me any time. I meant what I said about helping you search for job openings.'

Marcus took the page and pocketed it without looking at the number.

'Thanks,' he said, and then, apparently as an afterthought, 'Thanks for the lift.'

He heaved himself out of the car. Mo watched as he walked unsteadily up the path to his door, hunched against the rain. He cut a pathetic figure, dressed as he still was in his suede shoes, skinny jeans and baggy shirt. Jenkins had asked him what he was thinking of, arriving at work dressed like that: an unnecessary reproof, Mo had thought, given what Jenkins was about to tell him.

Marcus opened his front door and entered his house without a backward glance. Mo shook his head sadly and turned the car round. Best to get back quickly – Jenkins had been very reluctant to let him take Marcus home. Jenkins was not to be crossed: he was already making noises about things being very different when they were in the private sector.

Marcus walked into the kitchen and drank two glasses of water. It didn't slake his thirst, and served only to increase the feeling of nausea. He was glad that Sophie was at work, but the silence in the house was oppressive. There was much to think about, but the pounding in his head made thought impossible. If there was any notion in his head, it was the muted awareness that he'd have to tell his news to Sophie.

He sat at the breakfast bar, head in hands. He closed his eyes: immediately his nausea intensified. He opened them, and noticed something on the bar. An envelope. It had his name on it. He tore it open; a single sheet of paper fell out. The writing on it was ragged, obviously written in haste.

Marcus. I don't know who this Bailey is who writes to you but I don't like the sound of him. What is he to you? No, I don't want to know. I've had enough. We're not going anywhere. We're finished. I've gone to stay with a colleague while I sort myself out. Don't try to find me. Don't try to contact me at work – I'll ask them to monitor all my incoming calls.

I'll call round in a few days to collect my things. There's a lot to sort out, like who gets what, but get this straight - I want my share of the house. It's my right.

You've got problems Marcus and I think you need help, but it won't be me doing the helping.

Sophie.

PS Your mother phoned. She wants you to phone her back.

The contents of the note filtered slowly through his hangover. He was disoriented rather than distressed. A second piece of bad news, following so closely after the first, didn't double his anguish: rather the effect was numbing. He felt a vague sense of isolation, but then he often did. This was overtaken by an overwhelming weariness. There was so much that would have to be done. He'd have to sell the house: in any case, with no income he could no longer afford the mortgage. Where would he live? The thought of hunting for rented accommodation wearied him further – and how could he pay rent if he didn't have a job? Would he have to return to live with mother and Gordon?

Mother. Sophie had said he was to ring her. Instinctively, he went to the phone in the lounge. The message indicator was flashing. He picked up the handset.

Three new messages. First message sent yesterday, 9.35 pm. 'Marcus, where are you? I phoned earlier but Sophia said you were out. Please ring me back as soon as you get in.' Second message sent yesterday, 11.30 pm. 'Marcus, are you staying somewhere overnight? Is anything wrong? I'm worried. Please phone me however late you get in.' Third message sent today, 10.05 am. 'Marcus, there's something wrong, I know. I rang you at work but they said you no longer work there. Please phone me, darling.' End of final message.

No. he couldn't phone her, not yet. There was too much information to give. He must plan what to say, and in what order. Perhaps he should write it down, then read it out, not let her interrupt until he had finished? Or maybe ask to speak to Gordon? He'd be far less emotional. He always listened carefully to things that he, Marcus, had to say. Not many people did that.

He wandered back into the kitchen. Dirty dishes were piled on the draining board – Sophie hadn't bothered to load the dishwasher last night. She always left it to him. It was part of their routine. But no longer. He felt a spasm of some unidentifiable emotion, a constriction in his chest. He sat at the breakfast bar trying to make sense of all that had happened. His routine had been disrupted, that was the problem, he decided. People need a routine.

There was a dull thump from downstairs. The post. It was being delivered later with every day, something that had long irritated him. He rose from the bed and went down to the front door. There was the usual pile of catalogues, and a large brown envelope. He didn't need to look at it. Bailey.

Marcus's suspicions of a conspiracy, buried by the events of the previous night and this morning, were renewed. Had Bailey known that Sophie would be leaving? Was his letter timed to arrive after her departure? Would he be playing into Bailey's hands by reading it? The envelope lay there, on the doormat, mute testimony to all that had gone wrong over recent weeks. Marcus stood looking at it. He forced himself to think rationally. No harm could come to him from just glancing at it, could it? And this was one letter that Sophie wouldn't read. He came to a decision: read it, shred it, then forget it. He had more pressing problems to deal with now.

He took the envelope up to his study and opened it.

*

Hello Marcus,

This is it: my last letter. I hope after reading my story over the past few weeks that you've come to understand something of the events that

183

shaped me and why I behaved the way I did. When you've read this last one I hope you'll feel able to contact me – my email address is at the end. I'm sure you'll agree that we have much to talk about.

The events in Rochdale never caught up with me. I stopped attending the Labour Party meetings and never saw Barney again. The attack on Ackroyd was put down to local yobs – his membership of the National Front never made the press. But I became an isolated figure once again and I knew I had to leave the town, make a fresh start, move as far away from Lancashire as possible. Luckily, a job was advertised at the college in Leamington, and even luckier, I managed to get it. I started there in September 1970.

I found a furnished flat in a decaying Regency terrace, and soon settled into my job. My colleagues were friendly, the GCE students were receptive and, thank God, I wasn't required to teach Liberal Studies. I felt myself, at last, to be on a career ladder. My Head of Department said that student applications for the following year were so numerous that temporary lecturers needed to be appointed quickly. I began to look forward to my second year as an established member of staff, an indispensible intermediary between the older lecturers and the new intake of inexperienced fresh-faced graduates.

But it didn't work out like that, Marcus. The new intake were new graduates from the nearby Warwick University, all known to each other, all resident in Leamington, and all characterised by shoulder length hair and what the older lecturers called hippie clothing. My attempts to offer them a personal induction into the procedures of the college and the tricks of the teaching trade were met not impolitely, but with studied insouciance. I was a bit put out at first, but it was impossible to harbour a grudge against people who seemed so relaxed and friendly. I began to spend time hovering on the edges of their conversations, gradually becoming acclimatised to the nuances of their speech and learning to appreciate their humour. I began to emulate them: I grew my hair, first over my ears, then over my collar; I dug out my old jeans to wear to work, hurriedly ditching them and buying a flaired pair when I realised the old ones were passé. I began to participate in their conversations, hesitantly at first, then with growing confidence as I learned not to be earnest, not to be *heavy*.

Gradually, I became part of their circle. They introduced me to jazz and blues – they derided the musical tastes of the students whom they called teeny-boppers, but it didn't stop them attending the 'A' Level students' parties, where they abandoned their studied coolness and flung themselves about to the Rolling Stones. Some of them seemed very friendly with the female students, to the extent of taking them to the pub at lunchtime and on occasion not returning in the afternoon. I didn't participate in this activity, not at first, despite being aware that some of the girls stayed behind after my lectures to chat to me, chat which became increasingly coy and innuendo-laden.

It had to come, of course, Marcus. Drugs, I mean. It was cannabis at first. I was worried about the illegality of the practice, fearful of the devastating effect on my career that would result

185

should I ever be prosecuted. It wasn't the same for the Warwick Set, as I privately called them; they saw their time at the college as a pleasant and fairly lucrative post-graduation interlude, seemingly having no concern for the future. As one of them put it to me – 'We're just letting things all hang out for a while, man.'

Gradually, when invited to evenings in their flats, I became used to the use of dope as a social lubricant (it certainly made it easy to appreciate Miles Davies) and it was on one of those evenings when they asked me to take the acid test. I can't say I enjoyed my first trip, but the following day, at college, it became apparent that they now saw me as a fully-fledged member of their circle, and I knew I was honour bound to join them at the lunch-time pub sessions with the students.

That's what started me off, Marcus. I began to experience my own belated summer of love at the ripe old age of 29. I lost my inhibitions, became a hedonist, a Lothario, and enjoyed every minute – girls from the town, female colleagues, and, I'm now ashamed to say, students. I had a succession of live-in partners, but none of these lasted long. I was keen to play the field: after all, I had a lot of catching up to do, hadn't I?

Over the next few years, the Warwick Set all left the college, to be replaced by younger lecturers. Would it sound conceited, Marcus, if I were to say that the newcomers were in thrall to me? After all, I was by then a lecturer of some experience. And to be sure, I advised them and counselled them. But most of all I enjoyed leading them ...

Two pages into the letter and Marcus was bored. Bored, but also mystified and annoyed. Why was Bailey telling him all this? So, he'd taken drugs – so what? Marcus was unimpressed: he'd never understood what was so great about drugs, never having taken them himself. Why couldn't he give a straightforward account of what had happened, instead of muddling it up with descriptions of the sort of music he was listening to and the weird people he'd been with? And if it was all a way of letting him know that he once lived in Leamington and taught at the college there - well, Marcus knew that.

He was suddenly aware that he was cold, shivering in fact. He noticed that rain was beating against the window – how long had it been raining? He couldn't turn on the central heating, not in May. It was something he had agreed with Sophie.

Coffee. That would warm him. And he had eaten nothing since the peanuts and pretzels at the pub last night. Perhaps his stomach could take a biscuit with the coffee. He'd carry on reading the letter while eating and drinking.

Down to the kitchen. While waiting for the kettle to boil he fished for chocolate cookies in the biscuit barrel that stood on the breakfast bar. Only one left – shit! He must remember to ask Sophie to ... no! More of life's certainties crumbled around him. All desire for coffee left him. He stumbled upstairs, where Bailey's letter was waiting for him in front of his computer.

*

Would it sound unbearably conceited, Marcus, if I were to say that the newcomers were in thrall to me? But, after all, I was by then a lecturer of some experience. And to be sure, I advised them and counselled them. But most of all I enjoyed leading them up the primrose path. Tempting though it is, I won't recount all the things I got up to. They probably wouldn't shock your generation. But I was having the time of my life, and I felt I deserved it. After all, I'd had to wait until I was 30 before it started happening for me.

So, I'll fast forward (do you use that term, Marcus? Or did it go out with the demise of the video-tape?) five years to 1978. I'm certain of the year because the new librarian at the college arrived the day after I'd been to the flicks to see *Saturday Night Fever* which had just gone on general release. (*Saturday Night Fever*, Marcus? Bee Gees? Disco?) No, I wasn't into it myself, but the chick I was living with at the time thought it was cool. So did all the students. They were talking about it in the college library the following day, and my first sight and sound of the new librarian was of him going from table to table asking them to be quiet.

They didn't take much notice. He wasn't exactly an imposing figure, and his voice was soft with a faint rural burr to it - I found out later that he originated from Norfolk. He was of average height, had a big arse, but his clothes hung on him. He was short in the leg and wore baggy corduroy trousers, a check shirt and a tweed jacket that had seen better days. The way he dressed, and the fact that he was balding, led me to suppose he was in his early 40s at least. What hair he possessed was bushy and sprang out at the sides: he also wore sideboards and

188

Granny glasses. But I soon discovered that he was only 25, ten years younger than I.

You've probably got there already, Marcus. Yes, his name was Bob Sidelski. Surprising as it may seem –

*

Marcus put down the letter. Yes, as soon as read the word 'librarian' he suspected it was his father about whom Bailey was writing. His mother had told him about his job at the college, and of course it was mentioned in the reports of the trial. But she had never described what his father had looked like. In fact she said very little about him other than that he was a lovely, gentle man. And she always referred to him as Robert, not Bob.

It didn't come as a shock, seeing his father's name in Bailey's handwriting. He'd suspected for some time that this was where Bailey's story was leading. But he was surprised to learn that Bailey had met his father as early as 1978. That was 10 years before his father's death. Somehow his mother had given the impression that the two men became acquaintances only by the late 1980s. Very confusing. Perhaps he ought to draw a time-line to sort out the proper sequence of events.

Thoughts of his redundancy and of Sophie's leaving were, for the moment, minor irritants. He reached for pen and paper and scribbled down the dates that Bailey had so far revealed, then picked up the letter.

*

Surprising as it may seem, Bob became very popular amongst my crowd. He wasn't one for booze or dope, he didn't like jazz or blues, and he seemed to have no interest in women. But he had a quiet, dry sense of humour: he didn't say much, but when he did, people fell about. It's often said that if you can make a woman laugh then you're half-way there: well, women certainly seemed to warm to him, even the students, despite his unprepossessing looks and unkempt appearance. On the rare occasions he came to a party he was soon at the centre of a circle of females, but he never made a move for any of them. And when the party started to swing he'd leave, without ceremony, back to his bed-sit in Willes Road. I used to go there occasionally when I felt the need for some thoughtful mature company – I was living with a very young chick at the time. Incidentally, I asked the chick what it was that women found so appealing about him and she said he was funny and cool. Cool was not the way I'd have described him at the time, but now I know better how women think, Marcus.

I wouldn't say that Bob and I became bosom pals, but over the years we developed a relationship based on mutual respect for each other's intelligence, spiced with gentle mocking banter. I teased him about his appearance and his monastic lifestyle (at least I assumed it was monastic: he never spoke of any relationship, not even a one-night stand), and he affected disdain for my concern for *my* appearance ('Quite a Lord Fauntleroy, aren't you?' he said on one occasion) and for the rapid turn-over of my female partners. He was always very polite to them, of course, on the occasions when he met them with me at the pub, and they all liked him, but not to the extent where I ever saw him as a potential rival.

He treated your mother with the same politeness when he met her the first time she came to the pub with me. This was the year she joined the college as a mature student (well, she was 22, if you can call that mature). It would have been in about 1983, I think, and –

*

What? Mum in a pub with Bailey? This was a lie. Mum would never have been out with Bailey. Yes, she'd said that he'd kept – what was the word she used? – *pursuing* her, but this was when she was going out with Dad, and Bailey had continued to pursue her after she and Dad had started to live together. Mum had told him that story many times. And it couldn't be true that Dad and Bailey were ever friends.

And there was something else not right. Marcus peered at the letter again. 1983, Bailey had said. That couldn't be true either. Mum had said she joined the college in 1987 – she'd been very explicit about that. Perhaps he ought to draw two time-lines, one showing the sequence of events as told by this mother, the other the events according to Bailey. The first flicker of doubt began to nag at him. He jotted down *1983- Mum in pub with Bailey??* and resumed reading.

*

It would have been in about 1983, I think, and at that time your mother was just another member of my English class. But I fancied her, of course – she was a stunning-looking lady – and the word 'lady' is most apposite: she'd had quite a

191

privileged up-bringing, and was still living with her widowed mother in a wealthy village just outside Stratford. She spoke with the sort of accent you rarely hear these days, Marcus, apart from some of the toffs in today's government. For a 22 year old she was naive to the point of innocence compared to some of the teenagers in her classes; a throwback to the 1950s. She always dressed modestly, usually in a blouse and skirt, or a dress in summer, and was carefully coiffured. Even in the pub she used to sit erect in her seat, legs demurely crossed at the knee like those girls one used to see photographed at debutantes' parties. They were very nice legs. In the first term of her course she was a rather isolated figure, rarely able to join the mixed crowd of lecturers and students in the pub of an evening because she had to get the bus back to her village. I began to feel protective towards her, while still lusting after her. Have you experienced that strange mixture of protectiveness and lust, Marcus? If so, you'll know it's a heady combination.

Assuming that ladies like her who'd had a sheltered upbringing required careful wooing, I played the part of the perfect gentleman. But it seemed this wasn't what she wanted: quite the reverse, in fact. I'll draw a veil over the details of what happened (she is your mother, after all). But the result was that by the start of her second year of her course she'd moved into my flat. It was –

*

192

Marcus read the last sentence twice. Impossible. Unbelievable. It had to be a lie. The letter was all lies. Bailey was trying to provoke him. But why? But then, again, that nagging flicker of doubt. He scribbled on his pad – *mum, 2nd year, 23? 1984? Living with Bailey?* – then resumed reading.

There were only two more sides of writing.

When he'd finished reading them, his distress over Sophie's departure and his redundancy had evaporated. But the ache in his chest had returned, and it spread up to his throat and down to his guts. The emotions he felt were now only too identifiable, a combination of hurt and anger. Then the anger took over. He'd been betrayed. The rage was gradually replaced by a feeling of pent-up energy. He had to take revenge, revenge for the savage undermining of his understanding of the past, and he had to do it now. He turned on his computer and logged on to *thetrainline* website. But in the process of looking up train times to Stratford he realised he needed to be present when Sophie returned for her things: why should *she* have things so easy?

But if he were to remain here, how could he confront his mother? Yes! Of course! He grabbed the envelope containing Bailey's letter, scribbled over his own name and address and substituted his mother's, using a thick felt pen. He was half way down the stairs on his way to the post office when it occurred to him that his mother might throw the letter away unread as soon as she realised who it was from. A better idea came to him. Back in the study, he stuck an address-label over his mother's name and wrote on it 'Gordon Whittaker'.

Now, all that remained was to reply to his mother's phone messages. She needed to be reassured he was okay otherwise she might think of doing something

silly like coming up to Milton Keynes. He didn't want
her to know about Sophie – not yet, anyway.

Chapter 26

Warwickshire Saturday 2 June

After a fine start to the day, it had begun to cloud over. Not fair-weather cumulus clouds, rather the gradual fading of the sun behind a milky haze which was becoming denser and greyer with every hour. And a wind was getting up: the leaves of the oak tree on the village green were rustling as though it were autumn; the Union Jack bunting festooned around the village hall flapped and tugged at the twine that secured it.

Outside the hall, Gordon stood in an embarrassed huddle with the other men, all affecting insouciance as their wives engaged in an increasingly fractious debate about whether the tables should remain in the hall or be carried across to the green. Debbie Cartwright and Jan Barlow were on opposing sides and were the most vociferous. Jan was insisting that anyone who'd heard the weather forecast would know that it would be madness to hold the celebrations outside, while Debbie kept repeating that the forecast was not to be relied on. Jan said that the children would be soaked and their costumes would be ruined: Debbie said the whole point of the day was to let the children march through the village and end up on the green; how else could all the parents see them, they couldn't all cram into the village hall, could they?

'For God's sake,' David Barlow muttered to Gordon, 'How much longer have we got to listen to this? Women! Why don't they toss a coin?'

'Why don't you suggest that, then?'

'More than my life's worth, matey.'

I bet it is, thought Gordon: that's what comes of having a wife and a mistress on opposing sides of the argument - such a suggestion would incur the wrath of both of them. It was a problem that he'd never had, even in his younger days, and now, overweight, florid and bald, was never likely to experience. In any case he'd only ever had eyes for Meryl. When they first got together he worried that she saw him only as the supportive social worker that he then was, and that once she was restored to emotional health she might desert him for someone more attractive, richer, more her class. But it was not to be, for the demands placed on them by bringing up Marcus had if anything increased her dependence on him.

He looked over at her, standing on the fringe of the group of arguing women. She wasn't participating in the meteorological debate. Normally in a situation such as this she would be supporting Jan Barlow, not because she necessarily agreed with her, but because she automatically took the side of anyone who crossed swords with Debbie Cartwright. Gordon had hoped that helping with the organisation of the celebrations might distract her from her renewed concerns about Marcus, but since his phone call on Thursday she'd been distant, abstracted.

A raised voice. 'Oh, well, have it your own way. But don't blame me if everyone gets soaked to the skin.'

Jan Barlow had evidently lost the debate, and marched away, muttering to herself. Gordon glanced at David: he was stony-faced. No doubt tonight the poor bugger would be subject to indignant rants about the impossibility of that bloody woman, unless of course he was in that bloody woman's company.

'Okay, boys, it's been decided.' There was an air of triumphalism in Debbie's shout. 'You can start moving

196

the tables now. Come on, chop chop! We've wasted enough time already.'

The men hurried into the village hall and under Debbie's directions began the process of furniture removal. The activity served to lighten the atmosphere: jocular comments were exchanged about the relative fitness and strength of the participants, frequent reference being made to the prowess of each on the golf course or cricket field. Gordon, being a member of neither club, was unable to participate. The furniture movers were exclusively the wealthy incomers to the village, with whom Gordon exchanged the odd 'Good morning' but had little social contact. Those few of the original gentry who remained in the village were now far too old for such physical exertion. There were no proletarian inhabitants – the houses in the small council estate had been in private ownership since the Thatcher years, and the original tenants had taken the opportunity to realise their assets and move elsewhere.

After only two trips from the hall to the green Gordon began to feel breathless. David, his partner at the other end of the tables, had set a cracking pace. By the time of the third trip Gordon said that he needed a short rest.

'Not very fit, are you, matey?' observed David.

'I'm not as young as you lot,' said Gordon, wishing he had the courage to add that he was not David's matey.

'You could do with losing a bit of weight. Look, I'll find someone else to shift this stuff with me. You have your rest –' (this said with a discernible sneer) '– then why don't you go and help the girls with the chairs? You should be able to manage those.'

Left by himself on the green, detached from the activity and bustle all around him, Gordon reflected on his ambivalent attitude to the village. This wasn't just

197

because of the social changes that had occurred since he and Meryl had moved there, it was also the result of his retirement. When he was working, he'd been defined by his profession: his life had been shaped by its demands. The village was then a tranquil haven to which he returned from Studley every evening; he'd had no wish to socialise because he was usually exhausted. Meryl had the WI, the parish council and the church to occupy her, and he was happy to see her so engaged.

But as the years passed, he found he was being worn down by the intractable problems of his clients and by the constant sniping that his profession had to endure from the press and politicians. When the chance of early retirement came along, he'd taken it gratefully. But now, without a job, he was no longer the person he once was. He had no identity: as far as the villagers were concerned he was just Meryl's husband. He began to realise that his colleagues had been his friends, and without them he was isolated. The village was no longer a refuge, it had become a place of exile. For Meryl's sake, he'd tolerated it, because she was content. Or had been, up until the day she'd learned that Bailey was writing to Marcus. Now, with Meryl so often distrait and sometimes distraught, he realised he needed a friend in whom he could confide. But there was no one.

Aware of the onset of self-pity, he shook himself and made his way to the hall. His offer of help with the removal of the chairs was accepted gratefully by Debbie, and the next half hour was spent in the company of the matrons of the village, most of whom treated him with amused tolerance as he worked alongside them. Meryl was with them, of course, and he assumed it was her being there that made them so accepting of his presence. Many of the women were slightly in awe of her.

When the tables and chairs were finally arranged on the green to Debbie's satisfaction, the men were released from their duties with the reminder that they should be on hand again by early afternoon to assist with the various activities and then to move the furniture back into the hall ready for the evening. The women dispersed, the younger ones to the school where the children would soon assemble to have their costumes fitted under Jan Barlow's supervision, the middle-aged to the hall to prepare the stage for the evening's entertainment. Meryl joined the latter group, despite Debbie's role as stage manager, producer and director.

Some of the men wandered off, somewhat warily, in the general direction of *The Bell*. Gordon had no wish to join them: a light lunch at home followed by a quick snooze seemed an inviting prospect. Meryl would be making do with the rye bread and apple that she'd brought with her; she was eating less and less, Gordon had observed.

He walked slowly down the lane that led to their house. The wind was blowing the May blossom from the branches and swaying the cow parsley on the verges, but Gordon was unaware of his surroundings. Now he was alone, he had nothing to distract him from thinking of Marcus's phone call on Thursday. Meryl was still worrying about it, and privately Gordon had to concede that there might be cause for worry.

When Gordon had picked up the phone and realised it was Marcus, he'd said what he always said after the first few words of greeting – 'I'll hand you over to your mother.' But Marcus had said there was no need, Gordon could pass on the message to Mum. He'd then started talking in a slow monotone, saying that he'd been out the previous night at a party with some colleagues and he'd stayed here overnight which was why he hadn't got Mum's messages until that morning, and Sophie had also spent the night away, at a friend's, which was why she didn't pass on Mum's message to phone her, but she left a note for him about it but he didn't see it until he got in and –

Gordon had interrupted at that point and said that Meryl was standing next to him and would like a word. But Marcus was not to be diverted: it was as though he was delivering a scripted news bulletin. He'd gone on to explain that the reason he'd been at a party was that he was leaving his job with the Council and it was a sort of goodbye celebration, and that he would be getting a new job of course, and that he'd tell them all about it next week because he was planning to come down and see them and it would probably be on Wednesday because the train services would be disrupted on Monday and Tuesday because of the Jubilee Bank Holidays.

At that point Gordon had given up his attempts to speak and handed the phone to Meryl who was by then in a state of considerable agitation. She'd snatched the phone and said 'Darling, how are you? I've been so worried –' but had then stopped, her face crumpling. Apparently Marcus had said that he'd told Gordon all the news for him to pass on to her, and that he, Marcus, had to go now and that he'd see her soon.

Gordon had spent the rest of the day trying to comfort and reassure Meryl. It wasn't so much the content of Marcus's message that had upset her, more that he'd not wished to speak to her. She was all for getting in the car and setting out immediately for Milton Keynes, and had only been dissuaded by Gordon's repeated reminders that Marcus was coming down to see them, and moreover that as Sophie would be at work she wouldn't be accompanying him.

For the first time, he found himself welcoming the prospect of the protracted Jubilee junketing. It would keep Meryl occupied, and her involvement in its organisation precluded any further notions of her going to see Marcus. It sounded as though the lad needed some breathing space. It was strange about his leaving his job: 'would be getting a new one', he'd said. That sounded very much as though he had yet to find one. That worried Gordon: Marcus needed all the security and stability that employment provided.

He walked up the path towards his front door registering as he always did that the exterior woodwork needed repainting, and some was rotting. A few months ago he'd suggested that the widows should be replaced by double-glazed UPVC fittings: this had elicited the usual reaction from Meryl whenever she was confronted with the possibility of modernisation. All very well, thought Gordon, but he was reaching the age when he was beginning to notice how draughty the house was. Meryl never seemed to feel the cold.

He let himself in, picked up the post scattered on the doormat, carried it into the kitchen and set about making his lunch. In winter he spent a lot of time in the kitchen, savouring the warmth from the ancient Aga, but on cool summer days such as this there was no such comfort. He considered retrieving the one-bar electric fire from the cupboard under the stairs, but decided against it. It was June, for God's sake.

He settled down with a ham sandwich and a cup of tea, and thumbed through the post without any expectations that any of it would be for him – mail was invariably for Meryl; seed catalogues and gardening magazines, usually. But today there was something that bore his name: a rather battered brown envelope, obviously re-used, for the original address had been scrawled over and his own substituted, written by a thick felt pen. His name stood out from all the scrawl, in capital letters on an address label. He recognised the writing immediately.

He ripped open the envelope. 'Hello Marcus' the letter began. What the hell was this? He turned to the end of the letter. It was signed 'Derek'. Derek? Oh, God, surely not ...

After reading the first few paragraphs his suspicion was confirmed. And it was evident that Marcus had been receiving and reading these letters for some time. Why had Marcus forwarded this one to him? Should he destroy it, unread? Do what Marcus had promised Meryl he would do? But Marcus must have a reason for his actions – and if he were to arrive on Wednesday and speak and act on the assumption that he, Gordon, was party to the letter's contents, what ghastly scenario might result? He had no option. The letter had to be read.

The first few pages elicited no emotional response other than distaste for the fellow's philandering and his evident self-regard. He felt a flicker of annoyance on reading the account of Bailey's first meeting Sidelski and then Meryl; this immediately superseded by outright anger, for Meryl had always kept the details of these events from Marcus. Should she be told about this? No: it would destroy what remained of her equilibrium.

He read on. On reaching the last pages, he dropped the letter in shock and disbelief. He found himself chewing his ham sandwich furiously, gulping at his tea, pacing round the kitchen. Perhaps he'd misinterpreted what Bailey had written? He picked up the letter, read the last pages again. But there was no doubt about it.

The bastard! No wonder Marcus had sounded so strange on the phone; no wonder he had been so reluctant to speak to his mother. The poor little sod! He must be feeling as though a bomb had exploded under him, destroying the already fragile foundations of his childhood and adolescence. Gordon raged inwardly: he pictured himself knocking Bailey to the ground, kicking him until he screamed for mercy, gouging at his eyes, stamping on his balls: no torture was severe enough to punish him for the damage that he'd inflicted on Marcus by writing those paragraphs and the agony that Meryl would go through when she learned ...

Then, a second shock wave hit him as he suddenly realised that if what Bailey had written was true, then he himself had been deceived, and that it was Meryl who was guilty of the deception. And she'd kept the secret to herself for all the years they'd been together. Surely not? No, not Meryl. Bailey must be lying, trying to stake a claim for Marcus in revenge for his cuckolding by Robert, as if he'd not exacted the ultimate revenge already, all those years ago.

But the seeds of doubt had been sown. He knew that he couldn't live with the uncertainty, that he'd have to confront Meryl with the letter. He dreaded the thought of it, dreaded the effect that it would have on her, dreaded the effect that her response might have on him. The state of mild discontent that he'd been living in for years now seemed a halcyon age: the present was angst-ridden, the future a potential nightmare.

Chapter 27

Shropshire, Tuesday 5 June

Derek was an egalitarian. He adhered to this philosophy more out of loyalty to the days of his youthful idealism rather than from current conviction, but he had convinced himself that the existence of the Royal Family was an affront to the ideals of modern democracy and that the Golden Jubilee celebrations were an obscenity of sycophantic excess.

Gabrielle, less ideological by nature, thought that Royalty was merely an irritating irrelevance to be tolerated given the lack of appeal of any alternative system. The four day hiatus in the normal routines of life – no postal delivery, limited train services, TV scheduling disrupted, were mildly annoying, but not such as to induce republican fervour. But she had a sneaking admiration for the way a sense of community had been engendered in the town, not that she'd attended any of the events. While Derek was getting wet at the allotment, she had rather guiltily watched the river pageant on TV. The BBC's coverage had been appalling, she thought, but she had to admire the stoicism of the elderly couple who took to a boat in the cold and rain and even managed, for the odd fleeting moment, to look cheerful. When she told Derek about it he'd humphed that with a bit of luck it would finish off the old buggers, and in the case of the Duke it nearly did.

Derek's one concession to the occasion had been to view the rock concert with her, but the survivors from the 1960s had for the most part been embarrassing to watch. 'Christ, he's losing it completely,' had been his comment as Paul McCartney, jowls drooping and face ashen under thinning dyed hair, croaked his way through the songs that had once uplifted a generation. After that Derek had retreated to bed.

They'd not even been able to seek refuge in the company of the Taylors, for Giles and Davina had gone to visit their son in Norfolk. Gabrielle envied them. When younger, she had been able to shake off the occasional lack of fulfilment at being childless – being committed to her job had helped – but now, with retirement, she had moments of dread at the prospect of an old age without the comfort and support that children could bring. And she was younger than Derek: he would undoubtedly go first. She was past the menopause when they got together, so procreation had been an impossibility: she had no regrets at the time, being thankful that she had at last found someone with whom to share her life. An ungainly child and a shy, shapeless young woman, never one of a teenage crowd, she'd resigned herself to spinsterhood when in her twenties: she'd thrown herself into her work, had felt uncomfortable in the company of men, and consequently, as her few friends got married, had had little in the way of a social life.

She was always aware of what an incongruous couple she and Derek must seem. She noticed the appraising stares that women gave when they first met him, these often followed by covert second glances at herself, as if to check that this dowdy old biddy was indeed the partner of such a well-preserved man. If only they knew, she thought, only too aware that she could never tell them the circumstances of their meeting.

And if only they knew how content they were. She'd enjoyed the process of weaning Derek away from the bleakness of his past, watching him gaining in self-assurance, losing his misanthropy. There were still occasions when he showed flashes of the temper with which he knew he was cursed: sometimes she saw him, brows furrowed, lips working, as he fought to control it, talking himself down as he'd been taught to do. Sometimes she wondered if she were making a rod for her own back: would he still love her, would he still need her, if he became so secure in his own skin that new horizons might start to seem tempting? He constantly reassured her that this would never be, but she'd noticed recently that he'd begun to cast an eye towards attractive women, women like Davina. Gabrielle hadn't been entirely truthful when she'd said she was only teasing him about his fancying their friend.

But over the long four days of the Jubilee, Derek had grown more and more withdrawn. At first she'd assumed he was fretting because of the weather – his one visit to the allotment on Saturday had been too short to undertake all the tasks he'd set himself – but there was obviously something else niggling at him. He'd been short in his responses to her concerned enquiries as to whether he was feeling unwell. She tried not to worry, but his silence was beginning to concern her. She resolved to give him a few more days: if he didn't snap out of it she'd have to insist on his telling her what was troubling him.

It came as a relief therefore when earlier this morning she'd had a call from Davina: she and Giles had returned sooner than expected from visiting their son, and did Gabrielle fancy meeting up for coffee in town? - oh yes, she'd checked, the cafe was open despite the public holiday, and no, Giles wouldn't be coming because he wanted to get on with the book he was planning to write. Gabrielle seized the opportunity for an excuse to leave the house. When she told Derek where she was going his response was an abstracted 'What? Oh, right, okay,' before turning back to his crossword.

'It's good to be back,' said Davina, putting down her cup of latte. 'Norfolk's nice to visit when the weather's good, but we were cooped up in Nigel's cottage the whole time, and it's very poky. To be honest, Gabby, close confinement with Nigel's wife is not the most relaxing of experiences. And Giles was itching to get back to his bloody book.'

'I'm glad to see you. We've been shut up indoors as well. Derek's been fretting because he couldn't spend time at the allotment, and all there was on TV and in the papers was the Jubilee.'

Davina forked a generous portion of carrot cake into her mouth. How does she manage to eat so much and yet stay so slim? thought Gabrielle. Not thin and scrawny like most women of her age: she had a narrow waist, slim hips, a neat little bum that she showed to good effect in tight-fitting jeans. She noticed that as she chewed, Davina was staring at her.

'Are you all right, Gabby? You're looking a bit tired, if you don't mind my saying.'

'Me? I'm okay.'

'Are you sure?' Another portion of carrot cake was forked from her plate.

'Well, I am bit tired. Haven't been sleeping very well.'

'That's not a problem you usually have, is it?'

'No.' Gabrielle sipped her espresso.

'And how's Derek?'

'He's okay.'

'I've been longing to get you alone so I can ask you – *is* Derek writing a novel? And who is this young man he's writing to? He's very reticent about it all. A bit of

207

an enigma, your husband. A very attractive enigma, if you don't mind my saying.'

Gabrielle was not at all happy about the direction in which this conversation was heading. She'd come out to get respite from Derek, not to talk about him. She groped for a response to Davina's questions. Not finding one, she remained silent.

Davina looked round the cafe: it was almost empty. They were alone, apart from two elderly ladies sitting at the next table. She leaned towards Gabrielle and said quietly 'Gabby; we've become good friends, haven't we? The four of us, I mean. We're very fond of you two, you know.'

Oh God, what was coming now? 'Fond of' – what did that mean? Gabrielle thought again about the obvious mutual attraction between Derek and Davina – was she going to suggest ...? No, surely not.

'Yes, it's good to make new friends at our time of life,' she said lamely.

The two ladies at the next table began what was obviously going to be a protracted process of leaving. Davina watched them with evident impatience. Once they'd reached the door, she pushed aside her plate and cup and leaned across the table.

'Gabby. I want to say something important. I've been wanting to say it for some time. Giles was against it, but I've persuaded him it needs to be said. Close friends should be honest with each other, shouldn't they?'

Gabrielle felt the onset of something approaching panic. She had to forestall whatever ghastly suggestion that Davina might be about to make. She swallowed hard.

'Look, Davina.' Her voice was shaking. 'I know that Derek's an attractive man. And you're an attractive woman. But we, Derek and me, I mean, are very happy, and–'

'What *are* you on about, Gabby? Just hear me out, please. You see, Giles and I *know*. Know about Derek, I mean. What he ... what happened to him, back then. No, wait. We just want to let you know it makes no difference to how we feel about him. What happened, happened. All in the past. We're all different now to how we were when we were young. It's the Derek we met two years ago that we're fond of. Christ, I'm not putting this very well–'

'But how do you know? How did you find out?' Gabrielle was reeling. It was from shock, of course, but there was something else she couldn't define.

'Giles is a historian, isn't he? He's always using the internet for research, these days. He uses Google a lot. A few weeks ago he was stuck over some topic, so he started idly Googling people's names – he sometimes does that to try and track down old school friends. He entered Derek's name. It threw up a lot of Derek Baileys. One of them was in the context of a trial at Warwick Crown Court in the 80s. And that was it, that's how we know. Oh, don't worry, he didn't go on to research all the details.'

All Gabrielle could do was to stare at her friend. She had no idea what an appropriate response would be. And it seemed that Davina, having made her revelation, was now at a loss to know how to pursue the matter, for she stared back fixedly, chewing her bottom lip. Then she grabbed Gabrielle's hand.

'It doesn't change things, Gabby. I won't mention it again. Nor will Giles. Derek needn't know that we know, if you think that's best. But ... well, look, Giles and I have noticed how you always shy away from telling us how you and Derek met, and there are lots of other things you clam up about, aren't there? Mightn't it be best if ...?'

She seemed unable to continue with her question, and Gabrielle thought she knew why. Davina was groping for a way to voice the suggestion which she, Gabrielle, had put to Derek a few days ago – that for the friendship between the two couples to continue and grow, there needed to be complete openness, no secrets, no lies. She realised that it wasn't just shock that had hit her when Davina had revealed what she knew, but relief. She felt a sense of liberation.

Davina was still clutching her hand. Gabrielle gently freed it, took a sip of her cooling espresso, and sat back in her chair.

'Okay,' she said. 'I'll tell you how we met.'

*

She had met Derek in the library while searching for reading books suitable for adults rather than the Janet and John variety to which her reluctant students objected so violently. He approached her and asked if she needed any help. He'd only been working there for two weeks, he said, but he was already familiar with the library's limited stock. They struck up a conversation: she was surprised, then intrigued by his evident erudition. It was highly irregular to question an inmate about his background, but in response to her observation that he knew a lot about literature he volunteered that he had been a lecturer. He went on to say that after ten years of gardening, decorating, and sweating in the laundry, the Governor had decided that his good behaviour merited an occupation in keeping with his education. Apparently the other cons called him 'Prof' and asked for his assistance in writing letters, and even some of the screws had begun to treat him with grudging respect.

She found that she was visiting the library more than was strictly necessary. She'd begun to look forward to their conversations, and despite the ever-watchful presence of a warder, she found that she was developing an affection for him, and it seemed as though her feelings were reciprocated. Then he'd volunteered to help her in her literacy classes: the Governor agreed that he could, and it was during these sessions, working together, that she became aware that her affection was growing into something more.

She knew what he'd done, of course. She was a midlander, and his trial had been covered by the local press eight years previously. But, as she got to know him she found it hard to associate him with the offence he'd committed: it seemed totally out of character. He'd referred to it only once, saying that he deeply regretted what he'd done. She didn't pursue the matter, and it wasn't mentioned again.

Then, without warning, he had been transferred to Stafford. The Governor told him he should see it as a reward for good behaviour, for there he would be a Category C prisoner and would find the regime more relaxed. He told her how much he would miss her: for her part, she found herself bereft. After only a week she visited him there, and throughout the long years of his remaining sentence she continued to visit, twice a week, travelling out from her home in Birmingham. As the countdown to his parole approached, they dared to speak of their feelings for each other, and began to plan for a shared future.

*

'My God, Gabby. That's almost ... well, romantic, I suppose. What I mean is ... well, all that time before you ...'

'Before the relationship was consummated, you mean? Well, you're right. The funny thing was that once he'd been released and came to live with me, we were very shy with each other. It was like meeting for the first time all over again.'

'Yes, I suppose it would have been. How did you cope with people, friends I mean?'

'We didn't. Derek didn't want to make contact with his old friends, understandably. Most of them had moved on anyway. And I didn't really have any close friends, only colleagues. I'd been lonely for years, Davina. Just to live with someone was ... well, heaven, I suppose. To start with it was like looking after a child, he was so disoriented, so dependent on me. Then my mother died – oh, she never met Derek, in case you're wondering – and left me a bit of money. We decided to leave Birmingham; too many painful associations for him.'

'Why did you choose Ellesmere?'

'Peace and quiet. Far enough away from Birmingham, but not too isolated. It was a pin-in-the-map job, but after one visit we decided it was the place for us. So here we are.'

'Well, I'm glad you came, Gabby.'

'So am I.'

'And Derek?'

'Oh, he's happy. At least he seemed to be up until this weekend. He's gone back into his shell: don't know what's up with him. I've been worried; that's why I haven't been sleeping.'

'Are you going to tell him? Tell him that we know, I mean?'

'Oh yes. He'll be relieved, I think. And the news might jerk him out of the strange mood he's in.'

When she got in, he was still sitting in the armchair. The newspaper was on his lap, and when she entered he picked it up and started reading it, or, perhaps, pretended to read it. On the short walk home she hadn't allowed herself to have second thoughts about telling him Davina's news, but she had begun to wonder whether after all this would be the right time: rather than jerk him out of his mood the effect might be to make him even more withdrawn.

No, there must be no procrastination. If she didn't tell him now it would become ever more difficult to find an appropriate moment.

'Derek.'

He looked up. 'Oh, hi Gab. I was just going to make myself a coffee. Don't suppose you want one?'

'No. Listen. I've got something important to tell you. No, don't get up; your coffee can wait.'

'What's all this then?'

At least I've got his attention, she thought. The abstracted look had gone: he was looking at her with something approaching interest. She sat down opposite him.

'It's Davina. And Giles. They *know*, Derek. They know what happened to you. They found out by accident.'

He stared at her, eyes wide. 'How could they *possibly*?'

'The internet, Derek; Google; your trial. But never mind that. The point is, it makes no difference to them. To the way they think of you. So I told her how we met. It's all in the open; no more secrets. It's a relief, isn't it? We can relax in their company: no more

213

avoiding awkward questions, no more skirting round issues.'

He continued to stare at her, but said nothing. She found herself gabbling, reiterating how this was such a good thing, repeating what a difference it would make to their lives, to their friendship with the Taylors; and when he still said nothing she asked, pleadingly, whether he didn't agree, whether he wasn't as relieved as she?

'Yes.' he said eventually. 'I suppose so.'

She got up, kissed him, embraced him.

'Gab,' he said, gently disengaging himself, 'I've got something to tell *you*.'

'Yes? What is it? I know you've been worrying about something recently. No secrets, remember?'

'I wrote to Marcus last Wednesday. My last letter. I told him the end of the story, told him about the possibility ... you know. And I gave him my email address, asked him to contact me.'

'But why didn't you *tell* me? You've always told me before, whenever you've written.'

'I dunno, really. Perhaps I wanted to wait until he'd replied, so I could – '

'Present me with a *fait accompli*? But why?'

'I don't know. I'm sorry, Gab. But he hasn't emailed. That's six days since he must have got my letter. I've been sweating over all over this bloody Jubilee weekend.'

'But perhaps he's gone away.'

'Maybe. But I can't put up with any more waiting. So I've decided to go to Milton Keynes and call on him unannounced.'

The relief that Gabrielle had been feeling poured away like bathwater down a plughole.

'Oh, God, Derek; I think that's a crazy idea.'

214

Chapter 28

Milton Keynes and Warwickshire, Tuesday 5 June

She wasn't going to cry. She gripped the steering wheel tightly. *No, I'm not going to bloody cry.* She was angry and humiliated. Doubly humiliated, first by being rejected by that tosser, and then by having to return to the only place she could go. At least there was no need to tell Marcus what had happened: she'd said she'd return to sort out the finance, hadn't she? And he didn't know she'd gone to Ben's; there was no need for him to know where she'd been.

'Fuck you!' she yelled at the driver of an Audi whose horn blared at her in protest at her cutting him up on the roundabout. 'Fuck you!' she screamed again, and the obscenity was directed at not just the driver, but at Ben, and at Marcus, and the world in general.

There had been misunderstandings from the start. Ben had assumed it was just another one-nighter. She hadn't let on her intentions – she was too tired, too drained. There would be plenty of time to tell him the next day. So she'd said 'Just for a few nights, Ben. Had a bit of a row with Marcus. Need a bit of time away from him, okay?'

He'd expected sex, of course. Sophie couldn't cope with that. She'd said she was exhausted, needed a good night's sleep. He'd tried his inadequate best to seduce her; in the end she had to fight him off. He'd retreated, affronted, to the far side of the bed, which suited Sophie fine, but sleep had eluded her. How could she broach her idea of it being a longer stay than just a few nights?

Friday, Saturday and most of Sunday passed without her feeling able to raise the matter. In fact she'd found it hard to talk to him about anything, except work. Before, they'd only ever had a few hours in each other's company. Now, she'd found the days dragging: there was nothing to do. The mornings were spent reading the papers, followed by pub lunches, but then what? Watch TV? Nothing on but the Jublilee. Go for a walk? The weather was foul, and in any case neither of them cared for walking. Go to bed? She couldn't face that. Sitting around in his lounge was depressing: she hadn't noticed before how the surfaces needed dusting, the carpet needed hoovering, the windows needed cleaning. It had been a relief to get out to the Indian restaurant on the Friday and Saturday evening. But she couldn't escape the bathroom – soap scum in the bath and hand basin, his manky toothbrush and matted hairbrush. And the toilet! Stained bowl, dried piss on the seat. She was arsed if she was going to clean it. Okay, he was a single man, but his house reminded her of the squalor of a student flat.

And it wasn't just his house. He obviously used to make some effort to accommodate her when she'd come for her one-night stays, but after only a day his personal habits were revealed – he didn't wash his hands after using the toilet, didn't bath or shower but just applied more deodorant and after-shave, yawned and belched without covering his mouth, picked his nose when he thought she wasn't watching, and occasionally farted without offering an apology. To her disquiet, she'd found herself comparing his habits to those of the fastidious Marcus.

When Sunday evening came and neither of them could face the thought of another curry, he'd suggested that she rustle up an evening meal. 'Why me?' she'd asked: the response was that it would be nice to have someone cook for him for once; there were a few things in the fridge she could knock together. Biting her tongue, she'd looked in the fridge; there was nothing in it except ready meals, all past their sell-by date, and the remains of some rotting vegetables. She'd been aware that the kitchen wasn't too clean, but a more detailed inspection revealed its full horrors. There was grease over the cooker, in the sink and on the work-surfaces, mugs were stained with tannin, bits of dried food clung to the cutlery, the dishcloth was slimy, the drying cloth was filthy. He didn't possess a dishwasher. It was then that she had realised he'd have to change his ways if she were to contemplate staying for much longer.

Last night she'd sat him down, saying they needed to talk. He'd looked wary and asked what this was all about.

'I'd like you ... us, I mean, to make a few changes if I'm going to stay for longer.'

'Staying? What do you mean? How long were you thinking of staying?'

She told him she had left Marcus for good, that she needed somewhere to stay for a few weeks, that ... but he'd interrupted her. The floodgates opened – 'A few weeks? You must be joking! What about work? I'm your boss, remember; we can't cohabit, I've got my position to think of, no, there's no way you can stay here, whatever made you think you could? I've never said anything to give you that idea, haven't you got somewhere else you can go?'

That had settled it. She'd slept, or tried to sleep, on the settee last night; was up by 7, left his house by 8, and now 10 minutes later, was driving towards the house which until a few days ago she'd called home, and which would have to be again.

She let herself in. There was no sign of Marcus in the kitchen or lounge – was he still in bed? She went to the bottom of the stairs: the sound of running water came from the bathroom. She returned to the kitchen and sat down to wait, still not knowing how to tell him that she'd be staying with him. She remembered the note she'd left him and winced. The best thing was not to explain, not to apologise, just say that she'd changed her mind. But what sort of a ménage would it now be? They could hardly live more separate lives than they'd already been doing for the past few weeks. Eventually they'd split up, she was still set on that, wasn't she? But she felt too weary to start the process of financial disentanglement immediately. Leave it for a few months, or maybe longer. It might take her that long to find a new job. She'd decided to give in her notice. No way would she continue working for that disgusting little shit who'd taken advantage of his position to get the occasional shag. Perhaps she could accuse him of sexual harassment, get him sacked? Then there'd be no need for her to resign. But she knew she didn't have the energy to do it, and knew that during the process her work-colleagues would make her life intolerable.

She felt as though she'd been sitting here for hours. Marcus was taking his usual time in the bathroom, no doubt soaping and showering himself, carefully shaving, then washing his hair, making sure he was clean. She got up to make a cup of coffee. As she started drinking it, Marcus came down the stairs.

She glanced at him briefly as he entered: their eyes met for a second: Marcus was the first to look away.

'If you've come to collect your things than you can get on with it. But if you want to start talking about money that will have to wait. Mo's invited me to spend the day with him and I'll be staying there tonight.'

'Mo? Who's Mo?' *Not a woman, surely?*

'Mo Asfraf. He's a colleague.'

'Never heard you speak of him before. But that's okay; we can talk tomorrow evening.'

'No, we can't. Tomorrow I'm going down to Warwickshire to see mother and Gordon. I might be there for a few days.'

'Have you taken some time off work, then?'

He turned to face her.

'I've taken some time off in lieu of notice. I've been made redundant. So I'll have to sell the house, just like you said. I don't have any savings and it won't be easy to find a new job, will it?'

It took a few moments for the implications of his news to hit her.

'But what will *I* do?' she wailed.

*

He'd found himself unable to tell her while she was involved with the Jubilee celebrations. There'd been too many distractions – she'd been glued to the television on Saturday, organising the barn dance on Sunday, clearing up and engaging in post-mortems all day yesterday. Such was her involvement that she was totally absorbed in the present and seemed to have forgotten her concern about Marcus's phone call. Though twitching with trepidation himself, a condition which had worsened with every day that passed, Gordon had decided to allow her a few days of relative tranquillity.

But now the time had come. They'd finished breakfast and had washed up. Meryl was making out a shopping list. Gordon went to his study, retrieved the envelope from his writing desk and took it to the kitchen. She looked up from her list and asked him what he would like for supper this evening.

219

'Never mind that now. I've got something I want you to read.'

He handed her the envelope. She peered at the scrawled and crossed-out addresses.

'What on earth's this?'

He sat down opposite her.

'I received it on Friday. It was sent to Marcus, but he's forwarded it to me.'

'I don't understand. Who was it from? Why should Marcus send it on to you?'

'Read it, Meryl. It'll soon become clear.'

He watched as she extracted the notepaper and began to read. After a few seconds she looked up at him. Her expression was one of puzzlement rather than concern.

'I still don't understand.'

'Go to the last page. See who wrote it.'

He found he could no longer watch her. He didn't need to. There was a gasp, then a low, keening wail.

'But Marcus *promised*. He said he wasn't reading them. He promised he'd shred them unopened. You told me he'd keep his promise, didn't you? You said he couldn't lie. Why has he started doing this?'

'Meryl, if you read the letter I think you'll find that Marcus has probably received a lot more letters before this one.'

'I don't want to read it. I'm not going to. No one can make me.' Her voice was quavering now. Gordon steeled himself to be firm.

'You must read it. It's important. It doesn't affect just you and Marcus; I'm involved as well. *Read it*, Meryl.'

It was rare for Gordon to speak assertively to Meryl, but when he did, she usually complied. She did so now, first sniffing occasionally as she read, then giving small yelps which culminated in a sob as she neared the end.

220

But she didn't read the final page: she dropped it on the table and it fluttered down to the floor.

She began scratching her head violently. 'How *could* he? He *promised* me. Doesn't he know what it's done to me? I told him, didn't I, from the first day when Bailey contacted him? I told him. After all I've done to shield him from ... from all that business.'

'But Meryl–'

'I know who's fault it is: it's that girl. It was her who told him to read them. She's always hated me. I know what happened: Marcus told her I'd told him to shred the letters, so just to spite me she made him read them. The little *bitch*.'

For the first time in all their years together Gordon was unable to act as comforter and counsellor. Looking at her, the tears now flowing, her head jerking from side to side in the way that usually heralded hysteria, he felt something bordering on distaste, and more than that, resentment; resentment that she was so self-centred as not to realise the effect of the letter on their marriage and the impact of Bailey's revelations on *him*.

He did something he'd never done before: he shouted at her.

'*Shut up*, Meryl! Stop thinking about yourself for once. How do you think *I* feel?'

She stared at him as though uncomprehending.

'Is it true, Meryl? All the things that Bailey has said? How long had you been living with Robert before you knew you were pregnant? Did you say it was his? Or just let him believe it was his? Was that why Bailey....? And for God's sake why didn't you tell *me*, right at the start? You must have had some idea by the time I met you who Marcus resembled – is that why you never kept any photos of Robert?'

'You don't understand!' She was almost screaming. 'I didn't know. I wasn't sure. I don't know now!'

'Oh, come on. You must have some idea.'

'I don't! Sometimes I can see Robert in him, the way he looks, but not the way he behaves. Some kids don't take after their parents, do they? I didn't *want* to know then and I don't now. Maybe if Robert had lived ... you must understand; I was young, in a mess. Nothing like that had ever happened in our family before.' She stood up. 'I can't talk about it any more. I'm going to take a pill, go to bed. I just want to sleep.'

Gordon grasped her shoulders. 'No, you're not. You've got to face up to things. You've got to decide what you're going to say to Marcus. He arrives tomorrow, in case you'd forgotten. So you're going to sit down and we're going to talk it through, however long it takes.'

Chapter 29

Shropshire, Wednesday 6 June

It was two o'clock and Davina was in Tesco's. For over a year she'd held out against shopping there in deference to Giles's antipathy to the place, but you couldn't deny its convenience, and as it was invariably she who did the food shop she'd started using it, in common with most people in the town. As she wheeled her trolley along the aisles she greeted several acquaintances, some of whom had been at the forefront of the campaign against the opening of the superstore on Canal Way when the planning application was first submitted back in 2008. None of them seemed ashamed to be seen there. Giles was one of the few in the town who insisted in continuing the boycott.

Giles was becoming a bit of a reactionary, she thought, as she stood at the delicatessen counter. In fact he seemed to be turning into a conservative in everything except politics. There were times when she suspected that he might even have become one of those who voted Labour but were secretly relieved when the Tories won. Oh yes, he was on the side of the underprivileged, that went without saying, but recently he'd begun to rail against those aspects of modern society - semi-literacy, declining attention-span, the dumbing-down of the media - which, she privately thought, were the result of some of the very changes in education he had supported when in academia. He'd subscribed to the progressive educational notions of the time, when attention to correct spelling, grammar and punctuation were regarded as a conspiracy to keep deprived kids out of higher education: now, he was constantly enraged by the fact that recent graduates couldn't string a sentence together or compose an email that made sense. They'd started arguing about this recently, and it *was* arguing, slanging matches in fact, not the calm debating of issues that one would expect of two retired academics.

'Yes?'

The remark was directed at her from the assistant behind the counter. She was being asked what she wanted. In those small independent shops that remained in the town the word 'madam' would have followed the 'yes'. Its absence didn't bother Davina, but had Giles been present he would have been offended on her behalf. He would call it lack of common courtesy: Davina would respond to the effect that absence of deference was to be welcomed, and another argument would begin.

She asked for smoked salmon pâté and six slices of organic ham, and after being served was told to have a nice day, another thing that would have resulted in a groan of anguish from Giles. As she headed towards the check-out she wondered why it was that her irritation with her husband became more pronounced when he was away – he was in Shrewsbury, meeting a landscape historian with whom he was collaborating on a book which had been in the gestation phase for nearly a year. When they were together she could still glimpse flashes of the younger Giles, the trendy lecturer, open-minded, ready to debate, to listen to the views of others and even concede that they might have a point. When he was absent all she could bring to mind was the older man, the one whose opinions were hardening into prejudices, the one who'd even begun to dress like an effete member of the privileged classes. Cravats and linen jackets, for God's sake!

There were long queues at the checkouts. She joined the end of the shortest, and resigned herself to waiting. As she waited, she continued picking at the scabs of her relationship with Giles.

Their most recent disagreement had been about Derek. The night Giles had made his Google discovery about Derek's past, he'd charged from his study into the lounge, more animated than Davina had seen him for years, and with what could only be described as relish gave Davina a detailed account of what he'd learned. He'd professed to be shocked. Perhaps he was, but as they continued to discuss the matter Davina had begun to suspect that there was a touch of schadenfreude in his reaction to Derek's downfall. Davina had been less surprised by what he'd learned: she'd noticed that there was always a reluctance on the Baileys' part to discuss their pasts, and had suspected there might be some mystery in their history. It was the hint of mystery that added to Derek's undoubted attractiveness.

Yesterday, Davina had been less than honest when she'd told Gabrielle that Derek's past made no difference to Giles, because his attitude was ambivalent - 'It may have been years ago Davina, but it was a crime, and a violent crime at that; can we really continue seeing them and behave as though nothing had happened?' Her response to this had been that Derek had paid his debt to society, and that he'd become a close friend, and she wasn't willing to abandon close friends; they had precious few in the town. Their disagreement was still unresolved. Davina was eager for the two couples to meet up again as soon as possible: the longer the meeting was left, the more awkward it would be. Giles was still holding out against it.

She reached the checkout and her attention turned to the matter in hand. She'd just finished re-loading her swiped items into her trolley and was groping in her purse for her credit card - why did she never remember to extract it before re-loading? - when there was a 'Hello, Davina' from behind her.

It was Derek. Her pleasure at seeing him was immediately tempered by discomfort: how should she handle this? Wait till he mentioned it, perhaps? But what if he didn't? Would the matter then become a great unmentionable, a blight on their friendship? All these thoughts crossed her mind in the time it took her to say 'Oh, hi, Derek; how are you?'

'I'm okay. How about you?'

But you don't look okay, she thought. He looked tired, and hadn't shaved: most unlike him not to have paid attention to his appearance.

'I'm fine,' she said. 'How's Gabby?'

'She's not too well. She started a migraine last night and it hasn't shifted yet. I've left her in bed.'

'Oh, poor Gabby. I didn't know she suffered from migraines.'

'She used to get them a lot. But this is the first one she's had for years.'

Davina was digesting this information when a world-weary voice from behind the till asked if she was going to pay by cash or card. She apologised, proffered her card, and, the transaction completed, turned to Derek. He appeared as ill-at-ease as she felt. Something had to be said.

'Have you got much to get, Derek?'

'Not a lot. Just what I can carry.' He indicated his reusable shopping bag.

'D'you fancy a coffee in town after you've finished?'

There was a moment's hesitation, then 'Yes, why not?'

'Good. You do your shopping while I take my stuff to the car. I'll wait for you there: I'm parked next to the nearest trolley-park.'

'Right. See you, then.'

She trundled her trolley to the car, hurriedly dumped her shopping in the boot, sat at the wheel, adjusted the driving mirror and peered at herself. Make-up okay, no grey roots showing, nothing stuck in her teeth. She would pass, she supposed, but not for the first time wished that her face had remained as youthful as her figure; well, as youthful as it appeared to the outside world when gravity was held in check by tight jeans and a close-fitting shirt. God, why was she thinking like this? It was only old Derek after all. But despite his age he, unlike Giles, seemed to have kept a toehold on his youth: it was partly the way he dressed, but mainly the way he carried himself – Giles was developing a pronounced stoop. And there was the way he looked at her sometimes; and the gentle teasing. There was always something unsettling about being in his presence even with Giles and Gabrielle there: she often caught herself behaving as she used to as a young woman, re-inventing herself, adapting her persona according to the company she was keeping instead of settling for the ways of the mature matron which she had become.

There was a tap on the window: she started: how long had she been wool-gathering? She opened the door.

'Shall we walk into town? It's not worth trying to find a parking space. Leave your bag in the car – so long as you don't mind walking back for it.'

'Fine by me.'

227

It was strange walking beside him as they made their way into town. It was the first time they'd been alone together, and the conversation stuttered. He enquired about Giles; she told him about the visit to Shrewsbury; he asked how Giles's book was going; she said he didn't seem to be making much progress. All the while they stared straight ahead, never glancing at each other. She was conscious that the space between them had taken on a particular significance: should friends be walking so far apart? But if she were to move closer, would it presume a greater degree of intimacy than in fact existed?

She was relieved when they reached the coffee shop. The fact that it was the place where only yesterday she'd met Gabrielle added piquancy to the situation. The place was crowded: they queued to place their order and took their seats to await its delivery.

'Derek; has Gabby told you what–'

'Gabby told me about your meeting–'

They spoke simultaneously. They grinned at each other.

'You first,' said Davina.

'There's not much to say, Davina. Gabby told me how Giles found out. It was a shock, of course. But it doesn't matter, so long as you're okay with it, and Gabby says you are. It all seems like a distant nightmare now. If you were to ask me if I was ashamed of it all then my honest answer would be – yes, intellectually, but not in my guts. I'm not tormented by guilt, not for what I did. The thing that's got to me most is having to live with the secret, being afraid that people would find out. Now you have, and so long as it makes no difference, well, I'm relieved.'

Davina reached across the table and touched his hand briefly.

'It makes no difference. We all have things in our pasts that we regret, don't we?'

'Yeah, but nothing like mine. What about Giles? Does he feel the same as you?'

Davina was saved from answering by the arrival of their coffee.

'D'you mind my asking, Derek, but are you okay? You look a bit ... well, tired. Not your usual self.'

'Didn't get much sleep last night. Gabby ... well, we've had a bit of a disagreement.

'What about? Nothing to do with what I told her, I hope.'

'No, no. She's not happy with something I want to do, that's all. It was the disagreement that brought on her migraine.'

'It must have been a major disagreement, then. You two always seem so together.'

As she spoke she was aware that a boundary might be about to be crossed. The relationship between the two couples had not reached that stage of intimacy where the partner of one confided details of any marital discord to the partner of the other.

Derek stirred his coffee and took several sips. He was silent for so long that Davina was about to apologise for being insensitive, but he then spoke.

'I told her I wanted to go away for a day to visit someone. She's vehemently against it.'

'Why? Who is it you want to visit? Oh, sorry Derek, I'm intruding. It's none of my business. Sorry.'

She touched his hand again, less briefly this time. He was looking at her, mouth working slightly as though uncertain how to respond.

How much should he tell her? Might *she* understand why it was so important for him to see Marcus? Would confiding in her be a betrayal of Gabby?

She was looking at him, concernedly. He'd been so immersed in his own thoughts that he'd forgotten how attractive she was – yes, her face was lined, but she wasn't haggard, and those large brown eyes were beguiling. They were inviting him to confide, despite what she'd just said.

'No, don't apologise. I'd like to tell you. It would be good to get someone else's perspective.'

'If you're sure–'

'Yes, I am. Look, do you remember outside the pub a few weeks back when I let slip about this lad I've been writing to? Telling him my life story? I said he was the grandson of a former colleague. That wasn't true. His name's Marcus Sidelski. He's 24.'

She looked puzzled for a moment, then realisation evidently dawned.

'Sidelski? You mean he's the grandson of the fellow you ...?'

'Yes, Robert Sidelski, but no, not his grandson.'

'You mean ...?'

'All I know for certain is that Marcus is the son of Meryl Shaw – that was her name before he was born – the girl I lived with before she moved in with Sidelski. She was pregnant when she was living with him. Marcus was born after Sidelski died. Meryl gave him Sidelski's name.'

'So Marcus is Robert Sidelski's son?'

'Not necessarily, Davina. That's what I want to find out. That's why I want to visit him. See what he looks like.'

Her eyes widened.

'Oh my God, Derek. Are you saying what I think you're saying?'

He nodded.

'Are you ... do you feel like telling me exactly what happened?'

Yes, Derek did want to. The story was well rehearsed, wasn't it? He'd written it all down in the final paragraphs of his last letter to Marcus, the letter to which he'd had no response. It had seemed so easy, writing it down. But was it really what had happened? To give a true account of the past requires one to include not just what one remembers, but what may have been forgotten. Now, faced with telling the story to one to whom it was new, he couldn't be sure that what he'd written was the whole truth and nothing but the truth. But he told it to her none the less.

When he finished speaking she took his hand, and this time remained holding it. He caught a whiff of her perfume; it added to her allure: Gabby never wore perfume.

'You poor man; living with that uncertainty for all these years. It must be hard to bear.'

'No, I didn't even consider the possibility while I was banged up, nor after I'd been released. And those first months living with Gabby were like being born again – I thought I'd put my past behind me. But once we'd moved here and settled down I began to wonder. I tracked down Marcus on the net. It was only when I started writing to him that I gradually came to realise that I needed to know.'

'And Gabby? You've told her how you feel, I assume? And she supports you?'

'Oh yes. Well, she did until I told her that I wanted to meet him. She's against it. She says that as Marcus hasn't contacted me it must mean he doesn't want to know, so I should leave it. She's insistent about that. That's why we argued – the first real disagreement we've had.'

'So, what are you going to do?'

This was the question that had been exercising Derek since the previous afternoon, the reason for his sleepless night. He was still no nearer an answer.

'I don't know. I just don't know.'

'Perhaps I oughtn't to say this Derek, but I think Gabby's being a bit unreasonable.'

It was what he'd been hoping she'd say. He squeezed her hand. He realised he wanted to remain in her company, to listen to more supportive words, to bask in the support he felt that Gabrielle was denying him. But Gabrielle would be wondering where he'd got to.

'I think I ought to be going, Davina, much as I'd like to stay.'

Davina released his hand.

'Yes, okay. I'm glad you've confided in me. Hope it helped.'

They left the coffee shop and began walking back to the car. Once they'd left the town centre Davina took his arm. He pressed her hand to his side. He was feeling something more than comfort. Their pace slowed as they approached Tesco's car park. When they reached the car Davina got in: Derek waited for her to hand him his shopping bag, but she opened the passenger door.

'Get in, just for a minute, won't you?'

He sat down beside her. She turned to him.

'Giles won't be home till at least 5. Would you like to come back?'

Chapter 30

Warwickshire, Wednesday 30 June

Gordon had felt unwell immediately he got out of bed. He'd slept badly, disturbed by dreams. In dreams everything seems possible; the mind is freed of constraints and is free to wander at will: he'd experienced almost simultaneously the euphoria that came from everything turning out all right, and the despair resulting from the worst outcome imaginable. Meryl had still been sleeping soundly, no doubt the result of the pills she'd taken before retiring.

Then, pottering about in the kitchen, his right leg had given way beneath him, something that was happening with increasing frequency, and he'd fallen over. It had shaken him up. He hadn't just fallen: he was now of the age where one 'had a fall'. He'd had to sit down for a while to recover. After a hurried breakfast, he'd woken Meryl, told her he'd be back in less than an hour, and set off in the car for Leamington. He hadn't known what he was expecting. He'd decided that when alone with Marcus he'd go along with however the lad wanted to play it: only later, with Meryl present, might he have to take on the role of conciliator. He was practised at that, but of course when a social worker he'd never been emotionally involved.

He'd watched Marcus alight from the carriage. He'd stumbled slightly and looked around in that lost manner that he'd always had as a little boy, as though he'd been transported to an alien land where the inhabitants were not to be trusted. Gordon had shouted and waved: Marcus saw him and hurried towards him in the duck-like waddle that had resulted in so much teasing when he was at school. But he'd made no response to Gordon's shouted greeting; there was no change of expression, no smile, no wave. There was no means of judging his state of mind. Marcus's facial expressions and body language were often inappropriate to the situations in which he found himself.

Now, with Marcus in the passenger seat, he had to make conversation. Mention Bailey's letter right at the outset, perhaps? No; he mustn't force the pace: in any case that discussion must wait until they were with Meryl. The trouble with being alone with Marcus was that he had no small talk.

'Bloody awful weather, isn't it?' he said. 'Depressing, don't you find?'

Marcus seemed to give the question careful consideration. Eventually he said 'Yes, it was raining in Milton Keynes. It started to rain exactly ten minutes before the taxi arrived to take me to the station. I think it may have rained throughout my journey, but I was reading a magazine so I can't be sure of that.'

'Marcus, what's all this about your leaving your job? What brought that on? I thought you enjoyed your work at the council.'

Silence for a few moments, then 'Reorganisation. At the council.'

Bloody hell, I bet the poor little sod's been made redundant. 'You're looking for a new job, I suppose? How's it going?'

'Mo has offered to assist me. He has a lot of expertise in Information Technology, and also many contacts. He once worked in private industry, and still networks with his former colleagues. Mo's particular expertise is in ...'

Marcus launched into a detailed account of Mo's curriculum vitae, and Gordon knew there was little chance of his giving a straightforward response to the question he'd been asked. Marcus's accounts of events were often big on detail, while at the same time failing to give the bigger picture. Listening to him as he chuntered on about this Mo fellow, Gordon wondered what form of communication he used with Sophie: the idea of Marcus engaging in day-to-day commonplaces with her, let alone whispering intimacies while engaged in ... well, the notion was as impossible to imagine as one's parents having sex. But of course Sophie was also in I.T.: perhaps they employed some sort of computer code when in bed together.

As he turned off into the lane that led to the village Gordon's guts began to churn with apprehension at the thought of the meeting between mother and son. He glanced at Marcus in the passenger seat, wondering how he was feeling, but his face was as impassive as it had been ever since he'd alighted from the train. When they reached the drive to the house, he said 'Go easy on your mother, Marcus. She's a bit fragile.' There was no response.

Meryl must have been watching from the window, for the front door opened as soon as Gordon drew up outside. She'd made an effort, Gordon was pleased to see, she'd put on her favourite summer dress despite the weather; her hair was brushed to a sleek sheen and she was carefully made up.

Marcus clambered out of the car: he'd hardly straightened up before Meryl launched herself down the steps and flung her arms round him.

'Marcus, darling! It's so good to see you! Are you all right? Was the journey horrid? How long are you staying? You can stay as long as you like, you know that: your old room's all ready for you. Have you brought much luggage? Gordon will take it up, won't you Gordon? Are you hungry? We'll have dinner at 6, but would you like a snack now? There's tea of course, or coffee if you'd prefer. Oh, it's so good to see you!'

During this verbal onslaught Marcus stood rigid, his arms by his sides, his face crushed against his mother's cheek. For God's sake give the lad some space, thought Gordon, let him go to his room and unpack, give him time to adjust. As if suddenly aware of his lack of response, Meryl released him and stood back.

'Darling, you don't look well, and you've lost weight. You've not been eating properly. We'll soon feed you up. Are you sure you're all right? You don't feel ill, do you? Because–'

'I'm *all right*. I'll go and unpack.' Marcus picked up the suitcase which Gordon had unloaded from the boot.'

'Let me help you, darling, I've made some space in the wardrobe – '

'*No!*'

'Let him go, Meryl. Don't fuss. There's plenty of time to talk later.

There was plenty of time, but very little talk, not in the sense that Gordon had meant. Once Marcus had unpacked he joined them in the lounge, and Meryl immediately launched into a renewed interrogation about his health, his job, his plans, to which Marcus's responses were monosyllabic when he bothered to reply at all. This had the effect of making Meryl resort to a garbled account of what she'd been doing in the village over the Jubilee weekend. As she spoke her voice got higher and her body movements more agitated. Marcus, who was sitting opposite her, turned his chair so he was facing Gordon. Gordon interrupted Meryl's flow to ask how Sophie was: Marcus delivered a measured bulletin about her job and her prospects for promotion, at the end of which he fell silent, allowing Meryl to her resume her account of her doings in a voice which began to border on the hysterical.

Gordon searched for ways in which the afternoon could be rescued from total disaster. Marcus was obviously determined to ignore his mother, and Meryl had started scratching at her head, the usual precursor to tears. Some form of displacement activity was called for.

'Meryl, Marcus hasn't eaten since breakfast. Might it be an idea to have dinner early? Does that suit you, Marcus?'

'Yes, that would be okay.'

'How about it, then Meryl? You've got a casserole prepared, haven't you? I'll come and give you a hand with the veg. Do you want a coffee in the meantime, Marcus?'

'Yes please.'

'Make yourself at home, then. *The Guardian*'s in the rack if you want to read it.'

'No thanks. Is your pc still in your study? I'd like to check my emails.'

'I'm afraid my computer's not state-of-the-art, but you're welcome to use it.'

'Why won't he talk to me?' wailed Meryl. 'He talks to *you*.'

Gordon hurriedly closed the kitchen door.

'You're pushing him too hard, Meryl. Cut him a bit of slack. He never was one for chit-chat: don't be afraid of silence; he'll come round. Try and relax. It'll be better when we're eating.'

It was a bit better. Preparing the meal, something to which Meryl always gave assiduous attention, helped calm her down. She pulled out all the stops of course; best dinner service, precisely placed table-settings, highly polished wine glasses, carefully folded table

237

napkins. Marcus devoured his casserole with relish – his table manners hadn't improved, Gordon noticed – and gulped his wine as though it were a pint of lager, but he began to respond to Meryl's chatter. Gordon had suggested she talk about his studies at school and university, a subject which never failed to engage him, and he treated her to a lecture about recent developments in computer science, of which she understood about one word in ten, but it was communication of a sort. By the time they started on the dessert he was even responding to her recollections of his school contemporaries.

When the meal was over Gordon left them talking while he loaded the dishwasher. While doing so he came to a decision. It was arrogance on his part to assume that he was required to act as an intermediary: the as-yet-unspoken matter, though of great importance to him, was after all primarily an issue to be resolved between mother and son: his presence might actually inhibit the conversation that the two needed to have.

He returned to the dining room.

'I feel like a bit of fresh air,' he said. 'I think I'll go for a bit of a stroll now it's stopped raining. Might even call in at *The Bell* for a quick half.'

Marcus hurriedly pushed back his chair and got up.

'I'll come with you,' he said.

The darkness that descended on her was like nothing she'd experienced before. It came with devastating speed as soon as the front door closed. She hadn't known what to say to him; how could she know, when he gave no indication of what he wanted from her? Why had he come, if he was determined to ignore her? Was it just to punish her? She didn't know him – she never had, really. She'd known bits of him, of course; the things he used to ask, his replies to what she'd asked, his all-too-predictable responses to events. She'd become an expert on the semaphore of his body language. But as to what was in his head – that had always been unfathomable.

Sitting at the dining room table in the silence of the empty house she surrendered to a tide of emotion, and howled. An agonised, animal howl of anguish, a howl of desperation for her situation, which she knew was irresolvable. The thing that she had secretly dreaded since the time she'd carried Marcus in her womb had finally come to pass. She could see no way forward. She'd lost him, and probably Gordon as well.

Then, surging up from her guts came a deep, visceral loathing for Bailey, for what he'd done to Robert, for what his letter had done to Marcus, but above all for what he'd done to her. Why hadn't Gordon believed her when she'd told him she didn't know, that she wasn't certain? Any words she might use to try and explain the reason for her uncertainty would sound as though she were describing the actions of a slut. And she hadn't been a slut, not even promiscuous, not by the standards of the time. It was all Bailey's doing, continuing to force his attentions on her as though it were his right, even after she'd told him she was leaving him. Who could blame her for seeking Robert's comfort in the weeks before she finally went to live with him?

The shrill tones of the telephone jangled from the lounge. She jumped: her chair clattered to the floor. She was shaking. She didn't want to answer; couldn't cope with intrusion. But it might be Gordon, or Marcus even, ringing from the pub. She hurried to the lounge on legs that were jelly, and picked up.

'Hello?'

'Is that Meryl? It's Sophie. Is Marcus there? He's not answering his mobile.'

No! No! Not that woman!

'No. Marcus isn't here.'

'Whaddya mean? You mean he hasn't come to stay with you, or d'ya mean he's gone out? If he's out, tell him to phone me.'

'How *dare* you.'

'Eh?'

'How *dare* you presume to think I'd want to speak to you after what you've done?'

'What? What the fuck are you on about?'

'Just the sort of language I'd expect from you. You know very well what I mean. You've done everything you can to turn Marcus against me, haven't you? I don't want to hear from you again. Goodbye.'

That was enough. She couldn't cope with any more, not this evening. Couldn't face seeing Marcus, even. She'd talk to him in the morning. All she wanted now was oblivion. It was only 7 o'clock, but she'd be in bed and asleep by the time Gordon and Marcus returned. It might take more than one sleeping pill, but why not? Just one extra wouldn't harm her, would it?

Chapter 31

Shropshire, Warwickshire, Milton Keynes
Thursday 7 June

There was no throbbing in her temples, no feeling of nausea. It boded well. Tentatively, she opened her eyes. The curtains were drawn, but not completely: a shaft of sunlight pierced the room and splashed across the duvet cover. She was able to look at it without the flashes at the periphery of her vision that were always a warning to close her eyes. It had passed: the migraine had gone. Relief flooded through her. She rarely had an attack these days, and this had been a bad one. Her anger at its arrival the previous morning had been matched only by her distress over the events that had caused it. But now she was better and able to think, she knew she would be faced again by the prospect of Derek visiting Marcus unannounced. No good would come of it, she was sure. She'd been stupid from the outset to acquiesce in Derek's project. His letters hadn't seemed to provide the catharsis he sought; indeed she'd noticed that his equilibrium had lessened with each that he'd posted.

She became conscious of birdsong outside: Derek must have opened the window when he'd got up. How rare it was to hear birds singing in this sodden summer. Then, from downstairs, the muffled sound of music. Most unlike Derek not to be listening to Radio 4. What time was it? She peered at the bedside clock – my God, nearly ten o'clock. Time to face the day. She heaved herself from the bed: a bit shaky, but still no nausea, just a faint residual headache. She pulled the curtains: outside, an unusual sight: a clear blue sky; leaves, still

241

with their late-spring freshness, shimmering in the sunlight.

There was the familiar creak of the kitchen door being opened and the sound of the music became more distinct: then, tentative footsteps on the stairs. The bedroom door opened.

'Oh, you're up. I was coming to check on you. How are you feeling?'

'Much better. Okay, in fact. Sorry about yesterday.'

'Not your fault, Gabby. Would you like a cup of tea in bed?'

'No thanks. I'm up now. I'll be down in a minute. A slice of toast would be nice.'

'Right. Will do.'

He made to leave, then stopped and turned to face her.

'Gabby, I'm sorry I hassled you last night when I got in. I forgot how ill you feel when you have one of your migraines. It was just that I wanted to tell you about – '

'Tell me over breakfast. Oh, I think I can face coffee with the toast. Not too strong.'

'Right.'

He pattered down the stairs, his descent far less measured than his ascent.

Gabrielle searched the wardrobe for clothes suitable for what promised to be a warm summer day. As she dressed she recalled Derek's attempt to talk to her the previous evening. He'd woken her on arriving home and began talking urgently, but his words were just part of the thumping clamour in her head: all she'd wanted was for him to stop. But she could remember the gist of what he'd said: he was sorry he was so late, he'd decided to go to the library before shopping and spent ages there and he hadn't got to Tesco until after five, and there he'd run into Davina and they'd had a coffee

242

and got talking ... it was at that point that Gabrielle, head in hands, had cried out that she couldn't talk now, all she wanted was to sleep.

Now, she could understand why he'd been so keen to talk. No doubt he'd discussed with Davina the fact of her and Giles knowing his past. Gabrielle was glad the conversation had taken place: it needed to happen if the couples were to take up the reigns of their friendship. Pity Giles hadn't been there as well; at least she assumed he hadn't been; Derek hadn't mentioned him.

'Here's your toast. Coffee won't be a minute.'

'Thanks. Do you think you could turn the radio down a bit? Why are you listening to Radio 2?'

'Sorry. It's not Radio 2, it's a CD. Felt like a bit of music for a change. Haven't listened to Aretha Franklin for years.'

He turned off the CD player.

Gabrielle didn't comment. She didn't share Derek's passion for the popular music of his youth; usually he indulged only when wearing headphones.

He passed her the marmalade, poured her coffee and then stood beside her in the manner of an over-attentive waiter.

'Anything else I can get you?'

'No, that's fine. Why don't you sit down? Tell me about your meeting with Davina.'

'Oh, you remember my telling you that, do you? It was quite late when I bumped into her: I'd been in the library all afternoon and–'

'Yes, Derek, I remember you telling me that as well.'

'Right.'

'Well, how did it go? I suppose you talked about them knowing about your history? Did she have much to say? Did you say how you felt about it? I bet you feel much better about it now it's all in the open: you certainly seem more cheerful.'

'Yes, we talked about it a bit. I wasn't with her for long, just a quick coffee.'

'Where was Giles?'

'Don't know; she didn't say. At home I suppose.'

Gabrielle was conscious of him watching her as she sipped her coffee. Then he reached across and took her hand.

'Gabby. When I was in the library I did a lot of thinking. I've decided you were right – about Marcus, I mean. It would be wrong to visit him without warning. I need to be sure he wants to see me. If he doesn't, then – well, I can live without knowing. I've been doing so for over 20 years.'

Gabrielle felt light-headed with relief. She squeezed his hand.

'Oh, I'm so glad. You can dispense with the past now, can't you? Live for the present. Cement our friendship with Giles and Davina. You know, I was thinking; it might be nice for the four of us to go on holiday together. It's time we started broadening our horizons, and they'd be good company. Why don't we suggest it?'

'Oh ... I dunno. Maybe. Not immediately.'

He kissed her, picked up her plate and took it to the sink. As he rinsed it he began singing – '*You make me feel like a natural woman*'.

Strange choice of song for a man, thought Gabrielle, but it was good to see him so cheerful again.

*

Meryl had been dead to the world when they got back from the pub, though it was only nine o'clock; much later than he'd intended, but the extended visit had been worth it: at last he'd managed to get Marcus to talk. Gordon had been encouraged by their conversation: he'd been eager to tell Meryl about it, but he couldn't rouse her. Let her sleep, he'd thought: it would be best for her to receive the news when she was refreshed. He'd tell her when he brought her a cup of tea in the morning.

But now, down in the kitchen at 10am, nursing a throbbing head and uncertain bowels (he'd had three pints in the pub, far more than he was used to) he wasn't so sure how she'd react. Perhaps she wouldn't see it as good news. For her it would hold the potential for further anguish. He must present it in a positive light – as something that Marcus wanted, as something that would end the uncertainty that haunted her, as something to bring closure (he hated the cliché, but it seemed apt in this situation) and allow them all to move forward. Christ, now he was thinking entirely in those bloody clichés – would he ever stop being a social worker?

Youthful footsteps clattered down the stairs and Marcus entered. He was in pyjamas and dressing gown - retrieved by Meryl the previous day from her stash of his teenage belongings - unshaven, unwashed probably, and hair awry: Gordon noticed that it was beginning to recede at the temples, and was that a thin patch on the top? He felt a pang of sympathy: the poor lad was only in his early 20s.

'Morning, Marcus. Sleep okay?'

'Yes, I did. It was probably the drink that made me go to sleep so quickly.'

Bloody hell, he only had three halves of cider. 'I'm just going to take this cuppa up to your Mum. I'll stay and talk to her for a while. Can you manage to get your own breakfast?'

'Yes. I can do that very well. I always get breakfast when I'm in Milton Keynes.'

As Marcus spoke his mobile phone chirruped in his dressing gown pocket: he extracted it, glanced at it, then put it back in his pocket. Gordon was pleased to see that unlike most of his age-group, Marcus gave precedence to those in his presence rather than instantly responding to the siren call of technology. In the pub his phone had summoned him three times, but each time he'd ignored it.

With care Gordon carried the tea upstairs - his leg was still inclined to give way under him - pushed open the door and put the cup and saucer on the bedside table. Meryl, who'd been making wakening noises when he'd got up, was now sitting up in bed.

'Tea, darling. How are you feeling this morning? It looks like it's going to be a nice day'

She looked at him, rather warily he thought, before saying that she wasn't too bad, and asking what time he got home last night, and how was Marcus, and did he talk at all in the pub, and did he say anything about her?

Gordon sat down on the bed.

'I managed to get him to talk, eventually, but God it was hard work. I had to make all the running. I told him how you were feeling–'

'What do you mean? Have you any *idea* how I'm feeling?'

'Yes, I think I do. I told him how difficult things were for you, how upset you'd been by his not keeping his promise not to read any of Bailey's letters, how you felt betrayed.'

'Then why did he–'

'Hang on, Meryl. You might not like this, but I went on to tell him that I could understand that he felt betrayed as well, betrayed by your not telling him the whole truth.'

'But I don't *know* the whole truth, haven't you understood that yet?'

'Yes I *do* understand. I was trying to get him to open up, and it worked. Look, you know how hard he finds it to express his emotions, but he did manage to give some idea of how he was feeling. It's the not knowing that's getting to him. I said that if that was the case then he should realise that it's just the same for you.'

'And what did he say to that?'

'Nothing. But he seemed to be thinking about it. Look, drink your tea.'

She took a sip.

'I think he'll come round, Meryl. But I honestly think the only way of resolving all this is to find out the truth, both for your sake and for Marcus's. You've been worrying about it for over 20 years, haven't you? I wish you'd told me.'

'But I *don't want to know*.'

'What difference would it make? Whatever the truth it couldn't make you unhappier than you already are.'

'And how do you suggest we find out?'

'There are ways, Meryl.'

'Oh no. Not a DNA test.'

'No. That would be difficult to arrange, wouldn't it, given that ... '

He tailed off: it wouldn't help to remind her that Robert had been cremated. And she'd never entertain the idea of Bailey being asked to provide a sample.

'How, then?

'I'm not sure. I'll have to give it some thought.'

But Gordon had already given it a lot of thought, and he knew exactly what he was going to do.

*

247

Sophie was eating a late dinner of left-overs from a tray, sitting in front of the TV which she wasn't watching. Work had been terrible: Ben had treated her like shit, in front of her colleagues, loading her with demeaning tasks and then criticising her for not completing them within the impossible time-scales that he'd set. He'd been alternately bombastic and sarcastic and her colleagues had made no attempt to hide their grins. Eventually she could take it no longer: after a remark to the effect that she wasn't as competent as she thought she was, she finally lost it and screamed that he was a fucking chauvinist wanker, after which she was asked to leave the office and not return until she received a letter inviting her to a disciplinary hearing.

She wasn't going to give them the pleasure. She'd already emailed her letter of resignation. And if they thought she was going to work out her notice – well, stuff them. There was no way she was going to sit in that office again.

So her boats were well and truly burnt. No job, soon no house, no real friends, and no Marcus. Not that she missed him, well, not really; it was just a bit too quiet without someone else in the house. More worrying were the financial implications of his departure: they didn't hold a joint bank account; all the regular bills were paid by direct debit from Marcus's. And he topped up her account for things like petrol and the weekly shop. How long would it be before she was entitled to Job-seekers Allowance? Ages, probably, given that she'd resigned. The chances of finding a new job in the present climate were remote. In the space of a few hours she'd become one of the undeserving poor, a skiver not a striver, one whose bedroom curtains were still drawn when hardworking families left to go to work. The parrotings of the *Daily Mail* took on a new, unwelcome resonance.

They needed to get the finances sorted. She needed to know when he intended putting the house on the market. She needed to know when he was coming back. So she'd started texting him yesterday, and, when he never replied, had tried phoning him. But his phone was either switched off or he chose not to pick up. She had to swallow her pride to phone his mother, and she was more shaken by Meryl's accusation than she cared to admit to herself. After that she'd tried phoning his mobile again – three times that evening – to no avail. She'd tried twice again this afternoon. Still no joy.

She jumped up and took her plate to the kitchen where it joined the morning's unwashed breakfast things on the draining board. She cast around for something to do, something to occupy her mind. There was nothing. She went up to the bedroom, changed into the tee-shirt that she used as night-attire. But it was still light outside at 9 pm: she couldn't go to bed yet. She found herself envying those who gained enjoyment from reading in bed: she didn't enjoy reading at all, whatever her location. She peered out of the window: in the garden next door Kevin and Jane were sitting side-by-side on recliners, wine glasses in hand, the remains of a barbecued meal on the table beside them. As she watched, Kevin reached out and stroked his wife's thigh: Jane smiled and placed her hand on his groin.

She hurriedly turned away. She couldn't cope with seeing the intimacies of others, not now, not while she was alone.

She decided to try phoning Marcus one more time.

*

Gordon left Marcus and Meryl sitting together in the garden. The evening's meal, eaten alfresco, had been far less tense than that of yesterday. The subject had yet to be broached, but this was something only Meryl or Marcus could do, and only when on their own. It was up to them now. He needed to get on with the task he'd set himself, so that he was ready with the plan of action once rapprochement had been achieved between mother and son.

He went to his study, extracted Bailey's letter from the filing cabinet, read it one more time and committed to memory Bailey's email address. He hoped that Marcus wouldn't want to spend too much time in the coming days using the computer.

Chapter 32

Warwickshire and Shropshire

Friday 8 June

Alone in the house at last, sitting in his study at the computer.

Meryl was driving Marcus to Stratford so he could investigate a Laptop. Marcus had gone reluctantly: he'd wanted to go to Leamington where he was sure there'd be better shops with more choice, but Meryl refused to take him there. She never visited Leamington; hadn't done so for 24 years. Gordon knew that for her the place was a minefield of memories, a few happy, many sad, and one of unspeakable horror. She had been pleased when the giant multi-laned interchange had been built where the road from Stratford to Warwick and Leamington crossed the M40: a nervous driver, it gave her the excuse never to negotiate it. That was the reason she'd given to Marcus for refusing his request. Gordon hadn't offered to take him: after making his decision yesterday, the need to act immediately was imperative: he had to send the email today, and he needed to be alone to do it.

He stared at the blank screen, not knowing quite what to say or how to say it. How could he write about a matter of such delicacy to someone he'd never met, someone of whom he'd heard only appalling things, and someone whose recent actions had not only threatened the fragile emotional stability of Meryl and Marcus, but his own peace of mind?

Despite a working life of close contact with dysfunctional clients, Gordon had always liked to think that most people sublimated their basic instincts in accordance with a natural humanitarian inclination and social conditioning: most didn't live by the law of the jungle; most treated others with a degree of tolerance. But Bailey? His whole history pointed to the contrary. How could such a person be approached? What guarantee was there that receiving the email that he, Gordon, was struggling to write, wouldn't provoke Bailey into another heinous act?

He decided to try and draft the email on paper before committing it to the keyboard. Resisting the temptation go down and make a coffee, he lit a cigarette, pulled a piece of scrap paper from the pile on his desk and began to scribble.

Half an hour later, a second cigarette extinguished, and having recovered from a fit of coughing, he turned to the keyboard and copied what he'd written.

Mr Bailey.

I am emailing you concerning matters relating to Marcus Sidelski. I should explain that I know your email address because Marcus passed on to me your recent letter to him. I should further explain that I am Marcus's step-father, and you will gather from that that I am married to Meryl, formerly Miss Shaw. From this you will be aware that I am fully conversant with the events of the late 1980s.

Let me re-assure you that my purpose in contacting you is not to seek retribution or even an apology. To be honest, I would be prefer not to have anything to do with you. But you should be aware that your letters to Marcus have had a devastating effect on him and his mother. However, there is a course of action which, were you to agree to it, might help them come to terms with the situation in which they find themselves.

I prefer not to go into details at this stage. I wish first to ascertain whether you are willing to correspond with me. I should add that Marcus is no longer resident in Milton Keynes and does not have access to his computer.

I look forward to hearing from you.
Gordon Whittaker

Reasonably satisfied with what he had written, he clicked on 'send'. Now he was condemned to hours, days perhaps, of waiting for a reply, if a reply ever came at all.

Saturday 9 June

Gabrielle was out shopping. Derek had had his morning run, breakfasted, leafed through the paper and was sitting at the desk in the parlour. It was force of habit that led him to be there: it had been an almost daily ritual to sit there and write to Marcus, or, in recent days, to check his emails in the hope that Marcus had responded.

But now the need to establish contact was diminished, gone, almost. He'd been honest when he'd told Gabrielle that he'd decided not to pressure Marcus, that he could live without knowing. But he hadn't told her the reason for his abrupt change of heart. What had happened on Wednesday afternoon offered him the opportunity to rebuild his life, to consort with someone who didn't have a complete picture of him, someone who hadn't heard it all before. He loved Gabrielle of course and would never leave her, but he now knew he needed something more, something other than affection and companionship. He had no idea how things might develop, but it was the fact of experiencing something like the blithe unpredictability of youth that was so

253

exciting. That was it – the prospect of excitement. Future possibilities had pushed to the background the need to explore his past.

Now, he was at a loss to know how to occupy himself. Writing to Marcus had become almost addictive. He had to do something to pass the time before Gabby returned. He turned on his pc. Might as well check for emails, though he knew they'd mostly be spam.

One was titled *Attention Mr Bailey*. He opened it. The salutation *'Mr Bailey'* was the sort of thing that usually heralded an invitation to change his energy supplier, or take out life insurance, or join Saga. He was about to delete it when the name Marcus Sidelski leapt out at him. He read it, and thoughts of illicit encounters evaporated.

He knew he had to reply.

Hello Gordon Whittaker.

Thank you for your email. Let me assure you that I am totally indifferent to your feelings towards me. However, if my writing to Marcus has caused him distress then I'm sorry. If, as you say, there is something I can do to help him, then I'm willing to consider it. You can take this as an expression of my willingness to correspond with you.

Derek Bailey

He clicked on 'send', thinking as he did so that he now had the prospect of two potential sources of excitement, and two things he must keep Gabby from knowing.

Monday 11 June

Marcus had hogged Gordon's computer throughout Sunday. He said he was investigating employment

254

opportunities in Warwickshire. That was positive, Gordon supposed, but begged many questions. Was he intending never to return to Milton Keynes? If so, what about all the belongings he had there? Shouldn't he be setting about selling his house? And what about his partner Sophie? But Gordon didn't want to disturb Marcus's newly-found sense of purpose by questioning him. In any case, he had more pressing matters to attend to, once he could get access to his computer.

Access had at last been obtained. Marcus had caught the bus to Leamington (the trip to Stratford had been as unsuccessful as he'd predicted), Meryl was having coffee with friends from the W.I. He had the house to himself for about an hour. He logged on.

An email from Bailey was in his in-box. The relief that he'd received a reply was immediately superseded by anger at the tone that Bailey had adopted. Arrogant bastard. Just the sort of thing he should have expected. But he mustn't let his feelings obstruct what he was determined to do. This time, he knew exactly what to say.

Mr Bailey.

Let me come straight to the point. As a result of your letter, Marcus has lost his sense of identity: he doesn't know who he is, and this is causing him much anguish. As for his mother, all the uncertainty that she tried to suppress for 25 years has erupted to such a point that I fear for her health.

I believe that the only chance for them both to come to terms with the past is for them to learn the truth. I have not told Marcus this, but I have discussed the matter with his mother and she will, I think, come round to accepting what I say.

There is of course a sure way of determining paternity, but I do not wish to put Marcus through this.

255

There are two alternatives. One would be for me to meet you in the hope that I might identify (or preferably not identify) any likeness that you might have to Marcus. The second alternative would be for you to see (and I mean 'see', not 'meet') Marcus so that you can attempt the identification – and you might of course be able to recognise any likeness to the unfortunate Robert Sidelski, whom I never met, and of whom no photograph exists. This would of course mean that you would subsequently have to inform me of what you believe, and I would have to take on trust that you were telling the truth.

If you were to agree to the second alternative we would have to plan a means whereby you can observe Marcus. Let me be quite clear: under no circumstances would I want Marcus to meet you.

I look forward to hearing your thoughts on this matter.

Gordon Whittaker

Wednesday 13 June

It was late afternoon: Gabrielle was in the kitchen preparing dinner. Derek had been itching to get to the computer since Monday morning (there had been no response from Whittaker over the weekend), but that day he'd had to join Gabrielle on one of her occasional shopping trips to Shrewsbury, and yesterday had been taken up with joint domestic tasks and dinner at the pub with the Taylors.

He'd approached the pub encounter with some trepidation. He knew that Gabrielle had similar qualms, but for her it was the prospect of their meeting the Taylors for the first time since they'd become acquainted with his past. For him, this was no longer a big deal: overriding it was the worry that his demeanour in front of Davina, and hers in front of him, might subtly have changed, such that it might be noticed by their respective partners.

In fact the meeting was much like all their previous encounters – maybe a slight hesitancy before normal discourse started, and had he detected a slight coolness on the part of Giles? But the matter of his past had not been mentioned: much of the conversation had hinged on whether they should continue to attend the Book Group when it started meeting again in September, and if not what alternatives there might be, and then, prompted by Gabrielle, a discussion about the sort of holiday they might take together.

Throughout the start of all this he'd been sensitive to how he looked at, spoke to, laughed with Davina. Was he being too distant, over-formal? Was he not giving enough of the jokey asides, or engaging in the gentle teasing that had come to characterise his exchanges with her? Was he avoiding eye-contact with her? Was she, in turn, giving less of herself than had become her custom? He'd begun to feel uncomfortable, then worried that perhaps she might be regretting what had happened.

But then he'd gone to the bar to order a round, and Davina, passing him on her way to the Ladies, had brushed his hand with hers and whispered 'Just relax'. After that it had been better. And when he'd returned home with Gabrielle they sat and watched TV; he was still so buoyed by Davina's reassurance that the pc on the desk no longer exerted its pull

Now, sitting in the parlour alone, anticipation was raised again. He just had to hope that Gabrielle wouldn't make an unexpected entry – she probably wouldn't, given the clattering that was coming from the kitchen. She was always fully engaged in the process whenever she prepared a meal.

257

He logged on.

He had to read the email three times before he grasped all its implications. Such had been his obsession with discovering his relationship with Marcus that he'd never considered that Meryl might have been plagued with the same doubts for all those years. Indeed, he'd rarely thought of her. She had been just another chick from his well-stocked henhouse, a small part of a past that had been crowded with people. He had not felt betrayed by her; it was Robert, his erstwhile friend, who had been the betrayer.

He was angered by the tone of Whittaker's email – pompous, sneering bastard – and for a moment considered deleting it, or replying to the effect that he could get stuffed. But he knew he'd go along with Whittaker's proposal. It was now just a matter of satisfying his curiosity. If Marcus bore no resemblance to him, then all well and good. If there were a likeness, then ... well, okay, he'd have sired a son: so what? He would still be an unknown, a stranger, and one probably so influenced by that git of a stepfather that he wouldn't want any contact with him. That was okay by Derek: there were now more important things in his life. Whittaker had proposed an interesting scenario: it would be something he'd enjoy recounting to Davina.

He had time to send a very brief reply.

Whittaker –

I'm prepared to go along with either of your suggestions. It's up to you to decide, and up to you to arrange the how and where. Just so long as you give me plenty of notice. And I can assure you that whatever else I am, I am not a liar.

Bailey.

Chapter 33

He'd reluctantly agreed to Gordon's insistence that it would have to be a Windows laptop. He would have preferred a Mac, but Gordon had taken one look at the prices and demurred. Marcus had said that once he'd got a job he'd pay him back of course, but Gordon had said that was jumping ahead a bit, wasn't it, and it might be a good idea to actually start making applications, wouldn't it?

Now, in the passenger seat beside Gordon on the way to the computer shop in Leamington, Marcus decided it was time to raise the other issue, a subject he'd delayed broaching while the two had been engaged in the Mac *v* PC debate.

'It will also be necessary to buy a hub, of course,' he said.

'A what?'

'A hub. So we can have a WiFi connection.'

'What do you want that for?'

'So we can use our computers at the same time. Otherwise I'll have to take my laptop up to your study and connect it to the telephone line, and you might be using your computer, so I'd have to wait, and in any case it would be much better if could I operate from my bedroom, but of course with WiFi I could get a signal anywhere in the house, and –'

'How much will this hub thing set me back?'

'Oh, not very much.'

'Let's wait till we get to the shop before we make that decision shall we?'

'But–'

'Hang on, Marcus, I need to concentrate on my driving for a minute.'

Marcus became aware they were approaching a large roundabout. Looking at the road signs he realised it was the junction with the M40, the one his mother had been so insistent that she was not prepared to negotiate when he'd asked her to take him to Leamington. That had been over a week ago. Since then Marcus had been to Leamington by bus, visited the computer shop and seen several that he'd liked. On his return he'd asked Gordon when they could go and buy one, but Gordon had been annoyingly vague about when the trip would be made. Then this morning he had emerged from his study and announced that they'd be going this morning, and could Marcus hurry up, please, they needed to leave in fifteen minutes.

That suited Marcus. For some days now he'd been feeling a new sense of purpose in his life, freed from demands of home-management and spared the mockery of his erstwhile colleagues, though he missed Mo and emailed him whenever he could get access to Gordon's study. He valued Mo's advice on employment opportunities, but had decided it would suit him to apply for jobs down here – Leamington, perhaps, or at a pinch Coventry. Gordon or Mum could drive him to work and pick him up, couldn't they? And he might even try driving lessons again: Gordon could teach him. That would be much better than going to a driving school.

He was finding he liked living back home, now that Mum had stopped questioning him all the time. She still fussed of course, and had insisted on taking him to Stratford to buy clothes ('Marcus, darling, you can't possibly live with only one change of underwear'). But she no longer mentioned Bailey, and that suited him, because he found he no longer really cared about Bailey or what he'd suggested in his letter: it was silly of him to have got so worked up about it, Bailey was probably lying and if not, did it really matter, now that he was back living with Mum and Gordon? It was much more important to get back on-line permanently; his Facebook friends would be wondering what had happened to him, and of course he could start looking for jobs properly and then he could meet new people and –

'Not long now, Marcus. Christ, Warwick High Street's a bugger to drive through these days.'

Marcus peered out at his surroundings. They were approaching another roundabout. There was some sort of big castle thing on the right. At the roundabout Gordon turned left.

'Marcus, before you get all wrapped up with buying your computer, there's something I want to ask you.'

'Yes, what do you want to ask?'

'Look, Marcus, are you absolutely certain you want to stay down here, living with me and your mother, I mean?'

'Yes. You see, I think the opportunities for jobs are much–'

'Then don't you think it's time you started doing something about selling your house in Milton Keynes? It'll be me and your mother who'll be paying the mortgage unless you get a job soon. When's the next payment due? Remember you've got nothing being paid into your account.'

Marcus didn't want to have to think about the house, not now. He had computers on his mind.

'Yes. I'll start doing something about it soon. As soon as I've got the computer set up.'

'It's not just our problem though, is it? What about your Sophie? She must be in a bit of a mess, what with

261

all your stuff in the house. And she'll need her share of the proceeds from the sale, unless she intends staying there of course. You've got to be fair to her, Marcus.'

Sophie. To hear the name spoken jolted Marcus. He didn't want to think about her. All the horrible things that had happened to him over the past weeks were her fault, he was now sure of that. She wasn't a very nice person, he'd decided. Now that he wasn't with her he was much happier. So he was ignoring her telephone calls; her texts remained un-read. She wasn't texting so frequently now. She was probably beginning to get the message.

'Yes,' he said. 'I'll start doing that, once I've got the computer set up.'

'Come on, Marcus. I'm dying for a coffee, and I'm hungry. You've made your choice. Leave it in the shop, we can pick it up after we've had some lunch. That'll be okay, won't it?'

'Certainly,' said the sales assistant.

'But what about the hub? You did agree – '

'Yes, yes, Marcus. After lunch. But come *on.*'

What was the hurry? Marcus wondered. He'd noticed that Gordon had been getting increasingly impatient. Didn't he realise that the purchase of a computer required a great deal of careful thought?

They'd gone only a few steps from the shop door when Gordon stopped and slapped his hand against his head.

'Bugger! Hang on, Marcus. I've left my scarf in the shop.'

He emerged thirty seconds later with his tattered striped scarf draped round his neck. It occurred to Marcus that he'd never seen it before today. Why did Gordon need to wear a scarf in June?

*

As he turned off the M40 and approached Warwick, Derek was surprised to realise that he felt not a trace of apprehension, no butterflies, not even excitement; just mild curiosity about what might transpire, and above all anticipation of the relief that would follow when the whole thing was over.

He was glad he'd eventually decided to tell Gabrielle about the visit. One secret was quite enough to keep. Once he'd reassured her that the meeting was instigated by Marcus's stepfather and that it was *his* wish to learn the truth, she accepted, albeit with reluctance, that he would go. Since then she'd been rather quiet, a bit less affectionate than usual perhaps, but she'd come round.

On the other hand Davina, at their fleeting meetings alone together that they'd managed (in Tesco's coffee bar so it would look like a chance encounter), had been supportive, even enthusiastic. He'd asked her if she might possibly accompany him, but she'd said it would be too risky: she couldn't think of an excuse to be away for a whole day. It was a pity, thought Derek: he could have done with her company, and the appreciative audience that she would have been for his account of the encounter to come.

As he drove along the approach road to Warwick he was vaguely aware of changes that had occurred since last he'd been here, a lot of housing development to the left, but he couldn't remember what had been there before. Back then he'd rarely ventured out of Leamington, and the landscape evoked no memories. Warwick High Street seemed to have changed little, apart from the raised pedestrian crossings. It was only when approaching the outskirts of Leamington that he was seized by the anticipation of nostalgia for the town where he'd once lived.

But once he'd passed the railway station, he found the place wasn't as he thought it was. He couldn't understand the road system: he assumed he'd be able to drive right up The Parade, but was constantly diverted by one-way systems. He found himself crossing The Parade several times, but was unable to turn onto it, barred from entry by 'no right turn' signs. Eventually he found a car-park. He had an hour to spare, and decided to walk round and revisit some of his old haunts. But they weren't there: this wasn't the place he'd carried in his head for 24 years. New supermarkets had sprung up, shopping malls had appeared behind the Regency frontages, most of the old small shops had gone and the few that remained were run by Asians. The pubs had either disappeared or had been transformed into up-market bars. Worst of all, *The Red House*, the pub he used to drink in most nights, and on summer evenings in its beer garden, was closed. A notice fixed to the door announced that a planning application had been lodged to turn it into flats. As he walked round, he tried to subtract all the changes from the townscape and to substitute the things that had been there before. That new block of flats – that was the coffee bar he used to frequent on Saturday mornings: that car park – that was the terrace of houses where Tony and his chick (what was her name? Yes, Mavis) used to live: that convenience store – that was the bookshop he used to browse in. It worked, up to a point, but after a while it became depressing, and he decided not to visit the street where he'd had his flat. If Davina, who had never been to the town, were with him then she would be seeing an entirely different place, and by acting as her guide he might have been a more dispassionate observer.

It was time to make the rendezvous: it was important that he arrived there first. He hurried up The

Parade and found the entrance to the Royal Priors Parade, a precinct that hadn't existed in his day. Just in time he remembered the denim cap that he was carrying: he put it on, entered Costa, ordered a coffee and took a seat by the window. It was 1.50 – ten minutes to spare.

He tried to avoid glancing at his watch every few minutes. For the first time that day he felt a shudder of uncertainty: was this in fact something he really wanted to do? After all, he wasn't doing it for his benefit, was he?

Then, through the window he saw it. A long, striped scarf draped round the neck of a fat, bald, fellow who was lumbering ponderously towards the door of the cafe. Behind him, a young man.

*

As soon as he pushed open the door Gordon spotted the denim cap. Its wearer was staring at him. Gordon acknowledged the stare with a brief nod, then hurried to the counter, Marcus trailing behind him. He directed Marcus to sit at a table near the counter, placed his order in a voice that shook slightly (Christ, he was feeling nervous), then, on receiving it, joined Marcus. Fortunately the lad was sitting facing the denim cap.

This was it, then. Why was he feeling so shaky? He wouldn't know the outcome until Bailey had emailed him – Gordon had insisted there was to be no contact in the coffee bar. That was Meryl's wish. When he'd left her this morning she was incoherent with trepidation. They'd agreed the previous evening that Marcus shouldn't be told the real purpose of the trip to Leamington, not until its outcome was known. Given Marcus's new-found tranquillity, Gordon was beginning to wonder if he should be told at all.

He glanced over towards Bailey. He'd removed the denim cap. The bastard had a full head of hair. He didn't look his age and he was slim, clad in tee-shirt and jeans. The shit. Gordon was everything that Bailey wasn't: his face, figure and lack of hair meant he'd always had to feign indifference to the fads and fashions of his contemporaries. There was no justice in this world.

Their eyes met briefly: Bailey was the first to look away and Gordon felt he'd scored a minor victory. He appraised him: there seemed to be nothing of Marcus in him, but then Gordon wasn't adept at spotting likenesses in people. Meryl often accused him of being unobservant.

Bailey glanced towards him; Gordon turned his attention to his coffee and panini. Marcus was devouring his snack, still talking about his bloody computer, spluttering bits of carrot cake over the table. He belched, took a slurp of coffee, then stood up, looking around him.

'What's the matter, Marcus?'

'I need the toilet. Where is it?'

'Over there.'

Marcus scuttled away. In his absence, Gordon felt self-conscious. Bailey was but a few yards away, probably staring at him. He wished he had a newspaper to read. He pulled out his mobile phone and pretended to check for texts.

'Whittaker.'

Gordon started, looked up. Bailey was standing over him.

'I'm leaving. There's no point in emailing you when I get home. I can tell you now. He's not mine. He doesn't look much like the Bob Sidelski I remember, but he moves like him. And the clincher was his table manners. Hope you're satisfied.'

266

He strode to the door and disappeared. Immediately, Gordon felt about ten years younger.

When Marcus emerged from the toilet, Gordon stood up.

'Okay Marcus, let's go and collect your computer – unless you want to finish your coffee first.'

'No. I'm ready. You haven't forgotten about buying a hub, have you?'

Chapter 34

Gabrielle was on her knees, hoovering the stairs. It was a job she hated. The old hoover was heavy to lug about, and its tools not equal to the task of removing dried mud from the carpet. It wasn't often that Derek forgot to remove his trainers when coming in from his morning jog, but it had happened twice in the past week. He'd apologised profusely, but hadn't offered to clear up the mess. This morning he'd hurried off to the allotment immediately after breakfast, eager to make the most of a bright morning: more rain was forecast for the afternoon.

She scrubbed the final tread with the hoover tool, then scrambled up from her kneeling position and stood on the landing, hand clutching her aching back. She didn't resent Derek's hurried departure, for he was his old self again, in fact even more content than he used to be before starting his one-way correspondence with Marcus. There were no longer any moments of irritation, no flashes of temper. He was no longer tied to his computer, and had started to do a lot more reading. And a lot more singing: he listened to his records quite often.

She'd noticed the change in his mood even before he'd set out on his trip to Leamington. On his return he hadn't spoken much about it, beyond saying that he now knew for certain that Marcus wasn't his son, and that Marcus's step-father was a fat bald old geezer, and that he was surprised that Meryl had got together with someone like that. Gabrielle was surprised that he'd referred to Meryl: she'd been the great unmentionable for over 20 years. But since then he'd not mentioned Marcus or Meryl: it was as though they'd been expunged from his memory. Gabrielle was grateful for that. She'd got her old Derek back again.

In fact it was a slightly changed Derek. He was gentle, affectionate and attentive. He seemed to be doing everything he could to please her, apart from hoovering the stairs. He'd even taken over the shopping duties. Apparently he sometimes bumped into Davina in Tescos. On one occasion he'd had coffee with her there, though he hadn't mentioned this: Gabrielle had been told by Anthea from the book group, who'd seen them together.

Meetings with Giles and Davina in the pub had resumed. But these weren't quite as they used to be: Giles seemed a bit distant, he didn't engage with Derek so much as he used to. Gabrielle wondered if he was less forgiving of Derek's past than Davina obviously was. Davina on the other hand was paying more attention to Derek than hitherto: she laughed a lot at his jokes, made reference to conversations they'd had in Tesco's. And there was a lot of eye contact.

Were they? The possibility suddenly occurred to her. No; nonsense: and anyway there was no way they could have had the opportunity. She dismissed the idea. They'd just got to know each other a bit more, that was all. In any case, Derek seemed to be losing his libido, and about time too. He'd made no demands on her for weeks, and that suited her. She'd never enjoyed it as much as he obviously had. She always found it hard to fake enthusiasm: it was her passivity that often resulted in his flashes of temper. Now, thank God, they seemed to be settling into the sort of asexual serenity that befitted a couple in late middle age.

The back door slammed.

269

'Boots!' she shouted down the stairs.

'Okay. I've taken them off. D'you fancy a coffee?'

'Please.'

She made her way downstairs, carefully: her back was still giving her twinges. Derek was busy with the caffetiere, humming softly to himself.

'Did you get much done at the allotment?'

'Eh? Oh, yes, quite a bit.' Then - 'Gabby, will you be using the car next Wednesday?'

'Wednesday? I don't suppose so. Why?'

He went to the cupboard and selected two mugs.

Not looking at her, he said 'It's just that there's a book fair in Nantwich that day. I'd quite like to go and spend a few hours there.'

'Oh, that'll be nice. I might come along with you, if that's okay. I haven't been to Nantwich for years.'

He glanced at her, then looked away.

'Oh, I dunno, Gab. I might be tied up at the fair for quite a while. Wouldn't be much fun for you. Why don't we go together some other time; make a day of it?'

*

Meryl was walking back to the house after coffee with some of her WI friends. She had enjoyed it: now that the pressures of organising the Jubilee celebrations were behind them everyone was much more relaxed. Not Debbie Cartwright and Jan Barlow so much, though: Debbie had hosted the meeting and obviously resented having Jan in her house, while Jan took every opportunity to damn with faint praise Debbie's choice of decor. It had been amusing to listen to them; Meryl was looking forward to telling Gordon about it.

On a morning such as this, she thought, it was possible to believe that there might, after all, be a summer. The lane was festooned with greenery, lawnmowers could be heard whirring behind the high hedges, the twittering of birds was not drowned by the pattering of rain or the soughing of the wind. She might be able to get a few hours in the garden before the forecast downpour arrived. And even if she couldn't, it didn't matter. She was content. The weight of 25 years had been lifted from her shoulders. Marcus was hers.

And he would remain hers, for he had evidently decided to stay. He had a job interview coming up next week, and moreover it was in Stratford, not Coventry or Leamington, thank the Lord. He was full of it – in fact he spoke of little else. After his absence at university and in Milton Keynes she'd forgotten what he was like to live with; his long monologues, his formal speech, his literal interpretation of ironic remarks made by Gordon, his inflexible routines. One just had to be patient with him.

He seemed to have forgiven her for never having told him the exact truth about her past: he hadn't made this explicit, but he was with her as he'd always been as a boy and young teenager. He never mentioned Bailey or his letters. She and Gordon had agreed that there was no point in informing him of the certainty of his paternity, nor the devious means by which this information had been obtained. Only if his doubts resurfaced might it be necessary to tell him.

Best of all, he wasn't going back to *that woman*. He never spoke of her. Meryl hoped to God she'd be out this afternoon when Gordon and Marcus arrived in Milton Keynes to collect Marcus's belongings. Gordon had asked Marcus about that; would she be at work? Marcus hadn't responded directly, but said that he had his house key so it wouldn't matter if she were.

Once the pair returned, and Marcus's house had been put on the market (a visit to an Estate Agent was the other purpose of their trip) then all connections with Milton Keynes would be severed. Marcus could begin to build a life at home, make new friends, even meet a nice girl. Perhaps she might arrange introductions with the daughters of some of her friends, though most of them, she realised, were long married, some even divorced. A divorcee wouldn't be suitable for Marcus: he'd had quite enough dealings with hussies.

She was humming to herself as she reached her front gate. Looking up at the front of the house, she saw it through Gordon's eyes: yes, he was right; it could do with a bit of attention. And inside – yes, she resolved to get rid of some of the clutter, maybe buy some new furniture. It was time to make a break with the past. Gordon would be pleased. She felt a welling of affection for Gordon: what would she ever have done without him?

*

Derek rinsed the soap from his body and turned off the shower. As he dried himself he was still thinking about his lucky escape. It had never occurred to him that Gabrielle might want to join him in Nantwich. But she'd seemed happy enough with his suggestion of an alternative date.

Am I feeling guilty? he asked himself. No, he wasn't. Excitement overrode all other emotions. Life was good again. And hadn't he shown enough charity towards people recently? Like his telling Gabrielle, and Whittaker, that he was certain about Marcus? It was a white lie, intended to assuage their fears, an act of benevolence on his part. For he wasn't certain: he couldn't be sure. Certainly he had seen nothing of himself in the lad: not with those short legs and waddling walk. But he hadn't seen much of Bob

272

Sidelski either, except maybe the thinning hair. Hard to tell if it was frizzy like Bob's had been, for it was short and plastered with gel. And the table manners – just a joke, something to wind up Whittaker. As for himself; well, he no longer gave a toss. He had more pressing matters to attend to.

He must let Davina know that next week's trip was on. It had to be on Wednesday, the one occasion for God knows how long when Giles would be away on one of his visits to Shrewsbury. Davina could then book them into Travelodge – it was quite near to Nantwich. She'd assured him that that sort of anonymous motel would never look askance at a booking just for an afternoon – they'd be travellers, wouldn't they, just wanting a short rest from their journey? It probably happened all the time.

Naked, he appraised himself in the mirror. Not bad. Not the turn-on he once had been, but not a total turn-off either. But a pre-arranged illicit encounter was something he hadn't experienced for decades. It wasn't like the unexpected, unplanned coupling of three weeks ago. The time spent in anticipation could also be a time for worry, and worry wasn't always good for the libido. Perhaps he ought to get hold of some Viagra, just to be on the safe side?

*

Marcus, bouncing around in the passenger seat of the hired van on the road to Milton Keynes, wasn't really too worried about meeting Sophie, just so long as Gordon didn't leave him alone with her. With a bit of luck she wouldn't be in. It was mainly clothes he intended to take; she could have the computer: now he had a new one he didn't need the one they'd purchased together when they first moved into the house.

273

In fact he didn't think it necessary to take any of his things: as far as he was concerned all his old stuff could be left there. Mum had agreed to buy him new clothes, and he would pay her once he started working. But Gordon had been insistent: he said it wouldn't be fair to Sophie to leave her with all his belongings when the house was put on the market. Marcus couldn't understand why Gordon kept on about being fair to Sophie. It was all her fault, wasn't it?

He needed new clothes for his job interview next week. He was looking forward to the interview: he'd planned out exactly what he was going to say; he'd show them how up-to-date he was with all the latest developments in I.T. and they were bound to be impressed so long as they gave him the chance to tell them without interrupting him with irrelevant questions. It was only a small company which assembled computers to customers' requirements, but the job for which he was applying involved visiting customers in their own homes to sort out problems they were having, and this was something he'd enjoy. But of course it meant he'd have to learn to drive; Gordon had already given him two lessons, and they hadn't gone badly; it was much easier learning on the quiet lanes of Warwickshire than it had been in Milton Keynes.

It was good living back with Mum and Gordon. They'd lent him money to furnish his bedroom with shelves and a computer work station, and he'd organised the room to his own requirements and was looking forward to filing all his documents and photographs in alphabetical order. Everything would be to hand, and he'd hardly need to leave the room at all, except for meals of course, and for watching TV, and once he'd started earning he'd buy a small TV of his own. Then he'd be completely independent, and wouldn't have to listen to Mum going on about how he ought to get out more and meet people. She'd started suggesting he join her at her friends' for evening drinks and said that some of them had nice daughters who were longing to meet him, but that wasn't what –

'Getting near Milton Keynes now, Marcus,' said Gordon. 'You'll have to give me directions to get to your house.'

'Did you hear me Marcus?' said Gordon. 'I need you to give me directions.'

'Oh. Right. Yes. You follow the main road towards the town centre and just before you get to the sign to the station you turn left at the roundabout and then after about a mile you–'

'Woah! I can't remember all that. Just warn me when we're coming up to the turns.'

'Oh. Right.'

Typical Marcus, thought Gordon; silent for most of the journey and then a torrent of indigestible information delivered at breakneck speed. Gordon had addressed a few casual remarks to him soon after they'd set off, but his replies were monosyllabic when he bothered to reply at all. The lad was probably worrying about seeing Sophie: although he'd not said as much, it was obviously something he wasn't relishing. He'd refused to phone her to warn her of their visit, and had kept repeating, over and over again, that he had a key to the house so it wasn't necessary to contact her. Gordon assumed that they'd parted on bad terms. It was a pity if the relationship had foundered: Gordon had quite taken to Sophie on the one occasion he'd met her, though he'd never dared say this to Meryl.

He found the road system in Milton Keynes confusing, and Marcus was not entirely accurate in his directions: on several occasions he'd had to circumnavigate roundabouts twice before finding the correct exit. Eventually, Marcus said 'Turn right just here', and they entered the cul-de-sac where he'd lived.

There seemed to be a lot of activity. Two police cars and an ambulance were parked at the side of the narrow road. A policeman was standing on the pavement, talking to a young couple.

'Seems to be a bit of a problem here, Marcus,' said Gordon. 'D'you know those two?'

'Yes, it's Jane and Kevin. They live next door.'

'Well, I can't get past that ambulance. I'll park here and we'll walk. Which one is your house?'

'That one.' Marcus pointed. 'The ambulance is in front of it.'

Gordon glanced at Marcus but his face was a mask.

They got out of the van and walked towards the policeman and the young couple: the girl glanced towards them, then turned back to the constable.

'That's him!' they heard her say. 'That's Marcus, Sophie's partner!'

She ran up to them.

'Oh, Marcus; where have you been? Something terrible's happened. It's Sophie. We knew something was wrong 'cos we hadn't seen her for days and her car hadn't been moved. So we called the police – '

The constable interrupted her. 'Just a minute Miss. Leave this to me, will you?'

He turned to Marcus. 'Are you Marcus Sidelski, sir?'

Silence.

'Can you confirm you're Miss Blower's partner? That you live with her?'

Marcus remained silent, his mouth agape.

'Perhaps I can explain, constable,' said Gordon. 'Yes, this is Marcus. I'm his stepfather. And yes, he was Sophie Blower's partner, up until a few weeks ago.

They've separated, you see. Marcus lives with me and his mother now, in Warwickshire. What's all this about? What's happened?'

'I think it best if we moved away from here, sir. If you and Mr Sidelski would come and sit in the police car.'

'But can't you at least–'

Gordon was distracted by the front door of Marcus's house being opened. A paramedic emerged, followed by a second paramedic. Between them was a stretcher. Gordon had ample time to examine it as it was carried slowly towards the ambulance. The body on the stretcher was covered by a blanket. There was no means of telling who it was, because the face was also covered.

The girl standing beside them gave a muffled sob: her partner gasped. Gordon looked at Marcus. He was devoid of expression.

Chapter 35

Meryl was making good progress with clearing up the superficial clutter. She'd gone through her chests of drawers and wardrobes, extracting the clothes she hadn't worn for years and putting them in bags ready to take to the charity shop in Stratford. Her dressing table had been ruthlessly purged of those items of make-up that she was never likely to use again. Her filing cabinet no longer bulged with old letters, birthday cards, bills, receipts and ancient bank statements: all had been consigned to the blue plastic bag for collection by the council next Wednesday. She was feeling the lightness of spirit that comes from divesting oneself of possessions that are no longer needed.

She knew this was only a start. The more difficult task would come later, when she would have to decide which of the weightier items should go; the pictures, books and memorabilia she'd inherited from her father. It would require a hardening of the heart, and she would need Gordon's encouragement to go through with it. But once that was done she could progress to thinking about furniture, carpets and redecoration. The prospect of refurbishment began to seem quite exciting, though she knew Gordon would insist that attention should first be paid to double glazing and cavity wall insulation.

She deserved a cigarette, didn't she? She went to the kitchen, made a cup of coffee and sat, Consulate between her fingers, thinking that this really was the start of a new chapter; no, not so much a chapter, a completely new book. Pleased with the metaphor, she developed it by thinking of her past as a series of old volumes which were no longer of interest and which could be jettisoned with all the other lumber.

Gordon would be so pleased. She looked forward to his returning home so she could show him what she'd accomplished and tell him what she was resolved to do next. Then, the thought occurred to her – maybe Gordon had junk that needed disposal? His desk, at which she occasionally sat to write letters and deal with household accounts, was often overflowing with paper. Surely some of it was no longer needed? Perhaps she might at least go through it, sort it into piles and suggest that Gordon do his bit for minimalism? They would then be working together towards the same goal.

She extinguished her cigarette and went up to the study.

On entering, she found the desk was almost clear of clutter; just one pile of papers. She toyed with the thought of going through his filing cabinet, but that would be too daunting a task. She sat at the desk and idly leafed through the pile of papers. At the bottom was the envelope containing Bailey's letter.

She sat rigid for a moment, anticipating the onset of distress. But it didn't come. All that Bailey had said was now of no relevance. Looking at the other papers in the pile – utility bills, newspaper cuttings, instruction manuals for gadgets long since extinct – she realised they were all outdated: indeed Gordon had scored across them in red ink, this suggesting they were to be thrown out. No doubt Bailey's letter was awaiting the same fate. She would leave Gordon to dispose of them all.

She got up to leave. But on reaching the door she stopped, seized by a thought. She was, she realised, curious. Curious about one aspect of Bailey's letter. Oh yes, she'd skimmed through it, Gordon standing over her, on that awful day when she'd been confronted with it. But she hadn't taken some of it in. And she hadn't dared read the final pages, knowing what they were likely to contain. Gordon had had to paraphrase what was written.

But now she was strong. Whatever Bailey had said couldn't touch her, for all had been resolved. To read it would be an act of defiance in the face of someone who had tried to destroy her: it would provide – what was the word that Gordon sometimes used? – yes, closure.

She opened the envelope and leafed through the pages until she reached the final one.

*

and I don't really know what went wrong, Marcus. I suppose we began to tire of each other. No, that's not the whole truth. Let me be honest. Even though I'd taught her to question her upbringing, to widen her reading, to reject her mother's Tory politics – and yes, she did all these things – she still retained many features of her privileged background, the way she dressed, the way she spoke. It was her county accent that eventually began to grate.

And it seemed that she began to be irritated by me. She never went so far as to criticise me, but her body language in my presence spoke volumes. And then she began to withdraw her favours: she was always too tired, it seemed. I wasn't one to beg, Marcus, so I – well, let's say I forced the issue on one or two occasions. It's not something I'm proud of. But she was still a very sexy lady – was I expected to live like a monk in her presence? Might you behave the same way,

280

Marcus, if you were to find yourself in this situation?

This went on for two months. Then one evening, after a silent meal, she very calmly told me that she was moving out. No, she wasn't going back to mummy: she was moving in with Bob Sidelski. She had been 'seeing him', as she put it, for those two months.

I'm not going to attempt to describe my reaction to this news. Anger was paramount, of course. But I was buggered if I was going to let on how I felt: I had my pride. She moved in with Bob Sidelski the following day. The day after, Bob approached me at the college and tried to talk. I wasn't having any. I severed all contact with him: never went to the library, avoided the coffee bar if he was in there. Fortunately he stopped drinking in *The Red House*, as of course did your mother.

I resumed my bachelor life, of course: in fact I went wild. Shagged everything that moved. But all the while, my anger festered. To be cuckolded by the likes of Bob Sidelski, with his big arse and balding head and his down-at-heel attire! My colleagues were probably sniggering, or even worse, pitying me. Then, one day, walking into the college coffee bar, I saw him, in the company of some of my fellow lecturers. One of them looked up, spotted me, then turned and addressed a remark to Bob. The whole group burst into laughter. That was it. I'd had enough. Betrayal was one thing, scorn was another.

You probably know what happened next, Marcus. It was all described, in great detail, in the court proceedings. I spent the evening in the pub, tanking myself up, then went round to

281

Bob's flat, rang the bell. When he opened the door I pushed past him, charged into his kitchen. Your mother was there. Bob followed me in. Words were exchanged. I hit him, hard, twice, and he fell back, banging his head on the sink. I kicked him as he lay on the floor. Bad mistake, that. If I had left him there I might have got away with manslaughter.

We're nearly at the end, Marcus. The very week that I went for trial at the County Court, your mother gave birth. It was you, obviously. It was only later, in prison, that I had the time to think, to count back the weeks from the date of your birth and to realise that conception had taken place during the month that she was still living with me, but seeing Bob. The month when she was being bedded by both of us.

So now you know as much as I do. I won't pressurise you Marcus, but I hope that you can find it in your heart to contact me, and after that, who knows, maybe even meet me? I'll leave it up to you to decide. My email address is derekbailey@hotmail.co.uk

Derek

*

Carefully, she inserted the page back into the envelope. She was glad she had read it, for it served to confirm her view of Bailey. There was little if any remorse, a lot of self-justification. She was angered by his having referred to her being 'bedded' by him. These days it would be accurately described for what it was – rape.

Marcus, assuming he had read the letter carefully, must surely appreciate that little fault lay with her? She hadn't been sleeping around: she'd only started an affair with the gentle, understanding Robert when living with that arrogant bastard had become unbearable. But none of it mattered now. Her only regret was that she'd not confided in Gordon right from the outset, but he seemed to have forgiven her.

The telephone rang. She hurried downstairs and picked up: it was Gordon.

'Hello darling; are things okay with you?'

'Yes, fine. Are you on your way back? You must be nearly home by now.'

'No. We haven't set off yet. Just about to.'

'Why the delay? Surely it didn't take that long to load up Marcus's stuff?'

'We didn't get round to that. Listen, Meryl: there's been a bit of a problem. We'll have to return another day – '

'What sort of problem? What's happened?'

'It's too complicated to explain now. I'll tell you when we get back.'

'Are you all right? You sound a bit fraught. Is Marcus all right?'

'I'm okay. And Marcus ... he's absolutely fine. Never better, in fact. He can't wait to get back to his computer.'